"ONE OF THE STRONGEST SUSPENSE NOVELISTS TO EMERGE IN YEARS . . .

Enquiry is filled with suspense, high drama and the bristling hatred of revenge."
—*The New York Times*

"Absolutely the best-choice novel of suspense this year"
—*Newsday*

"A tight and tantalizing story, every bit as good as *Forfeit*"
—*Best Sellers*

"Interesting and plausible, strewn with highly diverting obstacles"
—*New Yorker*

"A winner all the way!"
—*Saturday Review*

Books by Dick Francis

Blood Sport
Bonecrack
Dead Cert
Enquiry
Flying Finish
For Kicks
Forfeit
High Stakes
In the Frame
Knockdown
Nerve
Odds Against
Rat Race
Risk
Slayride
Smokescreen

Published by POCKET BOOKS

Dick Francis

Enquiry

PUBLISHED BY POCKET BOOKS NEW YORK

POCKET BOOKS, a Simon & Schuster division of
GULF & WESTERN CORPORATION
1230 Avenue of the Americas, New York, N.Y. 10020

Copyright © 1969 by Dick Francis

Published by arrangement with Harper & Row, Publishers, Inc.
Library of Congress Catalog Card Number: 76-96007

ISBN: 0-671-83141-0

First Pocket Books printing November, 1975

10   9   8   7   6   5   4   3   2

Trademarks registered in the United States and other countries.

Printed in the U.S.A.

Part One

FEBRUARY

Chapter 1

Yesterday I lost my license.

To a professional steeplechase jockey, losing his license and being warned off Newmarket Heath is like being chucked off the medical register, only more so.

Barred from race riding, barred from racecourses. Barred, moreover, from racing stables. Which poses me quite a problem, as I live in one.

No livelihood and maybe no home.

Last night was a right so-and-so, and I prefer to forget those grisly sleepless hours. Shock and bewilderment, the feeling that it couldn't have happened, it was all a mistake. . . . This lasted until after midnight. And at least the disbelieving stage had had some built-in comfort. The full thudding realization which followed had none at all. My life was lying around like the untidy bits of a smashed teacup, and I was altogether out of glue and rivets.

This morning I got up and percolated some coffee and looked out the window at the lads bustling around in the yard and mounting and cloppeting away up the road to the Downs, and I got my first real taste of being an outcast.

Fred didn't bellow up at my window, as he usually did, "Going to stay there all day, then?"

This time, I was.

None of the lads looked up. . . . They more or less kept their eyes studiously right down. They were quiet, too. Dead quiet. I watched Bouncing Bernie heave his ten stone seven onto the gelding I'd been riding lately, and there was something apologetic about the way he lowered his fat bum into the saddle.

7

And he, too, kept his eyes down.

Tomorrow, I guessed, they'd be themselves again. To-morrow they'd be curious and ask questions. I understood that they weren't despising me. They were sympathetic. Probably too sympathetic for their own comfort. And embarrassed: that, too. And instinctively delicate about looking too soon at the face of total disaster.

When they'd gone, I drank my coffee slowly and won-dered what to do next. A nasty, very nasty, feeling of emptiness and loss.

The papers had been stuck as usual through my letter box. I wondered what the boy had thought, knowing what he was delivering. I shrugged. Might as well read what they'd said, the Goddamned reporters, God bless them.

The *Sporting Life,* short on news, had given us the headlines and the full treatment: "CRANFIELD AND HUGHES DISQUALIFIED."

There was a picture of Cranfield at the top of the page, and halfway down one of me, all smiles, taken the day I won the Hennessy Gold Cup. Some little subeditor letting his irony loose, I thought sourly, and printing the most cheerful picture he could dig out of the files.

The close-printed inches north and south of my happy face were unrelieved gloom.

"The Stewards said they were not satisfied with my explanation," Cranfield said. "They have withdrawn my license. I have no further comment to make."

Hughes, it was reported, had said almost exactly the same. Hughes, if I remembered correctly, had in fact said nothing whatsoever. Hughes had been too stunned to put one word consecutively after another, and if he had said anything at all it would have been unprintable.

I didn't read all of it. I'd read it all before, about other people. For "Cranfield and Hughes" one could substitute any other trainer and jockey who had been warned off. The newspaper reports on these occasions were always the same, totally uninformed. As a racing Enquiry was a private trial, the ruling authorities were not obliged to open the proceedings to the public or the press, and as they were not obliged to, they never did. In fact, like many another inward-looking concern, they seemed to be permanently engaged in trying to stop too many people from finding out what was really going on.

The *Daily Witness* was equally fogbound, except that Daddy Leeman had suffered his usual rush of purple prose to the head. According to him:

"Kelly Hughes, until now a leading contender for this season's jump jockeys' crown, and fifth on the list last year, was sentenced to an indefinite suspension of his license. Hughes, thirty, left the hearing ten minutes after Cranfield. Looking pale and grim, he confirmed that he had lost his license, and added, 'I have no further comment.'"

They had remarkable ears, those reporters.

I put down the paper with a sigh and went into the bedroom to exchange my dressing gown for trousers and a jersey, and after that I made my bed, and after that I sat on it, staring into space. I had nothing else to do. I had nothing to do for as far ahead as the eye could see. Unfortunately I also had nothing to think about except the Enquiry.

Put baldly, I had lost my license for losing a race. More precisely, I had ridden a red-hot favorite into second place in the Lemonfizz Crystal Cup at Oxford in the latter part of January, and the winner had been an unconsidered outsider. This would have been merely unfortunate had it not been that both horses were trained by Dexter Cranfield.

The finishing order at the winning post had been greeted with roars of disgust from the stands, and I had been booed all the way to the unsaddling enclosure. Dexter Cranfield had looked worried more than delighted to have taken first and second places in one of the season's big sponsored steeplechases, and the Stewards of the meeting had called us both in to explain. They were not, they announced, satisfied with the explanations. They would refer the matter to the Disciplinary Committee of the Jockey Club.

The Disciplinary Committee, two weeks later, were equally skeptical that the freak result had been an accident. Deliberate fraud on the betting public, they said. Disgraceful, dishonest, disgusting, they said. Racing must keep its good name clean. Not the first time that either of you has been suspected. Severe penalties must be inflicted as a deterrent to others.

Off, they said. Warned off. And good riddance.

It wouldn't have happened in America, I thought in depression. There all runners from one stable—or one owner, for that matter—were covered by a bet on any of them. So if the stable's outsider won instead of its favorite, the backers still collected their money. High time the same system crossed the Atlantic. Correction: more than high time; long, long overdue.

The truth of the matter was that Squelch, my red-hot favorite, had been dying under me all the way up the straight, and it was in the miracle class that I'd finished as close as second, and not fifth or sixth. If he hadn't carried so many people's shirts, in fact, I wouldn't have exhausted him as I had. That it had been Cranfield's other runner Cherry Pie who had passed me ten yards from the finish was just the worst sort of luck.

Armed by innocence, and with reason to believe that even if the Oxford Stewards had been swayed by the crowd's hostile reception the Disciplinary Committee were going to consider the matter in an atmosphere of cool common sense, I had gone to the Enquiry without a twinge of apprehension.

The atmosphere was cool, all right. Glacial. Their own common sense was taken for granted by the Stewards. They didn't appear to think that either Cranfield or I had any.

The first faint indication that the sky was about to fall came when they read out a list of nine previous races in which I had ridden a beaten favorite for Cranfield. In six of them, another of Cranfield's runners had won. Cranfield had also had other runners in the other three.

"That means," said Lord Gowery, "that this case before us is by no means the first. It has happened again and again. These results seem to have been unnoticed in the past, but this time you have clearly overstepped the mark."

I must have stood there looking stupid, with my mouth falling open in astonishment, and the trouble was that they obviously thought I was astonished at how much they had dug up to prove my guilt.

"Some of those races were years ago," I protested. "Six or seven, some of them."

"What difference does that make?" asked Lord Gowery. "They happened."

"That sort of thing happens to every trainer now and then," Cranfield said hotly. "You must know it does."

Lord Gowery gave him an emotionless stare. It stirred some primeval reaction in my glands, and I could feel the ripple of goose pimples up my spine. He really believes, I thought wildly, he really believes us guilty. It was only then that I realized we had to make a fight of it; and it was already far too late.

I said to Cranfield, "We should have had that lawyer," and he gave me an almost frightened glance of agreement.

Shortly before the Lemonfizz, the Jockey Club had finally thrown an old autocratic tradition out of the twentieth century and agreed that people in danger of losing their livelihood could be legally represented at their trials if they wished. The concession was so new that there was no accepted custom to be guided by. One or two people had been acquitted with lawyers' help who would presumably have been acquitted anyway; and if an accused person engaged a lawyer to defend him, he had in all cases to pay the fees himself. The Jockey Club did not award costs to anyone they accused, whether or not they managed to prove themselves innocent.

At first, Cranfield had agreed with me that we should find a lawyer, though both of us had been annoyed at having to shell out. Then Cranfield had by chance met at a party the newly elected Disciplinary Steward who was a friend of his, and had reported to me afterward, "There's no need for us to go to the expense of a lawyer. Monty Midgely told me in confidence that the Disciplinary Committee think the Oxford Stewards were off their heads reporting us, that he knows the Lemonfizz result was just one of those things, and not to worry, the Enquiry will only be a formality. Ten minutes or so, and it will be over."

That assurance had been good enough for both of us. We hadn't even seen any cause for alarm when, three or four days later, Colonel Sir Montague Midgely had turned yellow with jaundice and taken to his bed. It had been announced that one of the Committee, Lord Gowery, would deputize for him in any Enquiries which might be held in the next few weeks.

Monty Midgely's liver had a lot to answer for. Whatever he had intended, it now seemed all too appallingly clear that Gowery didn't agree with him.

The Enquiry was held in a large lavishly furnished room in the Portman Square headquarters of the Jockey Club. Four Stewards sat in comfortable armchairs along one side of a polished table, with a pile of papers in front of each of them, and a stenographer was stationed at a smaller table a little to their right. When Cranfield and I went into the room, the stenographer was fussing with a tape recorder, unwinding a lead from the machine which stood on his own table and trailing it across the floor toward the Stewards. He set up a microphone on a stand in front of Lord Gowery, switched it on, blew into it a couple of times, went back to his machine, flicked a few switches, and announced that everything was in order.

Behind the Stewards, across a few yards of plushy dark red carpet, were several more armchairs. Their occupants included the three Stewards who had been unconvinced at Oxford, the Clerk of the Course, the Handicapper who had allotted the Lemonfizz weights, and a pair of Stipendiary Stewards, officials paid by the Jockey Club and acting at meetings as an odd mixture of messenger boys for the Stewards and the industry's private police. It was they who, if they thought there had been an infringement of the rules, brought it to the notice of the Stewards of the meeting concerned, and advised them to hold an Enquiry.

As in any other job, some Stipendiaries were reasonable men and some were not. The Stipe who had been acting at Oxford on Lemonfizz day was notoriously the most difficult of them all.

Cranfield and I were to sit facing the Stewards' table, but several feet from it. For us, too, there were the same luxurious armchairs. Very civilized. Not a hatchet in sight. We sat down, and Cranfield casually crossed his legs, looking confident and relaxed.

We were far from soul mates, Cranfield and I. He had inherited a fortune from his father, an ex-soap manufacturer who had somehow failed to acquire a coveted peerage in spite of donating madly to every fashionable cause in sight, and the combination of wealth and disappointed social ambition had turned Cranfield *fils* into a roaring snob. To him, since he employed me, I was a servant; and he didn't know how to treat servants.

He was, however, a pretty good trainer. Better still, he had rich friends who could afford good horses. I had ridden for him semi-regularly for nearly eight years, and although at first I had resented his snobbish little ways, I had eventually grown up enough to find them amusing. We operated strictly as a business team, even after all that time. Not a flicker of friendship. He would have been outraged at the very idea, and I didn't like him enough to think it a pity.

He was twenty years older than I, a tallish thin Anglo-Saxon type with thin fine mousy hair, grayish-blue eyes with short fair lashes, a well-developed straight nose, and aggressively perfect teeth. His bone structure was of the type acceptable to the social cricle in which he tried to move, but the lines his outlook on life had etched in his skin were a warning to anyone looking for tolerance or generosity. Cranfield was mean-minded by habit and open-handed only to those who could lug him upward. In all his dealings with those he considered his inferiors, he left behind a turbulent wake of dislike and resentment. He was charming to his friends and polite in public to his wife. His three teen-age children echoed his delusions of superiority with pitiful faithfulness.

Cranfield had remarked to me some days before the Enquiry that the Oxford Stewards were all good chaps and that two of them had personally apologized to him for having to send the case on to the Disciplinary Committee. I nodded without answering. Cranfield must have known as well as I did that all three of the Oxford Stewards had been elected for social reasons only; that one of them couldn't read a number board at five paces, that another had inherited his late uncle's string of race horses but not his expert knowledge, and that the third had been heard to ask his trainer which his own horse was, during the course of a race. Not one of the three could read a race at anything approaching the standard of a racecourse commentator. Good chaps they might well be, but as judges frightening.

"We will show the film of the race," Lord Gowery said.

They showed it, projecting from the back of the room onto a screen on the wall behind Cranfield and me. We turned our armchairs round to watch it. The Stipendiary Steward from Oxford, a fat pompous bully, stood by the screen, pointing out Squelch with a long baton.

"This is the horse in question," he said as the horses lined up for the start. I reflected mildly that if the Stewards knew their job they would have seen the film several times already, and would know which was Squelch without needing to have him pointed out.

The Stipe more or less indicated Squelch all the way round. It was an unremarkable race, run to a well-tried pattern: hold back at the start, letting someone else make the pace; ease forward to fourth place and settle there for two miles or more; move smoothly to the front coming toward the second last fence, and press on home regardless. If the horse liked that sort of race, and if he were good enough, he would win.

Squelch hated to be ridden any other way. Squelch was, on his day, good enough. It just hadn't been his day.

The film showed Squelch taking the lead coming into the second last fence. He rolled a bit on landing, a sure sign of tiredness. I'd had to pick him up and urge him into the last, and it was obvious on the film. Away from the last, toward the winning post, he'd floundered about beneath me and if I hadn't been ruthless he'd have slowed to a trot. Cherry Pie, at the finish, came up surprisingly fast and passed him as if he'd been standing still.

The film flicked off abruptly and someone put the lights on again. I thought that the film was conclusive and that that would be the end of it.

"You didn't use your whip," Lord Gowery said accusingly.

"No, sir," I agreed. "Squelch shies away from the whip. He has to be ridden with the hands."

"You were making no effort to ride him out."

"Indeed I was, sir. He was dead tired, you can see on the film."

"All I can see on the film is that you were making absolutely no effort to win. You were sitting there with your arms still, making no effort whatsoever."

I stared at him. "Squelch isn't an easy horse to ride, sir. He'll always do his best, but only if he isn't upset. He has to be ridden quietly. He stops if he's hit. He'll only respond to being squeezed, and to small flicks on the reins, and to his jockey's voice."

"That's quite right," said Cranfield piously. "I always give Hughes orders not to treat the horse roughly."

As if he hadn't heard a word, Lord Gowery said, "Hughes didn't pick up his whip."

He looked enquiringly at the two Stewards flanking him, as if to collect their opinions. The one on his left, a youngish man who had ridden as an amateur, nodded noncommittally. The other one was asleep.

I suspected Gowery kicked him under the table. He woke up with a jerk, said, "Eh? Yes, definitely," and eyed me suspiciously.

It's a farce, I thought incredulously. The whole thing's a bloody farce.

Gowery nodded, satisfied. "Hughes never picked up his whip."

The fat bullying Stipe was oozing smugness. "I am sure you will find this next film relevant, sir."

"Quite," agreed Gowery. "Show it now."

"Which film is this?" Cranfield enquired.

Gowery said, "This film shows Squelch winning at Reading on January 3rd."

Cranfield reflected. "I was not at Reading on that day."

"No," agreed Gowery. "We understand you went to the Worcester meeting instead." He made it sound suspicious instead of perfectly normal. Cranfield had run a hot young hurdler at Worcester and had wanted to see how he shaped. Squelch, the established star, needed no supervision.

The lights went out again. The Stipe used his baton to point out Kelly Hughes riding a race in Squelch's distinctive colors of black and white chevrons and a black cap. Not at all the same sort of race as the Lemonfizz Crystal Cup. I'd gone to the front early on to give myself a clear view of the fences, pulled back to about third place for a breather at midway, and forged to the front again only after the last fence, swinging my whip energetically down the horse's shoulder and urging him vigorously with my arms.

The film stopped, the lights went on, and there was a heavy accusing silence. Cranfield turned toward me, frowning.

"You will agree," said Gowery ironically, "that you used your whip, Hughes."

"Yes, sir," I said. "Which race did you say that was?"

"The last race at Reading," he said irritably. "Don't pretend you don't know."

"I agree that the film you've just shown was the last race at Reading, sir. But Squelch didn't run in the last race at Reading. The horse in that film is Wanderlust. He belongs to Mr. Jessel, like Squelch does, so the colors are the same, and both horses are by the same sire, which accounts for them looking similar, but the horse you've just shown is Wanderlust. Who does, as you saw, respond well if you wave a whip at him."

There was a dead silence. It was Cranfield who broke it, clearing his throat.

"Hughes is quite right. That is Wanderlust."

He hadn't realized it, I thought in amusement, until I'd pointed it out. It's all too easy for people to believe what they're told.

There was a certain amount of hurried whispering going on. I didn't help them. They could sort it out for themselves.

Eventually Lord Gowery said, "Has anyone got a form book?" and an official near the door went out to fetch one. Gowery opened it and took a long look at the Reading results.

"It seems," he said heavily, "that we have the wrong film. Squelch ran in the sixth race at Reading, which is, of course, usually the last. However, it now appears that on that day there were seven races, the novice chase having been divided and run in two halves, at the beginning and end of the day. Wanderlust won the *seventh* race. A perfectly understandable mix-up, I am afraid."

I didn't think I would help my cause by saying that I thought it a disgraceful mix-up, if not criminal.

"Could we now, sir," I asked politely, "see the right film? The one that Squelch won."

Lord Gowery cleared his throat. "I don't, er, think we have it here. However," he recovered fast, "we don't need it. It is immaterial. We are not considering the Reading result, but that at Oxford."

I gasped. I was truly astounded. "But, sir, if you watch Squelch's race, you will see that I rode him at Reading exactly as I did at Oxford, without using the whip."

"That is beside the point, Hughes, because Squelch may not have needed the whip at Reading, but at Oxford he did."

"Sir, it *is* the point," I protested. "I rode Squelch at Oxford in exactly the same manner as when he won at Reading, only at Oxford he tired."

Lord Gowery absolutely ignored this. Instead, he looked left and right to his Stewards alongside and re-

marked, "We must waste no more time. We have three or
four witnesses to call before lunch."

The sleepy eldest Steward nodded and looked at his
watch. The younger one nodded and avoided meeting my
eyes. I knew him quite well from his amateur jockey
days, and had often ridden against him. We had all been
pleased when he had been made a Steward, because he
knew at first hand the sort of odd circumstances which
cropped up in racing to make a fool of the brightest, and
we had thought that he would always put forward or
explain our point of view. From his downcast semi-
apologetic face I now gathered that we had hoped too
much. He had not so far contributed one single word to
the proceedings, and he looked, though it seemed extraordinary, intimidated.

As plain Andrew Tring, he had been lighthearted, amusing, and almost reckless over fences. His recently inherited baronetcy and his even more recently acquired
Stewardship seemed on the present showing to have ham-
mered him into the ground.

Of Lord Plimborne, the elderly sleepyhead, I knew
very little except his name. He seemed to be in his
seventies and there was a faint tremble about many of his
movements, as if old age were shaking at his foundations
and would soon have him down. He had not, I thought,
clearly heard or understood more than a quarter of what
had been said.

An Enquiry was usually conducted by three Stewards,
but on this day there were four. The fourth, Wykeham,
second Baron Ferth, who sat on the left of Andrew Tring,
was not, as far as I knew, even on the Disciplinary Committee, let alone a Disciplinary Steward. But he had in
front of him a pile of notes as large as, if not larger than,
the others, and he was following every word with sharp
hot eyes. Exactly where his involvement lay I couldn't
work out, but there was no doubt that he cared about the
outcome.

He alone of the four seemed really disturbed that they
should have shown the wrong film, and he said quietly
but forcefully enough for it to carry across to Cranfield

and me, "I did advise against showing the Reading race, if you remember."

Gowery gave him an ice lance of a look which would have slaughtered thinner-skinned men, but against Ferth's inner furnace it melted impotently.

"You agreed to say nothing," Gowery said in the same piercing undertone. "I would be obliged if you would keep to that."

Cranfield had stirred beside me in astonishment, and now, thinking about it on the following day, the venomous little exchange seemed even more incredible. What, I now wondered, had Ferth been doing there, where he didn't really belong and was clearly not appreciated?

The telephone bell broke up my thoughts. I went into the sitting room to answer it and found it was a jockey colleague, Jim Enders, ringing up to commiserate. He himself, he reminded me, had had his license suspended for a while three or four years back, and he knew how I must be feeling.

"It's good of you, Jim, to take the trouble."

"No trouble, mate. Stick together, and all that. How did it go?"

"Lousy," I said. "They didn't listen to a word either Cranfield or I said. They'd made up their minds we were guilty before we ever went there."

Jim laughed. "I'm not surprised. You know what happened to me?"

"No. What?"

"Well, when they gave me my license back, they'd called the meeting for the Tuesday, see, and then for some reason they had to postpone it until the Thursday afternoon. So along I went on Thursday afternoon, and they hemmed and hawed and warned me as to my future conduct and kept me in suspense for a bit before they said I could have my license back. Well, I thought I might as well collect a *Racing Calendar* and take it home with me, to keep abreast of the times and all that, so, anyway, I collected my *Racing Calendar,* which is published at twelve o'clock on Thursdays—twelve o'clock, mind you— and I opened it, and what is the first thing I see but the notice saying my license has been restored. So how about *that?* They'd published the result of that meeting two hours before it had even begun."

"I don't believe it," I said.

"Quite true," he said. "Mind you, that time they were giving my license back, not taking it away. But, even so, it shows they'd made up their minds. I've always wondered why they bothered to hold that second Enquiry at all. Waste of everyone's time, mate."

"It's incredible," I said. But I did believe him, which before my own Enquiry I would not have done.

"When are they giving you your license back?" Jim asked.

"They didn't say."

"Didn't they tell you when you could apply?"

"No."

Jim shoved one very rude word down the wires. "And that's another thing, mate, you want to pick your moment right when you *do* apply."

"How do you mean?"

"When I applied for mine, on the dot of when they told me I could, they said the only Steward who had authority to give it back had gone on a cruise to Madeira and I would have to wait until he turned up again."

Chapter 2

When the horses came back from second exercise at midday, my cousin Tony stomped up the stairs and trod muck and straw into my carpet. It was his stable, not Cranfield's, that I lived in. He had thirty boxes, thirty-two horses, one house, one wife, four children, and an overdraft. Ten more boxes were being built, the fifth child was four months off, and the overdraft was turning puce. I lived alone in the flat over the yard and rode everything that came along.

All very normal. And, in the three years since we had moved in, increasingly successful. My suspension meant that Tony and the owners were going to have to find another jockey.

He flopped down gloomily in a green velvet armchair.

"You all right?"

"Yes," I said.

"Give me a drink, for God's sake."

I poured half a cupful of J & B into a chunky tumbler.

"Ice?"

"As it is."

I handed him the glass and he made inroads. Restoration began to take place.

Our mothers had been Welsh girls, sisters. Mine had married a local boy, so that I had come out wholly Celt, shortish, dark, compact. My aunt had hightailed off with a six-foot-four languid blond giant from Wyoming who had endowed Tony with most of his physique and double his brain. Out of U.S.A.A.F. uniform, Tony's father had reverted to ranch hand, not ranch owner, as he had led his in-laws to believe, and he'd considered it more important for his only child to get to ride well than to acquire any of that there fancy book learning.

Tony therefore played truant for years with enthusiasm, and had never regretted it. I met him for the first time when he was twenty-five, when his Pa's heart had packed up and he had escorted his sincerely weeping Mum back to Wales. In the seven years since then, he had acquired with some speed an English wife, a semi-English accent, an unimpassioned knowledge of English racing, a job as assistant trainer, and a stable of his own. And also, somewhere along the way, an unquenchable English thirst. For Scotch.

He said, looking down at the diminished drink, "What are you going to do?"

"I don't know, exactly."

"Will you go back home?"

"Not to live," I said. "I've come too far."

He raised his head a little and looked round the room, smiling. Plain white walls, thick brown carpet, velvet chairs in two or three greens, antique furniture, pink and orange striped curtains, heavy and rich. "I'll say you have," he agreed. "A big long way from Coedlant Farm, boyo."

"No further than your prairie."

He shook his head. "I still have grass roots. You've pulled yours up."

Penetrating fellow, Tony. An extraordinary mixture of raw intelligence and straws in the hair. He was right; I'd shaken the straws out of mine. We got on very well.

"I want to talk to someone who has been to a recent Enquiry," I said abruptly.

"You want to just put it behind you and forget it," he advised. "No percentage in comparing hysterectomies."

I laughed, which was truly something in the circumstances. "Not on a pain-for-pain basis," I explained. "It's just that I want to know if what happened yesterday was . . . well, unusual. The procedure, that is. The form of the thing. Quite apart from the fact that most of the evidence was rigged."

"Is that what you were mumbling about on the way home? Those few words you uttered in a wilderness of silence?"

"Those," I said, "were mostly 'They didn't believe a word we said.' "

"So who rigged what?"

"That's the question."

He held out his empty glass and I poured some more into it.

"Are you serious?"

"Yes. Starting from point A, which is that I rode Squelch to win, we arrive at point B, which is that the Stewards are convinced I didn't. Along the way were three or four little birdies all twittering their heads off and lying in their bloody teeth."

"I detect," he said, "that something is stirring in yesterday's ruins."

"What ruins?"

"You."

"Oh."

"You should drink more," he said. "Make an effort. Start now."

"I'll think about it."

"Do that." He wallowed to his feet. "Time for lunch. Time to go back to the little nestlings with their mouths wide open for worms."

"Is it worms today?"

"God knows. Poppy said to come, if you want."

I shook my head.

"You must eat," he protested.

"Yes."

He looked at me consideringly. "I guess," he said, "that you'll manage." He put down his empty glass. "We're here, you know, if you want anything. Company. Food. Dancing girls. Trifles like that."

I nodded my thanks, and he clomped away down the stairs. He hadn't mentioned his horses, their races, or the other jockeys he would have to engage. He hadn't said that my staying in the flat would be an embarrassment to him.

I didn't know what to do about that. The flat was my home. My only home. Designed, converted, furnished by me. I liked it, and I didn't want to leave.

I wandered into the bedroom.

A double bed, but pillows for one.

On the dressing chest, in a silver frame, a photograph of Rosalind. We had been married for two years when she went to spend a routine weekend with her parents. I'd been busy riding five races at Market Rasen on the Saturday, and a policeman had come into the weighing room at the end of the afternoon and told me unemotionally that my father-in-law had set off with his wife and mine to visit friends and had misjudged his overtaking distance in heavy rain and had driven head on into a truck and killed all three of them instantly.

It was four years since it had happened. Quite often I could no longer remember her voice. Other times she seemed to be in the next room. I had loved her passionately, but she no longer hurt. Four years was a long time.

I wished she had been there, with her tempestuous nature and fierce loyalty, so that I could have told her about the Enquiry, and shared the wretchedness, and been comforted.

That Enquiry . . .

Gowery's first witness had been the jockey who had finished third in the Lemonfizz, two or three lengths behind Squelch. About twenty, round-faced and immature, Master Charlie West was a boy with a lot of natural talent but too little self-discipline. He had a great opinion of himself, and was in danger of throwing away his future through an apparent belief that rules only applied to everyone else.

The grandeur of Portman Square and the trappings of the Enquiry seemed to have subdued him. He came into the room nervously and stood where he was told, at one end of the Stewards' table—on their left, and to our right. He looked down at the table and raised his eyes only once

or twice during his whole testimony. He didn't look across
to Cranfield and me at all.

Gowery asked him if he remembered the race.

"Yes, sir." It was a low mumble, barely audible.

"Speak up," said Gowery irritably.

The shorthand writer came across from his table and
moved the microphone so that it was nearer Charlie West.
Charlie West cleared his throat.

"What happened during the race?"

"Well, sir . . . Shall I start from the beginning, sir?"

"There's no need for unnecessary detail, West," Gowery said impatiently. "Just tell us what happened on the
far side of the course on the second circuit."

"I see, sir. Well . . . Kelly, that is, I mean, Hughes,
sir . . . Hughes . . . Well . . . Like . . ."

"West, come to the point." Gowery's voice held a fine-
honed edge. A heavy flush showed in patches on Charlie
West's neck. He swallowed.

"Round the far side, sir, where the stands go out of
sight, like, for a few seconds, well, there, sir . . . Hughes
gives this hefty pull back on the reins, sir. . . ."

"And what did he say, West?"

"He said, sir, 'O.K. Brakes on, chaps.' Sir."

Gowery said meaningfully, though everyone had heard
the first time and a pin would have crashed on the Wil-
ton, "Repeat that, please, West."

"Hughes, sir, said, 'O.K. Brakes on, chaps.' "

"And what did you take him to mean by that,
West?"

"Well, sir, that he wasn't trying, like. He always says
that when he's pulling one back and not trying."

"Always?"

"Well, something like that, sir."

There was a considerable silence.

Gowery said formally, "Mr. Cranfield . . . Hughes . . .
You may ask this witness questions, if you wish."

I got slowly to my feet.

"Are you seriously saying," I asked bitterly, "that at
any time during the Lemonfizz Cup I pulled Squelch back
and said 'O.K., brakes on, chaps'?"

He nodded. He had begun to sweat.

"Please answer aloud," I said.

"Yes. You said it."

"I did not."

"I heard you."

"You couldn't have done."

"I heard you."

I was silent. I simply had no idea what to say next. It was too like a playground exchange: you did, I didn't, you did, I didn't . . .

I sat down. All the Stewards and all the officials ranked behind them were looking at me. I could see that all, to a man, believed West.

"Hughes, are you in the habit of using this phrase?" Gowery's voice was dry acid.

"No, sir."

"Have you *ever* used it?"

"Not in the Lemonfizz Cup, sir."

"I said, Hughes, have you *ever* used it?"

To lie or not to lie . . . "Yes, sir, I have used it, once or twice. But not on Squelch in the Lemonfizz Cup."

"It is sufficient that you said it at all, Hughes. We will draw our own conclusions as to *when* you said it."

He shuffled one paper to the bottom of his pack and picked up another. Consulting it with the unseeing token glance of those who know their subject by heart, he continued, "And now, West, tell us what Hughes did after he had said these words."

"Sir, he pulled his horse back, sir."

"How do you know this?" The question was a formality. He asked with the tone of one already aware of the answer.

"I was just beside Hughes, sir, when he said that about brakes. Then he sort of hunched his shoulders, sir, and give a pull, sir, and, well, then he was behind me, having dropped out, like."

Cranfield said angrily, "But he finished in front of you."

"Yes, sir." Charlie West flicked his eyes upward to Lord Gowery, and spoke only to him. "My old horse couldn't act on the going, sir, and Hughes came past me again going into the second last, like."

"And how did Squelch jump that fence?"

"Easy, sir. Met it just right. Stood back proper, sir."

"Hughes maintains that Squelch was extremely tired at that point."

Charlie West left a small pause. Finally he said, "I don't know about that, sir. I thought as how Squelch would win, myself, sir. I still think as how he ought to have won, sir, being the horse he is, sir."

Gowery glanced left and right to make sure that his colleagues had taken the point. "From your position during the last stages of the race, West, could you see whether or not Hughes was making every effort to win?"

"Well, he didn't look like it, sir, which was surprising, like."

"Surprising?"

"Yes, sir. See, Hughes is such an artist at it, sir."

"An artist at what?"

"Well, at riding what looks from the stands as one hell of a finish, sir, while all the time he's smothering it like mad."

"Hughes is in the habit of not riding to win?"

Charlie West worked it out. "Yes, sir."

"Thank you, West," Lord Gowery said with insincere politeness. "You may go and sit over there at the back of the room."

Charlie West made a rabbit's scurry toward the row of chairs reserved for those who had finished giving evidence. Cranfield turned fiercely to me and said, "Why didn't you deny it more vehemently, for God's sake? Why the hell didn't you insist he was making the whole thing up?"

"Do you think they'd believe me?"

He looked uneasily at the accusing ranks opposite, and found his answer in their implacable stares. All the same, he stood up and did his best.

"Lord Gowery, the film of the Lemonfizz Cup does not bear out West's accusation. At no point does Hughes pull back his horse."

I lifted my hand too late to stop him. Gowery's and Lord Ferth's intent faces both registered satisfaction. They knew as well as I did that what West had said was borne out on the film. Sensing that Squelch was going to run out of steam, I'd given him a short breather a mile from home, and this normal everyday little act was now wide open to misinterpretation.

Cranfield looked down at me, surprised by my reaction.

"I gave him a breather," I said apologetically. "It shows."

He sat down heavily, frowning in worry.

Gowery was saying to an official, "Show in Mr. Newtonnards," as if Cranfield hadn't spoken. There was a pause before Mr. Newtonnards, whoever he was, materialized. Lord Gowery was looking slightly over his left shoulder, toward the door, giving me the benefit of his patrician profile. I realized with almost a sense of shock that I knew nothing about him as a person, and that he most probably knew nothing about me. He had been, to me, a figure of authority with a capital A. I hadn't questioned his right to rule over me. I had assumed naïvely that he would do so with integrity, wisdom, and justice.

So much for illusions. He was leading his witnesses in a way that would make the Old Bailey reel. He heard truth in Charlie West's lies and lies in my truth. He was prosecutor as well as judge, and was only admitting evidence if it fitted his case.

He was dispersing the accepting awe I had held him in like candy floss in a thunderstorm, and I could feel an unforgiving cynicism growing in its stead. Also I was ashamed of my former state of trust. With the sort of education I'd had, I ought to have known better.

Mr. Newtonnards emerged from the waiting room and made his way to the witnesses' end of the Stewards' table, sporting a red rosebud in his lapel and carrying a large blue ledger. Unlike Charlie West, he was confident, not nervous. Seeing that everyone else was seated, he looked around for a chair for himself, and, not finding one, asked.

After a fractional pause Gowery nodded, and the
official-of-all-work near the door pushed one forward. Mr.
Newtonnards deposited into it his well-cared-for pearl-
gray-suited bulk.

"Who is he?" I said to Cranfield. Cranfield shook his
head and didn't answer, but he knew, because his air of
worry had, if anything, deepened.

Andrew Tring flipped through his pile of papers, found
what he was looking for, and drew it out. Lord Plimborne
had his eyes shut again. I was beginning to expect that;
and in any case I could see that it didn't matter, since the
power lay somewhere between Gowery and Ferth, and
Andy Tring and Plimborne were so much window dressing.

Lord Gowery, too, picked up a paper, and again I had
the impression that he knew its contents by heart.

"Mr. Newtonnards?"

"Yes, my lord." He had a faint cockney accent overlaid
by years of cigars and champagne. Mid-fifties, I guessed;
no fool, knew the world, and had friends in show business. Not too far out: Mr. Newtonnards, it transpired, was
a bookmaker.

Gowery said, "Mr. Newtonnards, will you be so good
as to tell us about a certain bet you struck on the afternoon of the Lemonfizz Cup?"

"Yes, my lord. I was standing on my pitch in Tatter-
sall's when this customer come up and asked me for five
tenners on Cherry Pie." He stopped there, as if that was
all he thought necessary.

Gowery did some prompting. "Please describe this
man, and also tell us what you did about his request."

"Describe him? Let's see, then. He was nothing special.
A biggish man in a fawn coat, wearing a brown trilby and
carrying race glasses over his shoulder. Middle-aged, I
suppose. Perhaps he had a mustache. Can't remember,
really."

The description fitted half the men on the racecourse.

"He asked me what price I'd give him about Cherry
Pie," Newtonnards went on. "I didn't have any price

chalked on my board, seeing Cherry Pie was such an outsider. I offered him tens, but he said it wasn't enough, and he looked like moving off down the line. Well"— Newtonnards waved an expressive pudgy hand— "business wasn't too brisk, so I offered him eighteen to one. Couldn't say fairer than that, now, could I, seeing as there were only eight runners in the race? Worst decision I made in a long time." Gloom mixed with stoicism settled on his well-covered features.

"So when Cherry Pie won, you paid out?"

"That's right. He put down fifty smackers. I paid him nine hundred."

"Nine hundred pounds?"

"That's right, my lord," Newtonnards confirmed easily. "Nine hundred pounds."

"And we may see the record of this bet?"

"Certainly." He opened the big blue ledger at a marked page. "On the left, my lord, just over halfway down. Marked with a red cross. Nine hundred to fifty, ticket number nine seven two."

The ledger was passed along the Stewards' table. Plimborne woke up for the occasion and all four of them peered at the page. The ledger returned to Newtonnards, who shut it and let it lie in front of him.

"Wasn't that a very large bet on an outsider?" Gowery asked.

"Yes, it was, my lord. But then, there are a lot of mugs about. Except, of course, that once in a while they go and win."

"So you had no qualms about risking such a large amount?"

"Not really, my lord. Not with Squelch in the race. And anyway, I laid a bit of it off. A quarter of it, in fact, at thirty-threes. So my actual losses were in the region of four hundred and eighty-seven pounds ten. Then I took three hundred and two ten on Squelch and the others, which left a net loss on the race of one eight five."

Cranfield and I received a glare in which every unit of the one eight five rankled.

Gowery said, "We are not enquiring into how much

you lost, Mr. Newtonnards, but into the identity of the
client who won nine hundred pounds on Cherry Pie."

I shivered. If West could lie, so could others.

"As I said in my statement, my lord, I don't know his
name. When he came up to me, I thought I knew him
from somewhere, but you see a lot of folks in my game, so
I didn't think much of it. You know. Not until I was
driving home. Then it came to me, and I went spare, I
can tell you."

"Please explain more clearly," Gowery said patiently.
The patience of a cat at a mousehole. Anticipation making the waiting sweet.

"It wasn't him so much as who I saw him talking to.
Standing by the parade-ring rails before the first race.
Don't know why I should remember it, but I do."

"And who did you see this client talking to?"

"Him." He jerked his head in our direction. "Mr.
Cranfield."

Cranfield was immediately on his feet.

"Are you suggesting that I advised this client of yours
to back Cherry Pie?" His voice shook with indignation.

"No, Mr. Cranfield," said Gowery like the North Wind.
"The suggestion is that the client was acting on your
behalf, and that it was you yourself that backed Cherry
Pie."

"That's an absolute lie."

His hot denial fell on a lot of cold ears.

"Where is this mysterious man?" he demanded. "This
unidentified, unidentifiable nobody? How can you possibly trump up such a story and present it as serious
evidence? It is ridiculous. Utterly, utterly ridiculous."

"The bet was struck," Gowery said plonkingly, pointing
to the ledger.

"And I saw you talking to the client," confirmed Newtonnards.

Cranfield's fury left him gasping for words, and in the
end he, too, sat down again, finding like me nothing to say
that could dent the preconceptions ranged against us.

"Mr. Newtonnards," I said, "would you know this
client again?"

He hesitated only a fraction. "Yes, I would."

"Have you seen him at the races since Lemonfizz day?"

"No, I haven't."

"If you see him again, will you point him out to Lord Gowery?"

"If Lord Gowery's at the races." Several of the back ranks of officials smiled at this, but Newtonnards, to give him his due, did not.

I couldn't think of anything else to ask him, and I knew I had made no headway at all. It was infuriating. By our own choice, we had thrust ourselves back into the bad old days when people accused at racing trials were not allowed a legal defendant. If they didn't know how to defend themselves, if they didn't know what sort of questions to ask or in what form to ask them, that was just too bad. Just their hard luck. But this wasn't hard luck. This was our own stupid fault. A lawyer would have been able to rip Newtonnards' testimony to bits, but neither Cranfield nor I knew how.

Cranfield tried. He was back on his feet.

"Far from backing Cherry Pie, I backed Squelch. You can check up with my own bookmaker."

Gowery simply didn't reply. Cranfield repeated it.

Gowery said, "Yes, yes. No doubt you did. It is quite beside the point."

Cranfield sat down again, with his mouth hanging open. I knew exactly how he felt. Not so much banging the head against a brick wall as being actively attacked by a cliff.

They waved Newtonnards away and he ambled easily over to take his place beside Charlie West. What he had said stayed behind him, stuck fast in the officials' minds. Not one of them had asked for corroboration. Not one had suggested that there might have been a loophole in identity. The belief was written plain on their faces: if someone had backed Cherry Pie to win nine hundred pounds, it must have been Cranfield.

Gowery hadn't finished. With calm satisfaction, he picked up another paper and said, "Mr. Cranfield, I have here an affidavit from a Mrs. Joan Jones, who handled

the five-pound selling window on the Totalisator in the
paddock on Lemonfizz Cup day, that she sold ten win-
only tickets for horse number eight to a man in a fawn
raincoat, middle-aged, wearing a trilby. I also have here a
similar testimony from a Mr. Leonard Roberts, who was
paying out at the five-pound window in the same building, on the same occasion. Both of these Tote employees
remember the cient well, as these were almost the only
five-pound tickets sold on Cherry Pie, and certainly the
only large block. The Tote paid out to this man more than
eleven hundred pounds in cash. Mr. Roberts advised him
not to carry so much on his person, but the man declined
to take his advice."

There was another accusing silence. Cranfield looked
totally nonplused and came up with nothing to say. This
time, I tried for him. "Sir, did this man back any other
horses in the race, on the Tote? Did he back all, or two
or three or four, and just hit the jackpot by accident?"

"There was no accident about this, Hughes."

"But did he, in fact, back any other horses?"

Dead silence.

"Surely you asked?" I said reasonably.

Whether anyone had asked or not, Gowery didn't
know. All he knew was what was on the affidavit. He
gave me a stony stare and said, "No one puts fifty pounds
on an outsider without good grounds for believing it will
win."

"But, sir . . ."

"However," he said, "we will find out." He wrote a
note on the bottom of one of the affidavits. "It seems to
me extremely unlikely. But we will have the question
asked."

There was no suggestion that he would wait for the
answer before giving his judgment. And in fact he did
not.

Chapter 3

I wandered aimlessly round the flat, lost and restless. Reheated the coffee. Drank it. Tried to write to my parents, and gave it up after half a page. Tried to make some sort of decision about my future, and couldn't.

Felt too battered. Too pulped. Too crushed.

Yet I had done nothing.

Nothing.

Late afternoon. The lads were bustling round the yard setting the horses fair for the night, and whistling and calling to each other as usual. I kept away from the windows and eventually went back to the bedroom and lay down on the bed. The day began to fade. The dusk closed in.

After Newtonnards they had called Tommy Timpson, who had ridden Cherry Pie.

Tommy Timpson "did his two" for Cranfield and rode such of the stable's second strings as Cranfield cared to give him. Cranfield rang the changes on three jockeys: me, Chris Smith (at present taking his time over a fractured skull), and Tommy. Tommy got the crumbs and deserved better. Like many trainers, Cranfield couldn't spot talent when it was under his nose, and it wasn't until several small local trainers had asked for his services that Cranfield woke up to the fact that he had a useful emerging rider in his own yard.

Raw, nineteen years old, a stutterer, Tommy was at his worst at the Enquiry. He looked as scared as a two-year-old colt at his first starting gate, and although he couldn't help being jittery it was worse than useless for Cranfield and me.

Lord Gowery made no attempt to put him at ease but simply asked questions and let him get on with the answers as best he could.

"What orders did Mr. Cranfield give you before the race? How did he tell you to ride Cherry Pie? Did he instruct you to ride to win?"

Tommy stuttered and stumbled and said Mr. Cranfield had told him to keep just behind Squelch all the way round and try to pass him after the last fence.

Cranfield said indignantly, "That's what he *did*. Not what I told him to do."

Gowery listened, turned his head to Tommy, and said again, "Will you tell us what instructions Mr. Cranfield gave you *before* the race? Please think carefully."

Tommy swallowed, gave Cranfield an agonized glance, and tried again. "M-m-m-Mr. Cranfield s-s-said to take my p-p-pace from S-s-Squelch and s-s-stay with him as long as I c-c-could."

"And did he tell you to win?"

"He s-s-said of course g-g-go on and w-w-win if you c-c-can, sir."

These were impeccable instructions. Only the most suspicious or biased mind could have read any villainy into them. If these Stewards' minds were not suspicious and biased, snow would fall in the Sahara.

"Did you hear Mr. Cranfield giving Hughes instructions as to how he should ride Squelch?"

"N-no, sir. M-Mr. Cranfield did-didn't g-give Hughes any orders at all, sir."

"Why not?"

Tommy ducked it and said he didn't know. Cranfield remarked furiously that Hughes had ridden the horse twenty times and knew what was needed.

"Or you had discussed it with him privately, beforehand?"

Cranfield had no explosive answer to that, because of course we *had* discussed it beforehand. In general terms. In an assessment of the opposition. As a matter of general strategy.

"I discussed the race with him, yes. But I gave him no specific orders."

"So, according to you," Lord Gowery said, "you intended both of your jockeys to try to win?"

"Yes. I did. My horses are always doing their best."

Gowery shook his head. "Your statement is not borne out by the facts."

"Are you calling me a liar?" Cranfield demanded.

Gowery didn't answer. But, yes, he was.

They shooed a willing Tommy Timpson away and Cranfield went on simmering at boiling point beside me. For myself, I was growing cold, and no amount of central heating could stop it. I thought we must now have heard everything, but I was wrong. They had saved the worst until last, building up the pyramid of damning statements until they could put the final cap on it and stand back and admire their foursquare structure, their solid, unanswerable edifice of guilt.

The worst, at first, had looked so harmless. A quiet slender man in his early thirties, endowed with an utterly forgettable face. After twenty-four hours I couldn't recall his features or remember his voice, and yet I couldn't think about him without shaking with sick impotent fury.

His name was David Oakley. His business, enquiry agent. His address, Birmingham.

He stood without fidgeting at the end of the Stewards' table, holding a spiral-bound notebook which he consulted continually, and from beginning to end not a shade of emotion affected his face or his behavior or even his eyes.

"Acting upon instructions, I paid a visit to the flat of Kelly Hughes, jockey, of Corrie House training stables, Corrie, Berkshire, two days after the Lemonfizz Crystal Cup."

I sat up with a jerk and opened my mouth to deny it, but before I could say a word he went smoothly on.

"Mr. Hughes was not there, but the door was open, so I went in to wait for him. While I was there, I made certain observations." He paused.

Cranfield said to me, "What is all this about?"

"I don't know. I've never seen him before."

Gowery steamrollered on. "You found certain objects."

"Yes, my lord."

Gowery sorted out three large envelopes, and passed one each to Tring and Plimborne. Ferth was ahead of them. He had removed the contents from a similar envelope as soon as Oakley had appeared, and was now, I saw, watching me with what I took to be contempt.

The envelopes each held a photograph.

Oakley said, "The photograph is of objects I found on a chest of drawers in Hughes's bedroom."

Andy Tring looked, looked again, and raised a horrified face, meeting my eyes accidentally and for the first and only time. He glanced away hurriedly, embarrassed and disgusted.

"I want to see that photograph," I said hoarsely.

"Certainly." Lord Gowery turned his copy round and pushed it across the table. I got up, walked the three dividing steps, and looked down at it.

For several seconds I couldn't take it in, and when I did, I was breathless with disbelief. The photograph had been taken from above the dressing chest, and was sparkling clear. There was the edge of the silver frame and half of Rosalind's face, and from under the frame, as if it had been used as a paperweight, protruded a sheet of paper dated the day after the Lemonfizz Cup. There were three words written on it, and two initials.

"As agreed. Thanks. D.C."

Slanted across the bottom of the paper, and spread out like a pack of cards, were a large number of ten-pound notes.

I looked up, and met Lord Gowery's eyes, and almost flinched away from the utter certainty I read there.

"It's a fake," I said. My voice sounded odd. "It's a complete fake."

"What is it?" Cranfield said from behind me, and in his voice, too, everyone could hear the awareness of disaster.

I picked up the photograph and took it across to him,

and I couldn't feel my feet on the carpet. When he had grasped what it meant, he stood up slowly and in a low biting voice said formally, "My lords, if you believe this, you will believe anything."

It had not the slightest effect.

Gowery said merely, "That is your handwriting, I believe."

Cranfield shook his head. "I didn't write it."

"Please be so good as to write those exact words on this sheet of paper." Gowery pushed a plain piece of paper across the table, and after a second Cranfield went across and wrote on it. Everyone knew that the two samples would look the same, and they did. Gowery passed the sheet of paper significantly to the other Stewards, and they all compared and nodded.

"It's a fake," I said again. "I never had a letter like that."

Gowery ignored me. To Oakley he said, "Please tell us where you found the money."

Oakley unnecessarily consulted his notebook. "The money was folded inside this note, fastened with a rubber band, and both were tucked behind the photo of Hughes's girl friend, which you see in the picture."

"It's not true," I said. I might as well not have bothered. No one listened.

"You counted the money, I believe?"

"Yes, my lord. There were five hundred pounds."

"There was no money," I protested. Useless. "And anyway," I added desperately, "why would I take five hundred for losing the race when I would get about as much as that for winning?"

I thought for a moment that I might have scored a hit. Might have made them pause. A pipe dream. There was an answer to that, too.

"We understand from Mr. Jessel, Squelch's owner," Gowery said flatly, "that he pays you ten percent of the winning stake money through official channels by check. This means that all presents received by you from Mr. Jessel are taxed, and we understand that as you pay a high rate of tax your ten percent from Mr. Jessel would have in effect amounted to half, or less than half, of five hundred pounds."

They seemed to have enquired into my affairs down to the last penny. Dug around in all directions. Certainly I had never tried to hide anything, but this behind-my-back can opening made me feel naked. Also revolted. Also, finally, hopeless. And it wasn't until then that I realized I had been subconsciously clinging to a fairy-tale faith that it would all finally come all right, that because I was telling the truth I was bound to be believed in the end.

I stared across at Lord Gowery, and he looked briefly back. His face was expressionless, his manner entirely calm. He had reached his conclusions and nothing could overthrow them.

Lord Ferth, beside him, was less bolted down, but a great deal of his earlier heat seemed to have evaporated. The power he had generated no longer troubled Gowery at all, and all I could interpret from his expression was some kind of resigned acceptance.

There was little left to be said. Lord Gowery briefly summed up the evidence against us. The list of former races. The nonuse of the whip. The testimony of Charlie West. The bets struck on Cherry Pie. The riding orders given in private. The photographic proof of a payoff from Cranfield to Hughes.

"There can be no doubt that this was a most flagrant fraud on the racing public. . . . No alternative but to suspend your licenses. . . . And you, Dexter Cranfield, and you, Kelly Hughes, will be warned off Newmarket Heath until further notice."

Cranfield, pale and shaking, said, "I protest that this has not been a fair hearing. Neither Hughes nor I are guilty. The sentence is outrageous."

No response from Lord Gowery. Lord Ferth, however, spoke for the second time in the proceedings.

"Hughes?"

"I rode Squelch to win," I said. "The witnesses were lying."

Gowery shook his head impatiently. "The Enquiry is closed. You may go."

Cranfield and I both hesitated, still unable to accept that that was all. But the official near the door opened it, and all the ranks opposite began to talk quietly among themselves and to ignore us, and in the end we walked out. Stiff-legged. Feeling as if my head were a floating football and my body a chunk of ice. Unreal.

There were several people in the waiting room outside, but I didn't see them clearly. Cranfield, tight-lipped, strode away from me, straight across the room and out the far door, shaking off a hand or two laid on his sleeve. Dazed, I started to follow him, but was less purposeful, and was effectively stopped by a large man who planted himself in my way.

I looked at him vaguely. Mr. Jessel. The owner of Squelch.

"Well?" he said challengingly.

"They didn't believe us. We've both been warned off."

He hissed a sharp breath out between his teeth. "After what I've been hearing, I'm not surprised. And I'll tell you this, Hughes, even if you get your license back, you won't be riding for me again."

I looked at him blankly and didn't answer. It seemed a small thing after what had already happened. He had been talking to the witnesses in the waiting room. They would convince anyone, it seemed. Some owners were unpredictable anyway, even in normal times. One day they had all the faith in the world in their jockey, and the next day none at all. Faith with slender foundations. Mr. Jessel had forgotten all the races I had won for him because of the one I had lost.

I turned blindly away from his hostility and found a more welcome hand on my arm. Tony, who had driven up with me instead of seeing his horses work.

"Come on," he said. "Let's get out of here."

I nodded and went down with him in the lift, out into the hall, and toward the front door. Outside the door we could see a bunch of newspaper reporters waylaying Cranfield with their notebooks at the ready, and I stopped dead at the sight.

"Let's wait till they've gone," I said.

"They won't go. Not before they've chewed you up, too."

We waited, hesitating, and a voice called behind me, "Hughes."

I didn't turn round. I felt I owed no one the slightest politeness. The footsteps came up behind me and he finally came to a halt in front.

Lord Ferth. Looking tired.

"Hughes. Tell me. Why in God's name did you do it?"

I looked at him stonily.

"I didn't."

He shook his head. "All the evidence—"

"You tell me," I said rudely, "why decent men like Stewards so easily believe a lot of lies."

I turned away from him, too. Twitched my head at Tony and made for the front door. To hell with the press. To hell with the Stewards and Mr. Jessel. And to everything to do with racing. The upsurge of fury took me out of the building and fifty yards along the pavement in Portman Square, and only evaporated into grinding misery when we had climbed into the taxi Tony whistled for.

Tony thumped up the stairs to the darkened flat. I heard him calling.

"Are you there, Kelly?"

I unrolled myself from the bed, stood up, stretched, went out into the sitting room, and switched on the lights. He was standing in the far doorway, blinking, his hands full of tray.

"Poppy insisted," he explained.

He put the tray down on the table and lifted off the covering cloth. She'd sent hot chicken pie, a tomato, and about half a pound of Brie.

"She says you haven't eaten for two days."

"I suppose not."

"Get on with it, then." He made an instinctive line for

the whisky bottle and poured generously into two tumblers.

"And here. For once, drink this."

I took the glass and a mouthful, and felt the fire trickle down inside my chest. The first taste was always the best. Tony tossed his off and ordered himself a refill.

I ate the pie, the tomato, and the cheese. Hunger I hadn't consciously felt rolled contentedly over and slept.

"You can stay a bit?" I asked.

"Natch."

"I'd like to tell you about the Enquiry."

"Shoot," he said with satisfaction. "I've been waiting."

I told him all that had happened, almost word for word. Every detail had been cut sharply into my memory in the way that only happens in disasters.

Tony's astonishment was plain. "You were framed!"

"That's right."

"But surely no one can get away with that?"

"Someone seems to be doing all right."

"But was there *nothing* you could say to prove—"

"I couldn't think of anything yesterday, which is all that matters. It's always easy to think of all the smart clever things one *could* have said, afterward, when it's too late."

"What would you have said, then?"

"I suppose for a start I should have asked who had given that so-called enquiry agent instructions to search my flat. Acting on instructions, he said. Well, *whose* instructions? I didn't think of asking yesterday. Now I can see that it could be the whole answer."

"You assumed the Stewards had instructed him?"

"I suppose so. I didn't really think. Most of the time, I was so shattered that I couldn't think clearly at all."

"Maybe it *was* the Stewards."

"Well, no. I suppose it's barely possible they might have sent an investigator, though when you look at it in cold blood it wouldn't really seem likely, but it's a teardrop to the Atlantic that they wouldn't have supplied him with five hundred quid and a forged note and told him to photograph them somewhere distinctive in my flat. But that's what he did. So who instructed him?"

"Even if you'd asked, he wouldn't have said."

"I guess not. But at least it might have made the Stewards think a bit, too."

Tony shook his head. "He would still have said he found the money behind Rosalind's picture. His word against yours. Nothing different."

He looked gloomily into his glass. I looked gloomily into mine.

"That bloody little Charlie West," I said. "Someone got at him, too."

"I presume you didn't in fact say, 'Brakes on, chaps'?"

"I did say it, you see. Not in the Lemonfizz, of course, but a couple of weeks before, in that frightful novice chase at Oxford, the day they abandoned the last two races because it was snowing. I was hitting every fence on that deadly bad jumper that old Almond hadn't bothered to school properly, and half the other runners were just as green, and a whole bunch of us had got left about twenty lengths behind the four who were any use, and sleet was falling, and I didn't relish ending up with a broken bone at naught degrees centigrade, so as we were handily out of sight of the stands at that point I shouted, 'O.K., brakes on, chaps,' and a whole lot of us eased up thankfully and finished the race a good deal slower than we could have done. It didn't affect the result, of course. But there you are. I did say it. What's more, Charlie West heard me. He just shifted it from one race to another."

"The bastard."

"I agree."

"Maybe no one got at him. Maybe he just thought he'd get a few more rides if you were out of the way."

I considered it and shook my head. "I wouldn't have thought he was *that* much of a bastard."

"You never know." Tony finished his drink and absent-mindedly replaced it. "What about the bookmaker?"

"Newtonnards? I don't know. Same thing, I suppose.

Someone has it in for Cranfield, too. Both of us, it was. The Stewards couldn't possibly have warned off one of us without the other. We were knitted together so neatly."

"It makes me livid," Tony said violently. "It's wicked."

I nodded. "There was something else, too, about that Enquiry. Some undercurrent, running strong. At least, it was strong at the beginning. Something between Lord Gowery and Lord Ferth. And then Andy Tring, he was sitting there looking like a wilted lettuce." I shook my head in puzzlement. "It was like a couple of heavy animals lurking in the undergrowth, shaping up to fight each other. You couldn't see them, but there was a sort of quiver in the air. At least, that's how it seemed at one point. . . ."

"Stewards are men," Tony said with bubble-bursting matter-of-factness. "Show me any organization which doesn't have some sort of power struggle going on under its gentlemanly surface. All you caught was a whiff of the old brimstone. State of nature. Nothing to do with whether you and Cranfield were guilty or not."

He half convinced me. He polished off the rest of the whisky and told me not to forget to get some more.

Money. That was another thing. As of yesterday, I had no income. The Welfare State didn't pay unemployment benefits to the self-employed, as all jockeys remembered every snow-bound winter.

"I'm going to find out," I said abruptly.

"Find out what?"

"Who framed us."

"Up the Marines," Tony said unsteadily. "Over the top, boys. Up and at 'em." He picked up the empty bottle and looked at it regretfully. "Time for bed, I guess. If you need any help with the campaign, count on my Welsh blood to the last clot."

He made an unswerving line to the door, turned, and gave me a grimace of friendship worth having.

"Don't fall down the stairs," I said.

Part Two

MARCH

Chapter 4

Roberta Cranfield looked magnificent in my sitting room. I came back from buying whisky in the village and found her gracefully draped all over my restored Chippendale. The green velvet supported a lot of leg and a deep-purple size eight wool dress, and her thick long hair, the color of dead beech leaves, clashed dramatically with the curtains. She had white skin, incredible eyebrows, amber eyes, photogenic cheekbones, and a petulant mouth.

She was nineteen, and I didn't like her.

"Good morning," I said.

"Your door was open."

"It's a habit I'll have to break."

I peeled the tissue wrapping off the bottle and put it with the two chunky glasses on the small silver tray I had once won in a race sponsored by some candy manufacturers. Troy weight, twenty-four ounces; but ruined by the inscription L. HUGHES, WINNING JOCKEY, STARCHOCS SILVER STEEPLECHASE. Starchocs indeed. And I never ate chocolates. Couldn't afford to, from the weight point of view.

She flapped her hand from a relaxed wrist, indicating the room.

"This is all pretty lush."

I wondered what she had come for. I said, "Would you like some coffee?"

"Coffee and cannabis."

"You'll have to go somewhere else."

"You're very prickly."

"As a cactus," I agreed.

47

She gave me a half-minute unblinking stare with her liquid eyes. Then she said, "I only said cannabis to jolt you."

"I'm not jolted."

"No. I can see that. Waste of effort."

"Coffee, then?"

"Yes."

I went into the kitchen and fixed up the percolator. The kitchen was white and brown and copper and yellow. The colors pleased me. Colors gave me the sort of mental food I imagined others got from music. I disliked too much music, loathed the type of stuff you couldn't escape in restaurants and airliners, didn't own a record player, and much preferred silence.

She followed me in from the sitting room and looked around her with mild surprise.

"Do all jockeys live like this?"

"Naturally."

"I don't believe it."

She peered into the pine-fronted cupboard I'd taken the coffee from.

"Do you cook for yourself?"

"Mostly."

"Recherché things like shashlik?" An undercurrent of mockery.

"Steaks."

I poured the bubbling coffee into two mugs and offered her cream and sugar. She took the cream, generously, but not the sugar, and perched on a yellow-topped stool. Her copper hair fitted the kitchen, too.

"You seem to be taking it all right," she said.

"What?"

"Being warned off."

I didn't answer.

"A cactus," she said, "isn't in the same class."

She drank the coffee slowly, in separate mouthfuls, watching me thoughtfully over the mug's rim. I watched her back. Nearly my height, utterly self-possessed, as cool as the stratosphere. I had seen her grow from a demanding child into a selfish fourteen-year-old, and from there into a difficult-to-please débutante and from there to a glossy imitation model girl heavily tinged with boredom. Over the eight years I had ridden for her father, we had met briefly and spoken seldom, usually in parade rings and outside the weighing room, and on the occasions when she did speak to me she seemed to be aiming just over the top of my head.

"You're making it difficult," she said.

"For you to say why you came?"

She nodded. "I thought I knew you. Now it seems I don't."

"What did you expect?"

"Well . . . Father said you came from a farm cottage with pigs running in and out of the door."

"Father exaggerates."

She lifted her chin to ward off the familiarity, a gesture I'd seen a hundred times in her and her brothers. A gesture copied from her parents.

"Hens," I said. "Not pigs."

She gave me an upstage stare. I smiled at her faintly and refused to be reduced to the ranks. I watched the wheels tick over while she worked out how to approach a cactus, and gradually the chin came down.

"Actual hens?"

Not bad at all. I could feel my own smile grow genuine.

"Now and then."

"You don't look like . . . I mean . . ."

"I know exactly what you mean," I agreed. "And it's high time you got rid of those chains."

"Chains? What are you talking about?"

"The fetters in your mind. The iron bars in your soul."

"My mind is all right."

"You must be joking. It's chock-a-block with ideas half a century out of date."

"I didn't come here to——" she began explosively, and then stopped.

"You didn't come here to be insulted," I said ironically.

"Well, as you put it in that well-worn hackneyed phrase, no, I didn't. But I wasn't going to say that."

"What did you come for?"

She hesitated. "I wanted you to help me."

"To do what?"

"To—to *cope* with Father."

I was surprised, first that Father needed coping with, and second that she needed help to do it.

"What sort of help?"

"He's—he's so *shattered*." Unexpectedly there were tears standing in her eyes. They embarrassed and angered her, and she blinked furiously so that I shouldn't see. I admired the tears but not her reason for trying to hide them.

"Here are you," she said in a rush, "walking about as cool as you please and buying whisky and making coffee as if no screaming avalanche had poured down on you and smothered your life and made every thought an absolute bloody hell, and maybe you don't understand how anyone in that state needs help, and, come to that, I don't understand why *you* don't need help, but anyway Father *does*."

"Not from me," I said mildly. "He doesn't think enough of me to give it any value."

She opened her mouth angrily and shut it again and took two deep controlling breaths. "And it looks as though he's right."

"Ouch," I said ruefully. "What sort of help, then?"

"I want you to come and talk to him."

My talking to Cranfield seemed likely to be as therapeutic as applying itching powder to a baby. However, she hadn't left me much room for kidding myself that fruitlessness was a good reason for not trying.

"When?"

"Now. . . . Unless you have anything else to do."

"No," I said carefully. "I haven't."

She made a face and an odd little gesture with her hands. "Will you come now, then . . . please?"

She herself seemed surprised about the real supplication in that "please." I imagined that she had come expecting to instruct, not to ask.

"All right."

"Great." She was suddenly very cool, very employer's daughter again. She put her coffee mug on the drainboard and started toward the door. "You had better follow me in your car. It's no good me taking you; you'll need your own car to come back in."

"That is so," I agreed.

She looked at me suspiciously, but decided not to pursue it. "My coat is in your bedroom."

"I'll fetch it for you."

"Thank you."

I walked across the sitting room and into the bedroom. Her coat was lying on my bed in a heap. Black and white fur, in stripes going round. I picked it up and turned, and found she had followed me.

"Thank you so much." She presented her back to me and put her arms in the coat-putting-on position. On went the coat. She swiveled slowly, buttoning up the front with shiny black saucers. "This flat really is fantastic. Who is your decorator?"

"Chap called Kelly Hughes."

She raised her eyebrows. "I know the professional touch when I see it."

"Thank you."

She raised the chin. "Oh, well, if you won't say . . ."

"I would say. I did say. I did the flat myself. I've been whitewashing pigsties since I was six."

She wasn't quite sure whether to be amused or offended, and evaded it by changing the subject.

"That picture . . . that's your wife, isn't it?"

I nodded.

"I remember her," she said. "She was always so sweet to me. She seemed to know what I was feeling. I was really awfully sorry when she was killed."

I looked at her in surprise. The people Rosalind had been sweetest to had invariably been unhappy. She had had a knack of sensing it, and of giving succor without being asked. I would not have thought of Roberta Cranfield as being unhappy, though I supposed from twelve to fifteen, when she had known Rosalind, she could have had her troubles.

"She wasn't bad, as wives go," I said flippantly, and Miss Cranfield disapproved of that, too.

We left the flat and this time I locked the door, though such horses as I'd had had already bolted. Roberta had parked her Sunbeam Alpine behind the stables and across the doors of the garage where I kept my Lotus. She backed and turned her car with aggressive poise, and I left a leisurely interval before I followed her through the gates, to avoid a competition all the eighteen miles to her home.

Cranfield lived in an early-Victorian house in a hamlet four miles out of Lambourn. A country gentleman's residence, real-estate agents would have called it: built before the Industrial Revolution had invaded Berkshire and equally impervious to the social revolution a hundred years later. Elegant, charming, timeless, it was a house I liked very much. Pity about the occupants.

I drove up the back drive, as usual, and parked alongside the stable yard. A horse box was standing there with its ramp down, and one of the lads was leading a horse into it. Archie, the head lad, who had been helping, came across as soon as I climbed out of the car.

"This is a God-awful bloody business," he said. "It's wicked, that's what it is. Downright bloody wicked."

"The horses are going?"

"Some owners have sent boxes already. All of them will be gone by the day after tomorrow." His weather-beaten face was a mixture of fury, frustration, and anxiety. "All the lads have got the sack. Even me. And the missus and I have just taken a mortgage on one of the new houses up the road. Chalet bungalow, just what she'd always set her heart on. Worked for years, she has, saving for it. Now she won't stop crying. We moved in only a month ago, see? How do you think we're going to keep up the payments? Took every pound we had, what with the deposit and the solicitors, and curtains and all. Nice little place, too, she's got it looking real nice. And it isn't as if

the Guvnor really fiddled the blasted race. That Cherry
Pie, anyone could see with half an eye he was going to be
good someday. I mean, if the Guvnor had done it, like,
somehow all this wouldn't be so bad. I mean, if he
deserved it, well, serve him right, and I'd try and get a bit
of compensation from him because we're going to have a
right job selling the house again, I'll tell you, because
there's still two of them empty, they weren't so easy to
sell in the first place, being so far out of Lambourn. . . .
I'll tell you straight, I wish to God we'd never moved out
of the Guvnor's cottage, dark and damp though it may be.
. . . George," he suddenly shouted at a lad swearing and
tugging at a reluctant animal, "don't take it out on the
horse, it isn't *his* fault. . . ." He bustled across the yard
and took the horse himself, immediately quietening it and
leading it without trouble into the horse box.

He was an excellent head lad, better than most, and a
lot of Cranfield's success was his doing. If he sold his
house and got settled in another job, Cranfield wouldn't
get him back. The training license might not be lost
forever, but the stable's main prop would be.

I watched another lad lead a horse round to the waiting
box. He, too, looked worried. His wife, I knew, was on
the point of producing their first child.

Some of the lads wouldn't care, of course. There were
plenty of jobs going in racing stables, and one lot of digs
was much the same as another. But they, too, would not
come back. Nor would most of the horses, or many of the
owners. The stable wasn't being suspended for a few
months. It was being smashed.

Sick and seething with other people's fury as well as my
own, I walked down the short stretch of drive to the
house. Roberta's Alpine was parked outside the front door
and she was standing beside it looking cross.

"So there you are. I thought you'd ratted."

"I parked down by the yard."

"I can't bear to go down there. Nor can Father. In fact,
he won't move out of his dressing room. You'll have to
come upstairs to see him."

She led the way through the front door and across

thirty square yards of Persian rug. When we had reached the foot of the stairs, the door of the library was flung open and Mrs. Cranfield came through it. Mrs. Cranfield always flung doors open, rather as if she suspected something reprehensible was going on behind them and she was intent on catching the sinners in the act. She was a plain woman who wore no make-up and dressed in droopy woolies. To me she had never talked about anything except horses, and I didn't know whether she could. Her father was an Irish baron, which may have accounted for the marriage.

"My father-in-law, Lord Coolihan," Cranfield was wont to say; and he was wont to say it far too often. I wondered whether, after Gowery, he was the tiniest bit discontented with the aristocracy.

"Ah, there you are, Hughes," Mrs. Cranfield said. "Roberta told me she was going to fetch you. Though what good you can do I cannot understand. After all, it was you who got us into the mess."

"I what?"

"If you'd ridden a better race on Squelch, none of this would have happened."

I bit back six answers and said nothing. If you were hurt enough, you lashed out at the nearest object. Mrs. Cranfield continued to lash.

"Dexter was thoroughly shocked to hear that you had been in the habit of deliberately losing races."

"So was I," I said dryly.

Roberta moved impatiently. "Mother, do stop it. Come along, Hughes. This way."

I didn't move. She went up three steps, paused, and looked back. "Come on, what are you waiting for?"

I shrugged. Whatever I was waiting for, I wouldn't get it in that house. I followed her up the stairs, along a wide passage, and into her father's dressing room.

There was too much heavy mahogany furniture of a later period than the house, a faded plum-colored carpet, faded plum plush curtains, and a bed with an Indian cover.

On one side of the bed sat Dexter Cranfield, his back

bent into a bow and his shoulders hunched round his ears. His hands rolled loosely on his knees, fingers curling, and he was staring immovably at the floor.

"He sits like that for hours," Roberta said, on a breath beside me. And, looking at him, I understood why she had needed help.

"Father," she said, going over and touching his shoulder. "Kelly Hughes is here."

Cranfield said, "Tell him to go and shoot himself."

She saw the twitch in my face and, from her expression, thought that I minded, that I believed Cranfield, too, thought me the cause of all his troubles. On the whole, I decided not to crystallize her fears by saying I thought Cranfield had said shoot because shoot was in his mind.

"Hop it," I said, and jerked my head toward the door.

The chin went up like a reflex. Then she looked at the husk of her father, and back to me, whom she'd been to some trouble to bring, and most of the starch dissolved.

"All right. I'll be down in the library. Don't go without . . . telling me."

I shook my head, and she went composedly out of the room, shutting the door behind her.

I walked to the window and looked at the view. Small fields trickling down into the valley. Trees all bent one way by the wind off the Downs. A row of pylons, a cluster of council-house roofs. Not a horse in sight. The dressing room was on the opposite side of the house to the stables.

"Have you a gun?" I asked.

No answer from the bed. I went over and sat down beside him. "Where is it?"

His eyes slid a fraction in my direction and then back. He had been looking past me. I got up and went to the table beside his bed, but there was nothing lethal on it, and nothing in the drawer.

I found it behind the high mahogany bed head. A finely wrought Purdy more suitable for pheasants. Both barrels were loaded. I unloaded them.

"Very messy," I remarked. "Very inconsiderate. And anyway, you didn't mean to do it."

I wasn't at all sure about that, but there was no harm in trying to convince him.

"What are you doing here?" he said indifferently.

"Telling you to snap out of it. There's work to be done."

"Don't speak to me like that."

"How, then?"

His head came up a little, just like Roberta's. If I made him angry, he'd be halfway back to his normal self. And I could go home.

"It's useless sitting up here sulking. It won't achieve anything at all."

"*Sulking?*" He was annoyed, but not enough.

"Someone took our toys away. Very unfair. But nothing to be gained by grizzling in corners.'"

"*Toys* . . . You're talking nonsense."

"Toys, licenses, what's the difference. The things we prized most. Someone's snatched them away. Tricked us out of them. And nobody except us can get them back. Nobody else will bother."

"We can apply," he said without conviction.

"Oh, we can apply. In six months' time, I suppose. But there's no guarantee we'd get them. The only sensible thing to do is to start fighting back right now and find out who fixed us. Who, and why. And after that I'll wring his bloody neck."

He was still staring at the floor, still hunched. He couldn't even look me in the face yet, let alone the world. If he hadn't been such a climbing snob, I thought uncharitably, his present troubles wouldn't have produced such a complete cave-in. He was on the verge of literally not being able to bear the public disgrace of being warned off.

Well, I wasn't so sure I much cared for it myself. It was all very well knowing that one was not guilty, and even having one's closest friends believe it, but one could hardly walk around everywhere wearing a notice proclaiming,

"I am innocent. I never done it. It were all a stinking frame-up."

"It's not so bad for you," he said.

"That's perfectly true." I paused. "I came in through the yard."

He made a low sound of protest.

"Archie seems to be seeing to everything himself. And he's worried about his house."

Cranfield made a waving movement of his hand as much as to ask how did I think he could be bothered with Archie's problems on top of his own.

"It wouldn't hurt you to pay Archie's mortgage for a bit."

"*What?*" That finally reached him. His head came up at least six inches.

"It's only a few pounds a week. Peanuts to you. Life or death to him. And if you lose him, you'll never get so many winners again."

"You—you—" He spluttered. But he still didn't look up.

"A trainer is as good as his lads."

"That's stupid."

"You've got good lads just now. You've chucked out the duds, the rough and lazy ones. It takes time to weed out and build up a good team, but you can't get a high ratio of winners without one. You might get your license back but you won't get these lads back, and it'll take years for the stable to recover. If it ever does. And I hear you have already given them all the sack."

"What else was there to do?"

"You could try keeping them on for a month."

His head came up a little more. "You haven't the slightest idea what that would cost me. The wages come to more than four hundred pounds a week."

"There must still be quite a lot to come in in training fees. Owners seldom pay in advance. You won't have to dig very deep into your own pocket. Not for a month, anyway, and it might not take as long as that."

"What might not?"

"Getting our licenses back."

"Don't be so bloody ridiculous."

"I mean it. What is it worth to you? Four weeks' wages for your lads? Would you pay that much if there was a chance you'd be back in racing in a month? The owners would send their horses back if it was as quick as that. Particularly if you tell them you confidently expect to be back in business almost immediately."

"They wouldn't believe it."

"They'd be uncertain. That should be enough."

"There isn't a chance of getting back."

"Oh, yes, there damn well is," I said forcefully. "But only if you're willing to take it. Tell the lads you're keeping them on for a bit. Especially Archie. Go down to the yard and tell them now."

"Now."

"Of course," I said impatiently. "Probably half of them have already read the 'Situations Vacant' columns and written to other trainers."

"There isn't any point." He seemed sunk in fresh gloom. "It's all hopeless. And it couldn't have happened— it simply could *not* have happened—at a worse time. Edwin Byler was going to send me his horses. It was all fixed up. Now, of course, he's telephoned to say it's all off, his horses are staying where they are, at Jack Roxford's."

To train Edwin Byler's horses was to be presented with a pot of gold. He was a North Country businessman who had made a million or two out of mail order, and had used a little of it to fulfill a long-held ambition to own the best string of steeplechasers in Britain. Four of his present horses had in turn cost more than anyone had paid before. When he wanted, he bid. He only wanted the best, and he had bought enough of them to put him for the two previous seasons at the top of the Winning Owners' list. His string had grown from the beginning at Jack Roxford's, but I could understand that he was ready now for a change of trainer. Roxford had shown himself able enough, but was a nervy anxious sort of man, with flickering eyelids and an overplacatory manner. Stewards were unlikely to choose him for a personal friend. Byler was ready for a little ladder climbing, and Roxford would be no help at all. From Cranfield's point of view, I could see that to have been going to train Edwin Byler's horses, and now not to be going to, was a refined cruelty to pile on top of everything else.

To have been going to *ride* Edwin Byler's horses, as I would no doubt have done—that, too, was a thrust where it hurt.

"There's all the more point, then," I said. "What more do you want in the way of incentive? You're throwing away without a struggle not only what you've got but what you might have. . . . Why in the hell don't you get off your bed and behave like a gentleman and show some spirit?"

"Hughes!" He was outraged. But he still sat. He still wouldn't look at me.

I paused, considering him. Then, slowly, I said, "All right, then. I'll tell you why you won't. You won't because . . . to some degree . . . you are in fact guilty. You made sure Squelch wouldn't win. And you backed Cherry Pie."

That got him. Not just his head up, but up, trembling, onto his feet.

Chapter 5

"How dare you?"

"Frankly, just now I'd dare practically anything."

"You said we were framed."

"So we were."

Some of his alarm subsided. I stoked it up again.

"You handed us away on a plate."

He swallowed, his eyes flicking from side to side, looking everywhere except at me.

"I don't know what you mean."

"Don't be so weak," I said impatiently. "I rode Squelch, remember? Was he his usual self? He was not."

"If you're suggesting," he began explosively, "that I doped—"

"Oh, of course not. Anyway, they tested him, didn't they? Negative result. Naturally. No trainer needs to dope a horse he doesn't want to win. It's like swatting a fly with a bulldozer. There are much more subtle methods. Undetectable. Even innocent. Maybe you should be kinder to yourself and admit that you quite innocently stopped Squelch. Maybe you even did it subconsciously, wanting Cherry Pie to win."

"Bull," he said.

"The mind plays tricks," I said. "People often believe they are doing something for one good reason, while they are subconsciously doing it for another."

"Twaddle."

"The trouble comes sometimes when the real reason rears its ugly head and slaps you in the kisser."

"Shut up." His teeth and jaws were clenched tight.

I drew a deep breath. I'd been guessing, partly. And I'd guessed right.

I said, "You gave Squelch too much work too soon before the race. He lost the Lemonfizz on the gallops at home."

He looked at me at last. His eyes were dark, as if the pupils had expanded to take up all the iris. There was a desperate sort of hopelessness in his expression.

"It wouldn't have been so bad," I said, "if you had admitted it to yourself. Because then you would never have risked not engaging a lawyer to defend us."

"I didn't mean to overtrain Squelch," he said wretchedly. "I didn't realize it until afterward. I did back him, just as I said at the Enquiry."

I nodded. "I imagined you must have done. But you backed Cherry Pie as well."

He explained quite simply, without any of his usual superiority. "Trainers are often caught out, as you know, when one of their horses suddenly develops his true form. Well, I thought Cherry Pie might just be one of those. So I backed him, on the off chance."

Some off chance. Fifty pounds with Newtonnards and fifty pounds on the Tote. Gross profit, two thousand.

"How much did you have on Squelch?"

"Two hundred and fifty."

"Whew," I said. "Was that your usual sort of bet?"

"He was odds on . . . I suppose a hundred is my most usual bet."

I had come to the key question, and I wasn't sure I wanted to ask it, let alone have to judge whether the answer was true. However . . .

"Why," I said matter-of-factly, "didn't you back Cherry Pie with your own usual bookmaker?"

He answered without effort. "Because I didn't want Jessel knowing I'd backed Cherry Pie, if he won instead of Squelch. Jessel's a funny man, he takes everything personally; he'd as like as not have whisked Squelch away. . . ." He trailed off, remembering afresh that Squelch was indeed being whisked.

"Why should Jessel have known?"

"Eh? Oh, because he bets with my bookmaker, too, and the pair of them are as thick as thieves."

Fair enough.

"Well, who was the middle-aged man who put the bets on for you?"

"Just a friend. There's no need to involve him. I want to keep him out of it."

"Could Newtonnards have seen you talking to him by the parade ring before the first race?"

"Yes," he said with depression. "I did talk to him. I gave him the money to bet with."

And he still hadn't seen any danger signals. Had taken Monty Midgely's assurance at its face value. Hadn't revealed the danger to me. I could have throttled him.

"What did you do with the winnings?"

"They're in the safe downstairs."

"And you haven't been able to admit to anyone that you've got them."

"No."

I thought back. "You lied about it at the Enquiry."

"What else was there to do?"

By then, what indeed? Telling the truth hadn't done much for me.

"Let's see, then." I moved over to the window again, sorting things out. "Cherry Pie won on his merits. You backed him because he looked like coming into form rather suddenly. Squelch had had four hard races in two months, and a possibly overzealous training gallop. These are the straight facts."

"Yes . . . I suppose so."

"No trainer should lose his license because he didn't tell the world he might just possibly have a flier. I never see why the people who put in all work shouldn't have the first dip into the well."

Owners, too, were entitled. Cherry Pie's owner, however, had died three weeks before the Lemonfizz, and Cherry Pie had run for the executors. Someone was going to have a fine time deciding his precise value at the moment of his owner's death.

"It means, anyway, that you do have a fighting fund," I pointed out.

"There's no point in fighting."

"You," I said exasperatedly, "are so soft that you'd make a marshmallow look like granite."

His mouth slowly opened. Before that morning I had never given him anything but politeness. He was looking at me as if he'd never really noticed me, and it occurred to me that if we did indeed get our licenses back he would remember that I'd seen him in pieces, and maybe find me uncomfortable to have around. He paid me a retainer, but only on an annual contract. Easy enough to chuck me out and retain someone else. Expediently, and not too pleased with myself for it, I took the worst crags out of my tone.

"I presume," I said, "that you do want your license back?"

"There isn't a chance."

"If you'll keep the lads for a month, I'll get it back for you."

Defeat still showed in every sagging muscle, and he didn't answer.

I shrugged. "Well, I'm going to try. And if I give you your license back on a plate, it will be just too bad if Archie and the lads have gone." I walked toward the door and put my hand on the knob. "I'll let you know how I get on."

Twisted the knob. Opened the door.

"Wait," he said.

I turned round. A vestige of starch had returned, mostly in the shape of the reappearance of the mean lines round his mouth. Not so good.

"I don't believe you can do it. But as you're so cocksure, I'll make a bargain with you. I'll pay the lads for two weeks. If you want me to keep them on for another two weeks after that, you can pay them yourself."

Charming. He'd made two thousand pounds out of Cherry Pie and had overtrained Squelch and was the direct cause of my being warned off. I stamped on a violent inner tremble of anger and gave him a cold answer.

"Very well. I agree to that. But you must make a bargain with me, too. A bargain that you'll keep your mouth tight shut about your guilt feelings. I don't want to be sabotaged by you hairshirting it all over the place and confessing your theoretical sins at awkward moments."

"I am unlikely to do that," he said stiffly.

I wasn't so sure. "I want your word on it," I said.

He drew himself up, offended. It at least had the effect of straightening his backbone.

"You have it."

"Fine." I held the door open for him. "Let's go down to the yard, then."

He still hesitated, but finally made up his mind to it, and went before me through the door and down the stairs.

Roberta and her mother were standing in the hall, looking as if they were waiting for news at a pithead after a disaster. They watched the reappearance of the head of the family in a mixture of relief and apprehension, and Mrs. Cranfield said tentatively, "Dexter . . ."

He answered irritably, as if he saw no cause for anxiety in his having shut himself away with a shotgun for thirty-six hours, "We're going down to the yard."

"Great," said Roberta, practically smothering any tendency to emotion from her mother. "I'll come, too."

Archie hurried to meet us and launched into a detailed account of which horses had gone and which were about to go next. Cranfield hardly listened, and certainly didn't take it in. He waited for a gap in the flow, and, when he'd waited long enough, impatiently interrupted.

"Yes, yes, Archie, I'm sure you have everything in hand. That is not what I've come down for, however. I want you to tell the lads at once that their notice to leave is withdrawn for one month."

Archie looked at me, not entirely understanding.

"The sack," I said, "is postponed. Pending attempts to get wrongs righted."

"Mine, too?"

"Absolutely," I agreed. "Especially, in fact."

"Hughes thinks there is a chance we can prove ourselves innocent and recover our licenses," Cranfield said formally, his own disbelief showing like two heads. "In order to help me keep the stable together while he makes enquiries, Hughes has agreed to contribute one-half toward your wages for one month." I looked at him sharply. That was not all what I had agreed. He showed no sign of acknowledging his reinterpretation (to put it charitably) of the offer I had accepted, and went authoritatively on. "Therefore, as your present week's notice still has five days to run, none of you will be required to leave here for five weeks. In fact," he added grudgingly, "I would be obliged if you would all stay."

Archie said to me, "You really mean it?" and I watched the hope suddenly spring up in his face and thought that maybe it wasn't only my own chance of a future that was worth eight hundred quid.

"That's right," I said. "As long as you don't all spend the month busily fixing up to go somewhere else at the end of it."

"What do you take us for?" Archie protested.

"Cynics," I said, and Archie actually laughed.

I left Cranfield and Archie talking together, with most of the desperation evaporating from both of them, and walked away to my aerodynamic burnt-orange car. I didn't hear Roberta following me until she spoke in my ear as I opened the door.

"Can you really do it?" she said.

"Do what?"

"Get your license back."

"It's going to cost me too much not to. So I guess I'll have to, or . . ."

"Or what?"

I smiled. "Or die in the attempt."

It took me an hour to cross into Gloucestershire and almost half as long to sort out the geography of the village of Downfield, which seemed to consist mostly of cul-de-sacs.

The cottage I eventually found after six misdirections from local inhabitants was old but not beautiful, well painted but in dreary colors, and a good deal more trustworthy than its owner.

When Mrs. Charlie West saw who it was, she tried to shut the front door in my face. I put out a hand that was used to dealing with strong horses and pulled her by the wrist, so that if she slammed the door she would be squashing her own arm.

She screeched loudly. An inner door at the back of the hall opened all of six inches, and Charlie's round face appeared through the crack. A distinct lack of confidence was discernible in that area.

"He's hurting me!" Mrs. West shouted.

"I want to talk to you," I said to Charlie, over her shoulder.

Charlie West was less than willing. Abandoning his teenage wife—long straight hair, Dusty Springfield eyelashes, beige lipstick and all—he retreated a pace and quite firmly shut his door. Mrs. West put up a loud and energetic defense to my attempt to establish further contact with Master Charlie, and I went through the hall fending off her toes and fists.

Charlie had wedged a chair under the door handle.

I shouted through the wood, "Much as you deserve it, I haven't come here to beat you up. Come out and talk."

No response of any sort. I rattled the door. Repeated my request. No results. With Mrs. West still stabbing around like an agitated hornet, I went out of the front door and round the outside to try to talk to him through the window. The window was open, and the sitting room inside was empty.

I turned round in time to see Charlie's distant back view disappearing across a field and into the next parish. Mrs. West saw him, too, and gave me a nasty smile.

"So there," she said triumphantly.

"Yes," I said. "I'm sure you must be very proud of him."

The smile wobbled. I walked back down their garden path, climbed into the car, and drove away.

Round 1 slightly farcically to the opposition.

Two miles away from the village, I stopped the car in a farm gateway and thought it over. Charlie West had been a great deal more scared of me than I would have supposed, even allowing for the fact that I was a couple of sizes bigger and a fair amount stronger. Maybe Charlie was as much afraid of my fury as of my fists. He seemed almost to have been expecting that I would attempt some sort of retaliation, and certainly after what he had done, he had a right to. All the same, he still represented my quickest and easiest route to who, if not to why.

After a while, I started up again and drove on into the nearest town. Remembered I hadn't eaten all day, put away some rather good cold beef at three-thirty in a home-style café geared more to cake and scones, dozed in the car, waited until dark, and finally drove back again to Charlie's village.

There were lights on in several rooms of his cottage. The Wests were at home. I turned the car and retracked about a hundred yards, stopping half on and half off a grassy verge. Climbed out. Stood up.

Plan of attack: vague. I had had some idea of ringing the front doorbell, disappearing, and waiting for either Charlie or his dolly wife to take one incautious step outside to investigate. Instead, unexpected allies materialized in the shape of one small boy and one large dog.

The boy had a flashlight, and was talking to his dog, who paused to dirty up the roadside five yards ahead.

"What the hell d'you think you were at, you bloody great nit, scoffing our Mum's stewing steak? Gor blimey, mate, don't you ever learn nothing? Tomorrow's dinner gone down your useless big gullet and our Dad will give us both a belting this time, I shouldn't wonder—not just you, you senseless rotten idiot. Time you knew the bloody difference between me Mum's stewing steak and dogmeat, it is straight, though come to think of it there isn't all that much difference, 'specially as maybe your eyes don't look at things the same. Do they? I damn well wish you could talk, mate."

I clicked shut the door of the car and startled him, and he swung round with the light searching wildly. The beam caught me and steadied on my face.

The boy said, "You come near me and I'll set my dog

on you." The dog, however, was still squatting and showed no enthusiasm.

"I'll stay right here, then," I said amicably, leaning back against the car. "I only want to know who lives in that cottage over there, where the lights are."

"How do I know? We only come to live here the day before yesterday."

"Great . . . I mean, that must be great for you, moving."

"Yeah. Sure. You stay there, then. I'm going now." He beckoned to the dog. The dog was still busy.

"How would it be if you could offer your Mum the price of the stewing steak? Maybe she wouldn't tell your Dad, then, and neither your nor the dog would get a belting."

"Our Mum says we mustn't talk to strange men."

"Hmm. Well, never mind, then. Off you go."

"I'll go when I'm ready," he said belligerently. A natural-born rebel. About nine years old, I guessed.

"What would I have to do for it?" he said after a pause.

"Nothing much. Just ring the front doorbell of that cottage and tell whoever answers that you can't stop your dog eating the crocuses they've got growing all along the front there. Then when they come out to see, just nip off home as fast as your dog can stagger."

It appealed to him. "Steak probably costs a good bit," he said.

"Probably." I dug into my pocket and came up with a small fistful of pennies and silver. "This should leave a bit over."

"He doesn't really have to eat the crocuses, does he?"

"No."

"O.K., then." Once his mind was made up, he was jaunty and efficient. He shoveled my small change into his pocket, marched up to Charlie's front door, and told Mrs. West, who cautiously answered it, that she was losing her crocuses. She scolded him all the way down the path, and while she was bending down to search for the damage, my accomplice quietly vanished. Before Mrs. West exactly realized she had been misled, I had stepped briskly through her front door and shut her out of her own house.

When I opened the sitting-room door, Charlie said, without lifting his eyes from a racing paper, "It wasn't him again, then."

"Yes," I said, "it was."

Charlie's immature face crumpled into a revolting state of fear and Mrs. West leaned on the doorbell. I shut the sitting-room door behind me to cut out some of the din.

"What are you so afraid of?" I said loudly.

"Well . . . you . . ."

"And so you damn well ought to be," I said. I took a step toward him and he shrank back into his armchair. He was brave enough on a horse, which made this abject cringing all the more unexpected, and all the more unpleasant. I took another step. He fought his way into the upholstery.

Mrs. West gave the doorbell a rest.

"Why did you do it?" I said.

He shook his head dumbly, and pulled his feet up onto the chair seat in the classic womb position. Wishful regression to the first and only place where the world couldn't reach him.

"Charlie, I came here for some answers, and you're going to give them to me."

Mrs. West's furious face appeared at the window, and she started rapping hard enough to break the glass. With one eye on her husband to prevent him making another bolt for it, I stepped over and undid the latch.

"Get out of here!" she shouted. "Go on, get out."

"You get in. Through here. I'm not opening the door."

"I'll fetch the police."

"Do what you like. I only want to talk to your worm of a husband. Get in or stay out, but shut up."

She did anything but. Once she was in the room, it took another twenty minutes of fruitless slanging before I could ask Charlie a single question without her loud voice obliterating any chance of an answer.

Charlie himself tired of it first and told her to stop, but at least her belligerence had given him a breathing space.

He put his feet down on the floor again and said it was no use asking those questions, he didn't know the answers.

"You must do. Unless you told those lies about me out of sheer personal spite."

"No."

"Then why?"

"I'm not telling you."

"Then I'll tell you something, you little louse. I'm going to find out who put you up to it. I'm going to stir everything up until I find out, and then I'm going to raise such a stink about being framed that sulfur will smell like sweet peas by comparison, and you, Master Charlie West, *you* will find yourself without a license, not me, and even if you get it back you'll never live down the contempt everyone will feel for you."

"Don't you talk to my Charlie like that!"

"Your Charlie is a vicious little liar who would sell you, too, for fifty pounds."

"It wasn't fifty," she snapped triumphantly. "It was five hundred."

Charlie yelled at her and I came as near to hitting him as the distance between my clenched teeth. Five hundred pounds. He'd lied my license away for a handout that would have insulted a tout.

"That does it," I said. "And now you tell me who paid you."

The girl wife started to look as frightened as Charlie, and it didn't occur to me then that my anger had flooded through that little room like a tidal wave.

Charlie stuttered, "I d-d-don't know."

I took a pace toward him and he scrambled out of his chair and took refuge behind it.

"K-k-keep away from me. I don't know. I don't know."

"That isn't good enough."

"He really doesn't know," the girl wailed. "He really doesn't."

"He does," I repeated furiously.

The girl began to cry. Charlie seemed to be on the verge of copying her.

"I never saw—never saw the bloke. He telephoned."

"And how did he pay you?"

"In two—in two packages. In one-pound notes. A hundred of them came the day before the Enquiry, and I was to get . . ." His voice trailed away.

"You were to get the other four hundred if I was warned off?"

He nodded, a fractional jerk. His head was tucked into his shoulders, as if to avoid a blow.

"And have you?"

"What?"

"Have you had it yet? The other four hundred?"

His eyes widened, and he spoke in jerks. "No—but—of course—it—will—come."

"Of course it won't," I said brutally. "You stupid treacherous little ninny." My voice sounded thick, and each word came out separately and loaded with fury.

Both the Wests were trembling, and the girl's eye make-up was beginning to run down her cheeks.

"What did he sound like, this man on the telephone?"

"Just—just a man," Charlie said.

"And did it occur to you to ask why he wanted me warned off?"

"I said—you hadn't done anything to harm me—and he said—you never know—supposing one day he does. . . ."

Charlie shrank still further under my astounded glare. "Anyway—five hundred quid—I don't earn as much as you, you know." For the first time, there was a tinge of spite in his voice, and I knew that in truth jealousy had been a factor, that he hadn't done it entirely for the money. He'd got his kicks, too.

"You're only twenty," I said. "What exactly do you expect?"

But Charlie expected everything, always, to be run entirely for the best interests of Charlie West.

I said, "And you'll be wise to spend that money carefully, because, believe me, it's going to be the most expensive hundred quid you've ever earned."

"Kelly . . ." He was halfway to entreaty. Jealous,

greedy, dishonest, and afraid. I felt not the remotest flicker of compassion for him, only a widening anger that the motives behind his lies were so small.

"And when you lose your license for this—and I'll see that you do—you'll have plenty of time to understand that it *serves you right.*"

The raw revenge in my voice made a desert of their little home. They both stood there dumbly, with wide miserable eyes, too broken up to raise another word. The girl's beige mouth hung slackly open, mascara halfway to her chin, long hair straggling in wisps across her face and round her shoulders. She looked sixteen. A child. So did Charlie. The worst vandals are always childish.

I turned away from them and walked out of their cottage, and my anger changed into immense depression on the drive home.

Chapter 6

At two o'clock in the morning, the rage I'd unleashed on the Wests looked worse and worse.

To start with, it had achieved nothing helpful. I'd known before I went there that Charlie must have had a reason for lying about me at the Enquiry. I now knew the reason to be five hundred pounds. Marvelous. A useful scrap of information out of a blizzard of emotion.

Lash out when you're hurt. . . . I'd done that, all right. Poured out on them the roaring bitterness I'd smothered under a civilized front ever since Monday.

Nor had I given Charlie any reason to do me any good in future. Very much the reverse. He wasn't going to be contrite and eager to make amends. When he'd recovered himself, he'd be sullen and vindictive.

I'd been taught the pattern over and over. Country A plays an isolated shabby trick. Country B is outraged and exacts revenge. Country A is forced to express apologies and meekly back down, but thoroughly resents it. Country A now holds a permanent grudge, and harms Country B whenever possible. One of the classic variations in the history of politics and aggression. Also applicable to individuals.

To have known about the pitfalls and jumped in regardless was a mite galling. It just showed how easily good sense lost out to anger. It also showed me that I wasn't going to get results that way. A crash course in detection would have been handy. Failing that, I'd have to start taking stock of things coolly, instead of charging straight off again toward the easiest-looking target, and making another mess of it.

Cool stocktaking . . .

Charlie West hadn't wanted to see me because he had a guilty conscience. It followed that everyone else who had a guilty conscience wouldn't want to see me. Even if they didn't actually sprint off across the fields, they would all do their best to avoid my reaching them. I was going to have to become adept—and fast—at entering their lives when their backs were turned.

If Charlie West didn't know who had paid him, and I believed that he didn't, it followed that perhaps none of the others who had lied knew who had persuaded them to. Perhaps it had all been done on the telephone. Long-distance leverage. Impersonal and undiscoverable.

Perhaps I had set myself an impossible task and I should give up the whole idea and emigrate to Australia.

Except that they had racing in Australia, and I wouldn't be able to go. The banishment covered the world. Warned off. Warned off.

Oh God.

All right, so maybe I did let the self-pity catch up with me for a while. But I was privately alone in my bed in the dark, and I'd jeered myself out of it by morning.

Looking about as ragged as I felt, I got up at six and pointed the Lotus's smooth nose toward London, N.W.7., Mill Hill.

Since I could see no one at the races, I had to catch them at home, and in the case of George Newtonnards, bookmaker, home proved to be a sprawling pink-washed ranch-type bungalow in a prosperous suburban road. At 8:30 A.M. I hoped to find him at breakfast, but in fact he was opening his garage door when I arrived. I parked squarely across the entrance to his drive, which was hardly likely to make me popular, and he came striding down toward me to tell me to move.

I climbed out of the car. When he saw who it was, he stopped dead. I walked up the drive to meet him, shivering a little in the raw east wind and regretting I wasn't snug inside a fur-collared jacket like his.

"What are you doing here?" he said sharply.

"I would be very grateful if you would just tell me one or two things. . . ."

"I haven't time." He was easy, self-assured, dealing with a small-sized nuisance. "And nothing I can say will help you. Move your car, please."

"Certainly . . . Could you tell me how it was that you came to be asked to give evidence against Mr. Cranfield?"

"How it was . . . ?" He looked slightly surprised. "I received an official letter, requiring me to attend."

"Well, why? I mean, how did the Stewards know about Mr. Cranfield's bet on Cherry Pie? Did you write and tell them?"

He gave me a cool stare. "I hear," he said, "that you are maintaining you were framed."

"News travels."

A faint smile. "News always travels—toward me. An accurate information service is the basis of good bookmaking."

"How did the Stewards know about Mr. Cranfield's bet?"

"Mmm. Well, yes, that I don't know."

"Who, besides you, knew that you believed that Cranfield had backed Cherry Pie?"

"He did back him."

"Well, who besides you knew that he had?"

"I haven't time for this."

"I'll be happy to move my car . . . in a minute or two."

His annoyed glare gradually softened round the edges into a half-amused acceptance. A very smooth civilized man, George Newtonnards.

"Very well. I told a few of the lads—other bookmakers, that is. I was angry about it, see? Letting myself be taken to the cleaners like that. Me, at my age, I should know better. So maybe one of them passed on the word to the Stewards, knowing the Enquiry was coming up. But, no, I didn't do it myself."

"Could you guess which one might have done? I mean,

do you know anyone who has a grudge against Cranfield?"

"Can't think of one." He shrugged. "No more than against any other trainer who tries it on."

"Tries it on?" I echoed, surprised. "But he doesn't."

"Oh, yeah?"

"I ride them," I protested. "I should know."

"Yes," he said sarcastically. "You should. Don't come the naïve bit with me, chum. Your friend Chris Smith, him with the cracked skull, he's a proper artist at strangulation, wouldn't you say? Same as you are. A fine pair, the two of you."

"You believe I pulled Squelch, then?"

"Stands to reason."

"All the same, I didn't."

"Tell it to the Marines." A thought struck him. "I don't know any bookmakers who have a grudge against Cranfield, but I sure know one who has a grudge against *you*. A whopping great life-sized grudge. One time, he was almost coming after you with a chopper. You got in his way proper, mate, you did indeed."

"How? And who?"

"You and Chris Smith, you were riding two for Cranfield . . . about six months ago, it was . . . right at the beginning of the season, anyway . . . in a novice chase at Fontwell. Remember? There was a big holiday crowd in from the south coast because it was a bit chilly that day for lying on the beach. . . . Anyway, there was a big crowd all primed with holiday money . . . and there were you and Chris Smith on these two horses, and the public fancying both of them, and Pelican Jobberson asked you which was off, and you said you hadn't an earthly on yours, so he rakes in the cash on you and doesn't bother to balance his book, and then you go and ride a hell of a finish and win by a neck, when you could have lost instead without the slightest trouble. Pelican went spare and swore he'd be even with you when he got the chance."

"I believed what I told him," I said. "It was that

horse's first attempt over fences. No one could have pre-
dicted he'd have been good enough to win."

"Then why did you?"

"The owner wanted to, if possible."

"Did he bet on it?"

"The owner? No. It was a woman. She never bets
much. She just likes to see her horses win."

"Pelican swore you'd backed it yourself, and put him off
so that you could get a better price."

"You bookmakers are too suspicious for your own
good."

"Hard experience proves us right."

"Well, he's wrong this time," I insisted. "This bird
friend of yours. If he asked me . . . and I don't remember
him asking . . . then I told him the truth. And anyway,
any bookmaker who asks jockeys questions like that is
asking for trouble. Jockeys are the worst tipsters in the
world."

"Some aren't," he said flatly. "Some are good at it."

I skipped that. "Is he still angry after all these months?
And, if so, would he be angry enough not just to tell the
Stewards that Cranfield backed Cherry Pie, but to bribe
other people to invent lies about us?"

His eyes narrowed while he thought about it. He
pursed his mouth, undecided. "You'd better ask him yourself."

"Thanks." Hardly an easy question.

"Move your car now?" he suggested.

"Yes." I walked two steps toward it, then stopped and
turned back. "Mr. Newtonnards, if you see the man who
put the money on for Mr. Cranfield, will you find out who
he is . . . and let me know?"

"Why don't you ask Cranfield?"

"He said he didn't want to involve him."

"But you do?"

"I suppose I'm grasping at anything," I said. "But, yes,
I think I do."

"Why don't you just quieten down and take it?" he said
reasonably. "All this thrashing about . . . you got copped.

So, you got copped. Fair enough. Sit it out, then. You'll get your license back, eventually."

"Thank you for your advice," I said politely, and went and moved my car out of his gateway.

It was Thursday. I should have been going to Warwick to ride in four races. Instead, I drove aimlessly back round the North Circular Road wondering whether or not to pay a call on David Oakley, enquiry agent and imaginative photographer. If Charlie West didn't know who had framed me, it seemed possible that Oakley might be the only one who did. But even if he did, he was highly unlikely to tell me. There seemed no point in confronting him, and yet nothing could be gained if I made no attempt.

In the end, I stopped at a telephone box and found his number via enquiries.

A girl answered. "Mr. Oakley isn't in yet."

"Can I make an appointment?"

She asked me what about.

"A divorce."

She said Mr. Oakley could see me at eleven-thirty, and asked me my name.

"Charles Crisp."

"Very well, Mr. Crisp. Mr. Oakley will be expecting you."

I doubted it. On the other hand, he, like Charlie West, might in general be expecting some form of protest.

From the North Circular Road, I drove ninety miles up the M1 Motorway to Birmingham and found Oakley's office above a bicycle-and-radio shop half a mile from the town center.

His street door, shabby black, bore a neat small nameplate stating simply, "Oakley." There were two keyholes, Yale and Chubb, and a discreetly situated peephole. I tried the handle of this apparent fortress, and the door opened easily under my touch. Inside, there was a narrow passage with pale blue walls leading to an uncarpeted staircase stretching upward.

I walked up, my feet sounding loud on the boards. At

the top there was a small landing with another shabby black door, again and similarly fortified. On this door, another neat notice said, "Please ring." There was a bell push. I gave it three seconds' work.

The door was opened by a tall strong-looking girl dressed in a dark-colored leather trouser suit. Under the jacket she wore a black sweater, and under the trouser legs black leather boots. Black eyes returned my scrutiny, black hair held back by a tortoise-shell band fell straight to her shoulders before curving inward. She seemed at first sight to be about twenty-four, but there were already wrinkle lines round her eyes, and the deadness in their expression indicated too much familiarity with dirty washing.

"I have an appointment," I said. "Crisp."

"Come in." She opened the door wider and left it for me to close.

I followed her into the room, a small square office furnished with a desk, typewriter, telephone, and four tall filing cabinets. On the far side of the room there was another door. Not black; modern flat fiberboard, painted gray. More keyholes. I eyed them thoughtfully.

The girl opened the door, said through it, "It's Mr. Crisp," and stood back for me to pass her.

"Thank you," I said. Took three steps forward, and shut myself in with David Oakley.

His office was not a great deal larger than the anteroom, and no thrift had been spared with the furniture. There was dim brown linoleum, a bentwood coat stand, a small cheap armchair facing a gray metal desk, and over the grimy window, in place of curtains, a tough-looking fixed frame covered with chicken wire. Outside the window there were the heavy bars and supports of a fire escape. The Birmingham sun, doing its best against odds, struggled through and fell in wrinkled honeycomb shadows on the surface of an ancient safe. In the wall on my right another door, firmly closed. With yet more keyholes.

Behind the desk in a swivel chair sat the proprietor of all this glory, the totally unmemorable Mr. Oakley. Youngish. Slender. Mouse-colored hair. And this time sunglasses.

"Sit down, Mr. Crisp," he said. Accentless voice, entirely emotionless, as before. "Divorce, I believe? Give me the details of your requirements, and we can arrive at a fee." He looked at his watch. "I can give you just ten minutes, I'm afraid. Shall we get on?"

He hadn't recognized me. I thought I might as well take advantage of it.

"I understand you would be prepared to fake some evidence for me . . . photographs?"

He began to nod, and then grew exceptionally still. The unrevealing dark glasses were motionless. The pale straight mouth didn't twitch. The hand lying on the desk remained loose and relaxed.

Finally he said, without any change of inflection, "Get out."

"How much do you charge for faking evidence?"

"Get out."

I smiled. "I'd like to know how much I was worth."

"Dust," he said. His foot moved under the desk.

"I'll pay you in gold dust, if you'll tell me who gave you the job."

He considered it. Then he said, "No."

The door to the outer office opened quietly behind me.

Oakley said calmly, "This is not a Mr. Crisp, Didi. This is a Mr. Kelly Hughes. Mr. Hughes will be leaving."

"Mr. Hughes is not ready," I said.

"I think Mr. Hughes will find he is," she said.

I looked at her over my shoulder. She was carrying a large black-looking pistol with a very large black-looking silencer.

The whole works was pointing steadily my way.

"How dramatic," I said. "Can you readily dispose of bodies in the center of Birmingham?"

"Yes," Oakley said.

"For a fee, of course, usually," Didi added.

I struggled not to believe them, and lost. All the same . . .

"Should you decide after all to sell the information I need, you know where to find me." I relaxed against the back of the chair.

"I may have a liking for gold dust," he said calmly. "But I am not a fool."

"Opinions differ," I remarked lightly.

There was no reaction. "It is not in my interest that you should prove you were—shall we say—set up."

"I understand that. Eventually, however, you will wish that you hadn't helped to do it."

He said smoothly, "A number of other people have said much the same, though few, I must confess, as quietly as you."

It occurred to me suddenly that he must be quite used to the sort of enraged onslaught I'd thrown at the Wests, and that perhaps that was why his office . . . Didi caught my wandering glance and cynically nodded.

"That's right. Too many people tried to smash the place up. So we keep the damage to a minimum."

"How wise."

"I'm afraid I really do have another appointment now," Oakley said. "So, if you'll excuse me?"

I stood up. There was nothing to stay for.

"It surprises me," I remarked, "that you're not in jail."

"I am clever," he said matter-of-factly. "My clients are satisfied, and people like you . . . impotent."

"Someone will kill you, one day."

"Will you?"

I shook my head. "Not worth it."

"Exactly," he said calmly. "The jobs I accept are never what the victims would actually kill me for. I really am not a fool."

"No," I said.

I walked across to the door and Didi made room for me to pass. She put the pistol down on her desk in the outer office and switched off a red bulb which glowed brightly in a small switchboard.

"Emergency signal?" I enquired. "Under his desk."

"You could say so."

"Is that gun loaded?"

Her eyebrows rose. "Naturally."

"I see." I opened the outer door. She walked over to close it behind me as I went toward the stairs.

"Nice to have met you, Mr. Hughes," she said unemotionally. "Don't come back."

I walked along to my car in some depression. From none of the three damaging witnesses at the Enquiry had I got any change at all, and what David Oakley had said about me being impotent looked all too true.

There seemed to be no way of proving that he had simply brought with him the money he had photographed in my flat. No one at Corrie had seen him come or go: Tony had asked all the lads, and none of them had seen him. And Oakley would have found it easy enough to be unobserved. He had only had to arrive early, while everyone was out riding on the Downs at morning exercise. From seven-thirty to eight-thirty the stable yard would be deserted. Letting himself in through my unlocked door, setting up his props, loosing off a flash or two, and quietly retreating . . . The whole process would have taken him no more than ten minutes.

It was possible he had kept a record of his shady transactions. Possible, not probable. He might need to keep some hold over his clients, to prevent their later denouncing him in fits of resurgent civic conscience. If he did keep such records, it might account for the multiplicity of locks. Or maybe the locks were simply to discourage people from breaking in to search for records, as they were certainly discouraging me.

Would Oakley, I wondered, have done what Charlie West had done, and produced his lying testimony for a voice on the telephone? On the whole, I decided not. Oakley had brains where Charlie had vanity, and Oakley would not involve himself without tying his clients up tight, too. Oakley had to know who had done the engineering.

But stealing that information . . . or beating it out of him . . . or tricking him into giving it . . . as well as

buying it from him . . . every course looked as hopeless as
the next. I could only ride horses. I couldn't pick locks,
fights, or pockets. Certainly not Oakley's.

Oakley and Didi. They were old at the game. They'd
invented the rules. Oakley and Didi were senior league.

How did people get in touch with Oakley if they needed his brand of service?

He could scarcely advertise.

Someone had to know about him.

I thought it over for a while, sitting in my car in the car
park wondering what to do next. There was only one
person I knew who could put his finger on the pulse of
Birmingham if he wanted to, and the likelihood was that
in my present circumstances he wouldn't want to.

However . . .

I started the car, threaded a way through the one-way
streets, and found a slot in the crowded park behind the
Great Stag Hotel. Inside, the ritual of Business Lunch was
warming up, the atmosphere thickening nicely with the
smell of alcohol, the resonance of the fruity voices, the
haze of cigars. The Great Stag Hotel attracted almost
exclusively a certain grade of wary, prosperous, level-
headed businessmen needing a soft background for hard
options, and it attracted them because the landlord, Teddy
Dewar, was that sort of man himself.

I found him in the bar, talking to two others almost
indistinguishable from him in their dark-gray suits, white
shirts, neat maroon ties, 17 necks, and 38-inch waists.

A faint glaze came over his professionally noncommit-
tal expression when he caught sight of me over their
shoulders. A warned-off jockey didn't rate too high with
him. Lowered the tone of the place, no doubt.

I edged through to the bar on one side of him and
ordered whisky.

"I'd be grateful for a word with you," I said.

He turned his head a fraction in my direction and,
without looking at me directly, answered, "Very well. In a
few minutes."

No warmth in the words. No ducking of the unwelcome

situation, either. He went on talking to the two men about the dicky state of oil shares, and eventually smoothly disengaged himself and turned to me.

"Well, Kelly . . ." His eyes were cool and distant, waiting to see what I wanted before showing any real feeling.

"Will you lunch with me?" I made it casual.

His surprise was controlled. "I thought—"

"I may be banned," I said, "but I still eat."

He studied my face. "You mind."

"What do you expect? . . . I'm sorry it shows."

He said neutrally, "There's a muscle in your jaw. . . . Very well, if you don't mind going in straight away."

We sat against the wall at an inconspicuous table and chose beef cut from a roast on a trolley. While he ate, his eyes checked the running of the dining room, missing nothing. I waited until he was satisfied that all was well and then came briefly to the point.

"Do you know anything about a man called David Oakley? He's an enquiry agent. Operates from an office about half a mile from here."

"David Oakley? I can't say I've ever heard of him."

"He manufactured some evidence which swung things against me at the Stewards' Enquiry on Monday."

"Manufactured?" There was delicate doubt in his voice.

"Oh, yes," I sighed. "I suppose it sounds corny, but I really was not guilty as charged. But someone made sure it looked like it." I told him about the photograph of money in my bedroom.

"And you never had this money?"

"I did not. And the note supposed to be from Cranfield was a forgery. But how could we prove it?"

He thought it over.

"You can't."

"Exactly," I agreed.

"This David Oakley who took the photograph . . . I suppose you got no joy from him."

"No joy's right."

"I don't understand precisely why you've come to me." He finished his beef and laid his knife and fork tidily

together. Waiters appeared like genii to clear the table
and bring coffee. He waited still noncommittally while I
paid the bill.

"I expect it is too much to ask," I said finally. "After
all, I've only stayed here three or four times, I have no
claim on you personally for friendship or help . . . and yet
there's no one else I know who could even begin to do
what you could . . . if you will."

"What?" he said succinctly.

"I want to know how people are steered toward David
Oakley, if they want some evidence faked. He as good as
told me he is quite accustomed to do it. Well . . . how
does he get his clients? Who recommends him? I thought
that among all the people you know, you might think of
someone who could perhaps pretend he wanted a job
done . . . or pretend he had a friend who wanted a job
done . . . and throw out feelers, and see if anyone finally
recommended Oakley. And, if so, who."

He considered it. "Because if you found one contact,
you might work back from there to another . . . and
eventually perhaps to a name which meant something to
you?"

"I suppose it sounds feeble," I said resignedly.

"It's a very outside chance," he agreed. There was a
long pause. Then he added, "All the same, I do know of
someone who might agree to try." He smiled briefly, for
the first time.

"That's . . ." I swallowed. "That's marvelous."

"Can't promise results."

Chapter 7

Tony came clomping up my stairs on Friday morning after first exercise and poured half an inch of Scotch into the coffee I gave him. He drank the scalding mixture and shuddered as the liquor bit.

"God," he said. "It's cold on the Downs."

"Rather you than me," I said.

"Liar," he said amicably. "It must feel odd to you, not riding."

"Yes."

He sprawled in the green armchair. "Poppy's got the morning ickies again. I'll be glad when this lousy pregnancy is over. She's been ill half the time."

"Poor Poppy."

"Yeah. . . . Anyway, what it means is that we ain't going to that dance tonight. She says she can't face it."

"Dance?"

"The Jockeys' Fund dance. You know. You've got the tickets on your mantel over there."

"Oh . . . yes. I'd forgotten about it. We were going together."

"That's right. But now, as I was saying, you'll have to go without us."

"I'm not going at all."

"I thought you might not." He sighed and drank deeply. "Where did you get to yesterday?"

"I called on people who didn't want to see me."

"Any results?"

"Not many." I told him briefly about Newtonnards and David Oakley, and about the hour I'd spent with Andrew Tring.

It was because the road home from Birmingham led near his village that I'd thought of Andrew Tring, and my first instinct anyway was to shy away from even the thought of him. Certainly, visiting one of the Stewards who had helped to warn him off was not regulation behavior for a disbarred jockey. If I hadn't been fairly strongly annoyed with him, I would have driven straight on.

He was disgusted with me for calling. He opened the door of his prosperous sprawling old manor house himself, and had no chance of saying he was out.

"Kelly! What are you doing here?"

"Asking you for some explanation."

"I've nothing to say to you."

"You have indeed."

He frowned. Natural good manners were only just preventing him from retreating and shutting the door in my face. "Come in, then. Just for a few minutes."

"Thank you," I said without irony, and followed him into a nearby small room lined with books and containing a vast desk, three deep armchairs, and a color television set.

"Now," he said, shutting the door and not offering the armchairs, "why have you come?"

He was four years older than I, and about the same size. Still as trim as when he rode races, still outwardly the same man. Only the casual long-established changing-room friendliness seemed to have withered somewhere along the upward path from amateurship to Authority.

"Andy," I said, "do you really and honestly believe that that Squelch race was rigged?"

"You were warned off," he said coldly.

"That's far from being the same thing as guilty."

"I don't agree."

"Then you're stupid," I said bluntly. "As well as scared out of your tiny wits."

"That's enough, Kelly. I don't have to listen to this." He opened the door again and waited for me to leave. I didn't. Short of throwing me out bodily, he was going to have to put up with me a little longer. He gave me a furious stare and shut the door again.

I said, more reasonably, "I'm sorry. Really, I'm sorry. It's just that you rode against me for at least five years. . . . I'd have thought you wouldn't so easily believe I'd deliberately lose a race. I've never yet lost a race I could win."

He was silent. He knew that I didn't throw races. Anyone who rode regularly knew who would and who wouldn't, and in spite of what Charlie West had said at the Enquiry, I was not an artist at stopping one because I hadn't given it the practice.

"There was that money," he said at last. He sounded disillusioned and discouraged.

"I never had it. Oakley took it with him into my flat and photographed it there. All that so-called evidence— the whole bloody Enquiry, in fact—was as genuine as a lead sixpence."

He gave me a long doubtful look. Then he said, "There's nothing I can do about it."

"What are you afraid of?"

"Stop saying I'm afraid," he said irritably. "I'm not afraid. I just can't do anything about it, even if what you say is true."

"It is true . . . and maybe you don't think you are afraid, but that's definitely the impression you give. Or maybe . . . are you simply overawed? The new boy among the old powerful prefects. Is that it? Afraid of putting a foot wrong with them?"

"Kelly!" he protested; but it was the protest of a touched nerve.

I said unkindly, "You're a gutless disappointment," and took a step toward his door. He didn't move to open it for me. Instead, he put up a hand to stop me, looking as angry as he had every right to.

"That's not fair. Just because I can't help you . . ."

"You could have done. At the Enquiry."

"You don't understand."

"I do indeed. You found it easier to believe me guilty than to tell Gowery you had any doubts."

"It wasn't as easy as you think."

"Thanks," I said ironically.

"I don't mean . . ." He shook his head impatiently. "I mean, it wasn't all as simple as you make out. When Gowery asked me to sit with him at the Enquiry, I believed it was only going to be a formality, that both you and Cranfield had run the Lemonfizz genuinely and were surprised yourselves by the result. Colonel Midgely told me it was ridiculous having to hold the Enquiry at all, really. I never expected to be caught up in having to warn you off."

"Did you say," I said, "that Lord Gowery asked you to sit with him?"

"Of course. That's the normal procedure. The Stewards sitting at an Enquiry aren't picked out of a hat."

"There isn't any sort of rota?"

"No. The Disciplinary Steward asked two colleagues to officiate with him . . . and that's what put me on the spot, if you must know, because I didn't want to say no to Lord Gowery—" He stopped.

"Go on," I urged without heat. "Why not?"

"Well, because . . ." He hesitated, then said slowly, "I suppose in a way I owe it to you. . . . I'm sorry, Kelly, desperately sorry. I do know you don't usually rig races. . . . I'm in an odd position with Gowery and it's vitally important I keep in with him."

I stifled my indignation. Andrew Tring's eyes were looking inward, and from his expression he didn't very much like what he could see.

"He owns the freehold of the land just north of Manchester where our main pottery is." Andrew Tring's family fortunes were based not on fine porcelain but on smashable teacups for institutions. His products were dropped by dishwashers in schools and hospitals from Waterloo to Hong Kong, and the pieces in the world's dustbins were his perennial license to print money.

He said, "There's been some redevelopment round there and that land is suddenly worth about a quarter of a million. And our lease runs out in three years. . . . We have been negotiating a new one, but the old one was for ninety-nine years and no one is keen to renew for that long. . . . The ground rent is in any case going to be raised considerably, but if Gowery changes his mind and wants to sell that land for development, there's nothing we can do about it. We only own the buildings. . . . We'd lose the entire factory if he didn't renew the lease. And we can only make cups and saucers so cheaply because our overheads are small. If we have to build or rent a new factory, our prices will be less competitive and our world trade figures will slump. Gowery himself has the final say as to whether our lease will be renewed or not, and on what terms. . . . So you see, Kelly, it's not that I'm afraid of him . . . there's so much more at stake . . . and he's always a man to hold it against you if you argue with him."

He stopped and looked at me gloomily. I looked gloomily back. The facts of life stared us stonily in the face.

"So that's that," I agreed. "You are quite right. You can't help me. You couldn't, right from the start. I'm glad you explained. . . ." I smiled at him twistedly, facing another dead end, the last of a profitless day.

"I'm sorry, Kelly. . . ."

"Sure," I said.

Tony finished his fortified breakfast and said, "So there wasn't anything sinister in Andy Tring's lily-livered bit on Monday."

"It depends what you call sinister. But, no, I suppose not."

"What's left, then?"

"Damn all," I said in depression.

"You can't give up," he protested.

"Oh, no. But I've learned one thing in learning nothing, and that is that I'm getting nowhere because I'm me. First thing Monday morning, I'm going to hire me my own David Oakley."

"Attaboy," he said. He stood up. "Time for second lot, I hear." Down in the yard the lads were bringing out the horses, their hoofs scrunching hollowly on the packed gravel.

"How are they doing?" I asked.

"Oh . . . so-so. I sure hate having to put up other jocks. Given me a bellyful of the whole game, this business has."

When he'd gone down to ride, I cleaned up my already clean flat and made some more coffee. The day stretched emptily ahead. So would the next day and the one after that, and every day for an indefinite age.

Ten minutes of this prospect was enough. I searched around and found another straw to cling to: telephoned a man I knew slightly at BBC. A cool secretary said he was out, and to try again at eleven.

I tried again at eleven. Still out. I tried at twelve. He was in then, but sounded as if he wished he weren't.

"Not Kelly Hughes, the . . ." His voice trailed off while he failed to find a tactful way of putting it.

"That's right."

"Well . . . er . . . I don't think . . ."

"I don't want anything much," I assured him resignedly. "I just want to know the name of the outfit who make the films of races. The camera patrol people."

"Oh." He sounded relieved. "That's the Racecourse Technical Services. Run by the Levy Board. They've a virtual monopoly, though there's one other small firm operating sometimes under license. Then there are the television companies, of course. Did you want any particular race? Oh . . . the Lemonfizz Crystal Cup, I suppose."

"No," I said. "The meeting at Reading two weeks earlier."

"Reading . . . Reading . . . Let's see, then. Which lot would that be?" He hummed a few out-of-tune bars while he thought it over. "I should think . . . yes, definitely the small firm, the Cannot Lie people. Cannot Lie, Ltd. Offices at Woking, Surrey. Do you want their number?"

"Yes, please."

He read it to me.

"Thank you very much," I said.

"Any time . . . er . . . well . . . I mean . . ."

"I know what you mean," I said. "But thanks anyway."

I put down the receiver with a grimace. It was still no fun being everyone's idea of a villain.

The BBC man's reaction made me decide that the telephone might get me nil results from the Cannot Lie brigade. Maybe they couldn't lie, but they could certainly evade. And anyway, I had the whole day to waste.

The Cannot Lie office was a rung or two up the luxury ladder from David Oakley's, which wasn't saying a great deal. A large rather bare room on the second floor of an Edwardian house in a side street. A rickety lift large enough for one slim man or two starving children. A well-worn desk with a well-worn blonde painting her toenails on top of it.

"Yes?" she said when I walked in.

She had lilac panties on, with lace. She made no move to prevent my seeing a lot of them.

"No one in?" I asked.

"Only us chickens," she said. She had a South London accent and the smart back-chatting intelligence that often goes with it. "Which do you want, the old man or our Alfie?"

"You'll do nicely," I said.

"Ta." She took it as her due, with a practiced come-on-so-far-but-no-further smile. One foot was finished. She stretched out her leg and wiggled it up and down to help with the drying.

"Going to a dance tonight," she explained. "In me peep-toes."

I didn't think anyone would concentrate on the toes. Apart from the legs, she had a sharp-pointed little bosom under a white cotton sweater and a bright pink patent-leather belt clasping a bikini-sized waist. Her body looked about twenty years old. Her face looked as if she'd spent the last six of them bed hopping.

"Paint the other one," I suggested.

"You're not in a hurry?"

"I'm enjoying the scenery."

She gave a knowing giggle and started on the other foot. The view was even more hair-raising than before. She watched me watching, and enjoyed it.

"What's your name?" I asked.

"Carol. What's yours?"

"Kelly."

"From the Isle of Man?"

"No. The land of our fathers."

She gave me a bright glance. "You catch on quick, don't you?"

I wished I did. I said regretfully, "How long do you keep ordinary routine race films?"

"Huh? Forever, I suppose." She changed mental gear effortlessly, carrying straight on with her uninhibited painting. "We haven't destroyed any so far, that's to say. Course, we've only been in the racing business eighteen months. No telling what they'll do when the big storeroom's full. We're up to the eyebrows in all the others, with films of motor races, golf matches, three-day events, any old things like that."

"Where's the big storeroom?"

"Through there." She waved the small pink enameling brush in the general direction of a scratched once-cream door. "Want to see?"

"If you don't mind."

"Go right ahead."

She had finished the second foot. The show was over. With a sigh, I removed my gaze and walked over to the door in question. There was only a round hole where most doors have a handle. I pushed against the wood and the door swung into another large high room, furnished this time with rows of free-standing bookshelves, like a public library. The shelves, however, were of bare functional wood, and there was no covering on the planked floor.

Well over half the shelves were empty. On the others were rows of short wide box files, their backs labeled with neat typed strips explaining what was to be found within. Each box proved to contain all the films from one day's racing, and they were all efficiently arranged in chronological order. I pulled out the box for the day I rode Squelch and Wanderlust at Reading, and looked inside. There were six round cans of sixteen-millimeter film, numbered 1 to 6, and space enough for another one, Number 7.

I took the box out to Carol. She was still sitting on top of the desk, dangling the drying toes and reading through a women's magazine.

"What have you found, then?"

"Do you lend these films to anyone who wants them?"

"Hire, not lend. Sure."

"Who to?"

"Anyone who asks. Usually it's the owners of the horses. Often they want prints made to keep, so we make them."

"Do the Stewards often want them?"

"Stewards? Well, see, if there's any doubt about a race, the Stewards see the film on the racecourse. That van the old man and our Alfie's got develops it on the spot as soon as it's collected from the cameras."

"But sometimes they send for them afterward?"

"Sometimes, yeah. When they want to compare the running of some horse or other." Her legs suddenly stopped swinging. She put down the magazine and gave me a straight stare. "Kelly . . . Kelly *Hughes?*"

I didn't answer.

"Hey, you're not a bit like I thought." She put her blond head on one side, assessing me. "None of those sportswriters ever said anything about you being smashing-looking and dead sexy."

I laughed. I have a crooked nose and a scar down one cheek from where a horse's hoof had cut my face open, and among jockeys I was an also-ran as a bird-attracter.

"It's your eyes," she said. "Dark and sort of smiley and sad and a bit withdrawn. Give me the happy shivers, your eyes do."

"You read all that in a magazine," I said.

"I never!" But she laughed.

"Who asked for the film that's missing from the box?" I said. "And what exactly did they ask for?"

She sighed exaggeratedly and edged herself off the desk into a pair of bright pink sandals.

"Which film is that?" She looked at the box and its reference number, and did a Marilyn Monroe sway over to a filing cabinet against the wall. "Here we are. One official letter from the Stewards' Secretaries saying please send film of last race at Reading. . . ."

I took the letter from her and read it myself. The words were quite clear: "the last race at Reading." Not the sixth race. The last race. And there had been seven races. It hadn't been Carol or the Cannot Lie Company who had made the mistake.

"So you sent it?"

"Of course. Off to the authorities, as per instructions." She put the letter back in the files. "Did you in, did it?"

"Not that film, no."

"Alfie and the old man say you must have made a packet out of the Lemonfizz, to lose your license over it."

"Do you think so, too?"

"Stands to reason. Everyone thinks so."

"Man in the street?"

"Him, too."

"Not a cent."

"You're a nit, then," she said frankly. "Whatever did you do it for?"

"I didn't."

"Oh, yeah?" She gave me a knowing wink. "I suppose you have to say that, don't you?"

"Well," I said, handing her the Reading box to put back in the storeroom, "thanks anyway." I gave her half a smile and went across the expanse of mottled linoleum to the door out.

I drove home slowly, trying to think. Not a very profitable exercise. Brains seemed to have deteriorated into a mushy blankness.

There were several letters for me in the mailbox on my front door, including one from my parents. I unfolded it as I walked up the stairs, feeling as usual a million miles away from them on every level.

My mother had written the first half, in her round regular handwriting, on one side of a large piece of lined paper. As usual, there wasn't a period to be seen. She punctuated entirely with commas.

Dear Kelly,

Thanks for your note, we got it yesterday, we don't like reading about you in the papers, I know you said you hadn't done it son but no smoke without fire is what Mrs. Jones the post office says, and it is not nice for us what people are saying about you round here, all airs and graces they say you are and pride goes before a fall and all that, well the pullets have started laying at last, we are painting your old room for Auntie Myfanwy who is coming to live here with us, her arthritis is too bad for those stairs she has, well Kelly, I wish I could say we want you to come home but your Da is that angry and now Auntie Myfanwy needs the room anyway, well son, we never wanted you to go for a jockey, there was that nice job at the Townhall in Tenby you could have had, I don't like to say it but you have disgraced us son, there's horrid gossip it is going into the village now, everyone whispering, your loving Mother.

I took a deep breath and turned the page over to receive the blast from my father. His writing was much like my mother's, as they had learned from the same teacher, but he had pressed so hard with his ballpoint that he had almost dug through the paper.

Kelly,

You're a damned disgrace boy. It's soft saying you didn't do it. They wouldn't of warned you off if you didn't do it. Not lords and such. They know what's right. You're lucky you're not here I would give you a proper belting. After all that scrimping your Ma did to let you go off to the University. And people said you would get too ladidah to speak to us, they were right. Still, this is worse, being a cheat. Don't you come back here, your Ma's that upset, with what that cat Mrs. Jones saying things. It would be best to say don't send us any more money into the bank. I asked the manager but he said only you can cancel a banker's order so you'd better do it. Your Ma says it's as bad as you being in prison, the disgrace and all.

He hadn't signed it. He wouldn't know how to, we had so little affection for each other. He had despised me from childhood for liking school, and had mocked me unmercifully all the way to college. He showed his jolly side only to my two older brothers, who had had what he considered a healthy contempt for education: one of them had gone into the Merchant Navy, and the other lived next door and worked alongside my father for the farmer who owned the cottages.

When in the end I had turned my back on all the years of learning and taken to racing, my family had again all disapproved of me, though I guessed they would have been pleased enough if I'd chosen it all along. I'd wasted the country's money, my father said; I wouldn't have been given all those grants if they'd known that as soon as I was out I'd go racing. That was probably true. It was also true that since I'd been racing I'd paid enough in taxes to send several other farm boys through college on grants.

I put my parents' letter under Rosalind's photograph. Even she had been unable to reach their approval, because they thought I should have married a nice girl from my own sort of background, not the student daughter of a colonel.

They had rigid minds. It was doubtful now if they would ever be pleased with me, whatever I did. And if I got my license back, as like as not they would think I had somehow cheated again.

You couldn't take aspirins for that sort of pain. It stayed there, sticking in knives. Trying to escape it, I went into the kitchen to see if there was anything to eat.

A tin of sardines, one egg, the dried-up remains of some Port-Salut.

Wrinkling my nose at that lot, I transferred to the sitting room and looked at the television programs.

Nothing I wanted to see.

I slouched in the green velvet armchair and watched the evening slowly fade the colors into subtle grays. A certain amount of peace edged its way past the dragging gloom of the last four days. I wondered almost academically whether I would get my license back before or after I stopped wincing at the way people looked at me, or spoke to me, or wrote about me. Probably the easiest course would be to stay out of sight. Hiding myself away.

Like I was hiding away at that minute, by not going to the Jockeys' Fund dance.

The tickets were on the mantel. Tickets for Tony and Poppy, and for me and the partner I hadn't got around to inviting. Tickets which were not going to be used, which I had paid twelve fund-raising guineas for.

I sat in the dark for half an hour thinking about the people who would be at the Jockeys' Fund dance.

Then I put on my black tie and went to it.

Chapter 8

I went prepared to be stared at.

I was stared at.

Also pointed out and commented on. Discreetly, however, for the most part. And only two people decisively turned their backs.

The Jockeys' Fund dance glittered as usual with titles, diamonds, champagne, and talent. Later it might curl round the edges into spilled drinks, glassy eyes, raddled make-up, and slurring voices, but the gloss wouldn't entirely disappear. It never did. The Jockeys' Fund dance was one of the great social events of the steeplechasing year.

I left my coat in the cloakroom and walked along the wide passage to where the lights were low, the music hot, and the air thick with smoke and scent. The opulent ballroom of the Royal County Hotel, along the road from Ascot racecourse.

Around the dancing area there were numbers of large circular tables with chairs for ten or twelve round each, most of them occupied already. According to the chart in the hall, at table Number 32 I would find the places reserved for Tony and me, if in fact they were still reserved. I gave up looking for table 32 less than halfway down the room, because whenever I moved a new battery of curious eyes swiveled my way. A lot of people raised a hello, but none of them could hide their slightly shocked surprise. It was every bit as bad as I'd feared.

A voice behind me said incredulously, "Hughes!"

I knew the voice. I turned round with an equal sense of the unexpected. Roberta Cranfield. Wearing a honey-

99

colored silk dress with the top smothered in pearls and gold thread and her copper hair drawn high with a trickle of ringlets down the back of her neck.

"You look beautiful," I said.

Her mouth opened. "Hughes!"

"Is your father here?"

"No," she said disgustedly. "He wouldn't face it. Nor would Mother. I came with a party of neighbors but I can't say I was enjoying it much until you turned up."

"Why not?"

"You must be joking. Just look around. At a rough guess, fifty people are rubbernecking at you. Doesn't it make you cringe inside? Anyway, I've had quite enough of it myself this evening, and I didn't even *see* the damned race, let alone get myself warned off." She stopped. "Come and dance with me. If we're hoisting the flag, we may as well do it thoroughly."

"On one condition," I said.

"What's that?"

"You stop calling me Hughes."

"What?"

"Cranfield, I'm tired of being called Hughes."

"Oh!" It had obviously never occurred to her. "Then . . . Kelly . . . how about dancing?"

"Enchanted, Roberta."

She gave me an uncertain look. "I still feel I don't know you."

"You've never bothered."

"Nor have you."

That jolted me. It was true. I'd disliked the idea of her. And I didn't really know her at all.

"How do you do?" I said politely. "Come and dance."

We shuffled around in one of those affairs which look like formalized jungle rituals, swaying in rhythm but never touching. Her face was quite calm, remotely smiling. From her composure one would have guessed her to be entirely at ease, not the target of turned heads, assessing glances, half-hidden whispers.

"I don't know how you do it," she said.

"Do what?"

"Look so . . . so matter-of-fact."

"I was thinking exactly the same about you."

She smiled, eyes crinkling and teeth gleaming, and incredibly in the circumstances she looked happy.

We stuck it for a good ten minutes. Then she said we would go back to her table, and made straight off to it without waiting for me to agree. I didn't think her party would be pleased to have me join them, and half of them weren't.

"Sit down and have a drink, my dear fellow," drawled her host, reaching for a champagne bottle with a languid hand. "And tell me all about the bring-back-Cranfield campaign. Roberta tells me you are working on a spot of reinstatement."

"I haven't managed it yet," I said deprecatingly.

"My dear chap . . ." He gave me an inspecting stare down his nose. He'd been in the Guards, I thought. So many ex-Guards officers looked at the world down the sides of their noses: it came of wearing those blinding hats. He was blond, in his forties, not unfriendly. Roberta called him Bobbie.

The woman on the other side of him leaned over and drooped her heavy pink satin bosom perilously near her brimming glass.

"Do tell me," she said, giving me a thorough gaze from heavily made-up eyes, "what made you come?"

"Natural cussedness," I said pleasantly.

"Oh." She looked taken aback. "How extraordinary."

"Joined to the fact that there was no reason why I shouldn't."

"And are you enjoying it?" Bobbie said. "I mean to say, my dear chap, you are somewhat in the position of a rather messily struck-off doctor turning up four days later at the British Medical Association's grandest function."

I smiled. "Quite a parallel."

"Don't needle him, Bobbie," Roberta said.

Bobbie removed his stare from me and gave it to her

instead. "My dear Roberta, this cookie needs no little girls rushing to his defense. He's as tough as old oak."

A disapproving elderly man on the far side of the pink bosom said under his breath, "Thick-skinned, you mean."

Bobbie heard, and shook his head. "Vertebral," he said. "Different altogether." He stood up. "Roberta, my dear girl, would you care to dance?"

I stood up with him.

"No need to go, my dear chap. Stay. Finish your drink."

"You are most kind," I said truthfully. "But I really came tonight to have a word with one or two people. . . . If you'll excuse me, I'll try to find them."

He gave me an odd formal little inclination of the head, halfway to a bow. "Come back later, if you'd care to."

"Thank you," I said. "Very much."

He took Roberta away to dance and I went up the stairs to the balcony which encircled the room. There were tables all round up there, too, but in places one could get a good clear view of most people below. I spent some length of time identifying them from the tops of their heads.

There must have been about six hundred there, of whom I knew personally about a quarter. Owners, trainers, jockeys, Stewards, reporters, two or three of the bigger bookmakers, starters, judges, Clerks of Courses, and all the others, all with their wives and friends and chattering guests.

Jessel was there, hosting a party of twelve almost exactly beneath where I stood. I wondered if his anger had cooled since Monday, and decided if possible not to put it to the test. He had reportedly sent Squelch off to Pat Nikita, a trainer who was a bitter rival of Cranfield's, which had been rubbing it in a bit. The report looked likely to be true, as Pat Nikita was in the party below me.

Cranfield and Nikita regularly claimed each other's horses in selling races and were apt to bid each other up spitefully at auctions. It was a public joke. So in choosing Nikita as his trainer, Jessel was unmistakably announcing worldwide that he believed Cranfield and I had stopped his horse. Hardly likely to help convince anyone that we hadn't.

At one of the most prominent tables, near the dancing space, sat Lord Ferth, talking earnestly to a large lady in pale blue ostrich feathers. All the other chairs round the table were askew and unoccupied, but while I watched the music changed to a Latin rhythm, and most of the party drifted back. I knew one or two of them slightly, but not well. The man I was chiefly looking for was not among them.

Two tables away from Lord Ferth sat Edwin Byler, gravely beckoning to the waiter to fill his guests' glasses, too proud of his homemade wealth to lift the bottle himself. His cuddly little wife, on the far side of the table, was loaded with half the stock of Hatton Garden and was rather touchingly reveling in it.

Not to be going to ride Edwin Byler's string of superhorses. . . . The wry thrust of regret went deeper than I liked.

There was a rustle behind me and the smell of Roberta's fresh flower scent. I turned toward her.

"Kelly?"

She really looked extraordinarily beautiful.

"Kelly . . . Bobbie suggested that you should take me in to supper."

"That's generous of him."

"He seems to approve of you. He said——" She stopped abruptly. "Well, never mind what he said."

"Do you know him well?" I asked.

She fielded the implication deftly. "Oh, fairly. He lives in the next village to us. He asked me tonight . . . well, I suspect he asked me . . . to cheer me up a bit. Father had canceled our own party, and Bobbie rang me yesterday. He's a nice man."

"Yes," I agreed.

We went down the stairs and through an archway to

the supper room. The light there was of a heartier watt-age. It didn't do any damage to Roberta.

Along one wall stretched a buffet table laden with aspic-shining cold meats and oozing cream gâteaux. Ro-berta said she had dined at Bobbie's before coming on to the dance and wasn't hungry, but we both collected some salmon and sat down at one of the twenty or so small tables clustered into half of the room.

Six feet away sat three fellow jockeys resting their elbows among a debris of empty plates and coffee cups.

"Kelly!" one of them exclaimed in a broad northern voice. "My God. Kelly. Come over here, you old so-and-so. Bring the talent with you."

The talent's chin began its familiar upward tilt.

"Concentrate on the character, not the accent," I said.

She gave me a raw look of surprise, but when I stood up and picked up her plate, she came with me. They made room for us, admired Roberta's appearance, and didn't refer to anyone being warned off. Their girls, they explained, were powdering their noses, and when the noses reappeared, immaculate, they all smiled goodbye and went back to the ballroom.

"They were kind." She sounded surprised.

"They would be."

She fiddled with her fork, not looking at me. "You said the other day that my mind was in chains. Was that what you meant . . . that I'm inclined to judge people by their voices . . . and that it's wrong?"

"Eton's bred its rogues," I said. "Yes."

"Cactus. You're all prickles."

"Original sin exists," I said mildly. "So does original virtue. They both crop up regardless. No respecters of birth."

"Where did you go to school?"

"In Wales."

"You haven't a Welsh accent. You haven't any accent at all. And that's odd, really, considering you are only . . ." Her voice trailed away and she looked aghast at her self-betrayal. "Oh dear . . . I'm sorry."

"It's not surprising," I pointed out. "Considering your father. And anyway, in my own way I'm just as bad. I smothered my Welsh accent quite deliberately. I used to practice in secret, while I was still at school, copying the BBC news announcers. I wanted to be a Civil Servant, and I was ambitious, and I knew I wouldn't get far if I sounded like the son of a Welsh farm laborer. So in time this became my natural way of talking. And my parents despise me for it."

"Parents!" she said despairingly. "Why can we never escape them? Whatever we are, it's because of *them*. I want to be *me*." She looked astonished at herself. "I've never felt like this before. I don't understand. . . ."

"Well, I do," I said, smiling. "Only it happens to most people around fifteen or sixteen. Rebellion, it's called."

"You're mocking me." But the chin stayed down.

"No."

We finished the salmon and drank coffee. A large loudly chattering party collected food from the buffet and pushed the two tables next to us together so that they could all sit at one. They were well away on a tide of alcohol and bonhomie, loosened and expansive. I watched them idly. I knew four of them: two trainers, one wife, one owner.

One of the trainers, Trevor Norse, caught sight of me and literally dropped his knife.

"That's Kelly Hughes," he said disbelievingly. The whole party turned round and stared. Roberta drew a breath in distress. I sat without moving.

"What are you doing here?"

"Drinking coffee," I said politely.

His eyes narrowed. Norse was not amused. I sighed inwardly. It was never good to antagonize trainers; it simple meant one less possible source of income; but I'd ridden for Trevor Norse several times already, and knew that it was practically impossible to please him anyway.

A heavy man, six feet plus, laboring under the misapprehension that size could substitute for ability. He was much better with owners than with horses, tireless at cultivating the one and lazy with the other.

His brainless wife said abruptly, "I hear you're paying Dexter's lads' wages because you're sure you'll get your license back in a day or two."

"What's all that?" Norse said sharply. "Where did you hear all that nonsense?"

"Everyone's talking about it, darling," she said protestingly.

"Who's everyone?"

She giggled weakly. "I heard it in the ladies, if you must know. But it's quite true, I'm sure it is. Dexter's lads told Daphne's lads in the local pub, and Daphne told Miriam, and Miriam was telling us in the ladies. . . ."

"Is it true?" Norse demanded.

"Well, more or less," I agreed.

"Good Lord."

"Miriam said Kelly Hughes says he and Dexter were framed, and that he's finding out who did it." Mrs. Norse giggled at me. "My *dear,* isn't it all such fun?"

"Great," I said dryly. I stood up, and Roberta also.

"Do you know Roberta Cranfield?" I said formally, and they all exclaimed over her, and she scattered on them a bright artificial smile, and we went back and tried another dance.

It wasn't altogether a great idea, because we were stopped halfway round by Daddy Leeman of the *Daily Witness* who raked me over with avid eyes and yelled above the music was it true I was claiming I'd been framed. He had a piercing voice. All the nearby couples turned and stared. Some of them raised skeptical eyebrows at each other.

"I really can't stand a great deal more of this," Roberta said in my ear. "How can you? Why don't you go home now?"

"I'm sorry," I said contritely. "You've been splendid. I'll take you back to Bobbie."

"But you . . . ?"

"I haven't done what I came for. I'll stay a bit longer."

She compressed her mouth and started to dance again. "All right. So will I."

We danced without smiling.

"Do you want a tombola ticket?" I asked.

"No." She was astonished.

"You might as well. I want to go down that end of the room."

"Whatever for?"

"Looking for someone. Haven't been down that end at all."

"Oh. All right, then."

She stepped off the polished wood onto the thick carpet, and threaded her way to the aisle which led down to the gaily decorated tombola stall at the far end of the ballroom.

I looked for the man I wanted, but I didn't see him. I met too many other eyes, most of which hastily looked away.

"I hate them," Roberta said fiercely. "I hate people."

I bought her four tickets. Three of them were blanks. The fourth had a number which fitted a bottle of vodka.

"I don't like it much," she said, holding it dubiously.

"Nor do I."

"I'll give it to the first person who's nice to you."

"You might have to drink it yourself."

We went slowly back down the aisle, not talking.

A thin woman sprang up from her chair as we approached her table and, in spite of the embarrassed holding-back clutches of her party, managed to force her way out into our path. We couldn't pass her without pushing. We stopped.

"You're Roberta Cranfield, aren't you?" she said. She had a strong-boned face, no lipstick, angry eyes, and stiffly regimented graying hair. She looked as if she'd had far too much to drink.

"Excuse us," I said gently, trying to pass.

"Oh, no, you don't," she said. "Not until I've had my say."

"Grace!" wailed a man across the table. I looked at him more closely. Edwin Byler's trainer, Jack Roxford. "Grace, dear, leave it. Sit down, dear," he said.

Grace dear had no such intentions. Grace dear's feelings were far too strong.

"Your father's got exactly what he deserves, my lass, and I can tell you I'm glad about it. Glad." She thrust her face toward Roberta's, glaring like a madwoman. Roberta looked down her nose at her, which I would have found as infuriating as Grace did.

"I'd dance on his grave," she said furiously. "That I would."

"Why?" I said flatly.

She didn't look at me. She said to Roberta, "He's a bloody snob, your father. A bloody snob. And he's got what he deserved. So there. You tell him that."

"Excuse me," Roberta said coldly, and tried to go forward.

"Oh, no, you don't." Grace clutched at her arm. Roberta shook her hand off angrily. "Your bloody snob of a father was trying to get Edwin Byler's horses away from us. Did you know that? Did you know that? All those grand ways of his. Thought Edwin would do better in a bigger stable, did he? Oh, I heard what he said. Trying to persuade Edwin he needed a grand top-drawer trainer now, not poor little folk like us, who've won just rows of races for him. Well, I could have laughed my head off when I heard he'd been had up. I'll tell you. Serves him right, I said. What a laugh."

"Grace," said Jack Roxford despairingly. "I'm sorry, Miss Cranfield. She isn't really like this."

He looked acutely embarrassed. I thought that probably Grace Roxford was all too often like this. He had the haunted expression of the forever-apologizing husband.

"Cheer up, then, Mrs. Roxford," I said loudly. "You've got what you want. You're laughing. So why the fury?"

"Eh?" She twisted her head round at me, staggering a fraction. "As for you, Kelly Hughes, you just asked for what you got, and don't give me any of that crap we've been hearing this evening that you were framed, because you know bloody well you weren't. People like you and Cranfield, you think you can get away with murder, people like you. But there's justice somewhere in this world sometimes and you won't forget that in a hurry, will you now, Mr. Clever Dick."

One of the women of the party stood up and tried to persuade her to quieten down, as every ear for six tables around was stretched in her direction. She was oblivious of them. I wasn't.

Roberta said under her breath, "Oh God."

"So you go home and tell your bloody snob of a father," Grace said to her, "that it's a great big laugh him being found out. That's what it is, a great big laugh."

The nervous woman friend pulled her arm, and Grace swung angrily round from us to her. We took the brief opportunity and edged away round her back, and as we retreated we could hear her shouting after us, her words indistinct above the music except for "laugh" and "bloody snob."

"She's *awful*," Roberta said.

"Not much help to poor old Jack," I agreed.

"Is she always like that?"

"I don't know her, and I don't know Jack himself well, either. They seem an odd sort of couple. Loathe each other devotedly, perhaps."

"I do hate scenes," she said. "They're so messy."

"Do you think all strong emotions are messy?"

"That's not the same thing," she said. "You can have strong emotions without making scenes. Scenes are disgusting."

I sighed. "That one was."

"Yes."

She was walking, I noticed, with her neck stretched very tall, the classic signal to anyone watching that she was not responsible or bowed down, or amused at being involved in noise and nastiness. Rosalind, I reflected nostalgically, would probably have sympathetically agreed with dear disturbed Grace, led her off to some quiet mollifying corner, and reappeared with her eating out of her hand. Rosalind had been tempestuous herself and understood uncontrollable feelings.

Unfortunately at the end of the aisle we almost literally bumped into Jessel, who came in for the murderous glance from Roberta which had been earned by dear

Grace. Jessel naturally misinterpreted her expression and spat first.

"You can tell your father that I had been thinking for some time of sending my horses to Pat Nikita, and that this business has made me regret that I didn't do it a long time ago. Pat has always wanted to train for me. I stayed with your father out of a mistaken sense of loyalty, and just look how he repaid me."

"Father has won a great many races for you," Roberta said coldly. "And if Squelch had been good enough to win the Lemonfizz Cup, he would have done."

Jessel's mouth sneered. It didn't suit him.

"As for you, Hughes, it's a disgrace you being here tonight and I cannot think why you were allowed in. And don't think you can fool me by spreading rumors that you are innocent and on the point of proving it. That's all piffle, and you know it, and if you have any ideas you can reinstate yourself with me that way, you are very much mistaken."

He turned his back on us and bristled off, pausing triumphantly to pat Pat Nikita on the shoulder, and looking back to make sure we had noticed. Very small of him.

"There goes Squelch," I said resignedly.

"He'll soon be apologizing and sending him back," she said with certainty.

"Not a hope. Jessel's not the humble-pie kind. And Pat Nikita will never let go of that horse. Not to see him go back to your father. He'd break him down first."

"Why are people so jealous of each other?" she exclaimed.

"Born in them," I said. "And almost universal."

"You have a very poor opinion of human nature," she said disapprovingly.

"An objective opinion. There's as much good as bad."

"You can't be objective about being warned off," she protested.

"Er . . . no," I conceded. "How about a drink?"

She looked instinctively toward Bobbie's table, and I shook my head. "In the bar."

"Oh . . . still looking for someone?"

"That's right. We haven't tried the bar yet."

"Is there going to be another scene?"

"I shouldn't think so."

"All right, then."

We made our way slowly through the crowd. By then the fact that we were there must have been known to almost everyone in the place. Certainly the heads no longer turned in open surprise, but the eyes did, sliding into corners, giving us a surreptitious once-over, probing and hurtful. Roberta held herself almost defiantly straight.

The bar was heavily populated, with cigar smoke lying in a cloud over the well-groomed heads and the noise level doing justice to a discothèque. Almost at once, through a narrow gap in the cluster, I saw him, standing against the far wall, talking vehemently. He turned his head suddenly and looked straight at me, meeting my eyes briefly before the groups between us shifted and closed the line of sight. In those two seconds, however, I had seen his mouth tighten and his whole face compress into annoyance; and he had known I was at the dance, because there was no surprise.

"You've seen him," Roberta said.

"Yes."

"Well . . . who is it?"

"Lord Gowery."

She gasped. "Oh, no, Kelly."

"I want to talk to him."

"It can't do any good."

"You never know."

"Annoying Lord Gowery is the last—positively the last—way of getting your license back. Surely you can see that?"

"Yes . . . He's not going to be kind, I don't think. So would you mind very much if I took you back to Bobbie first?"

She looked troubled. "You won't say anything silly? It's Father's license as well, remember."

"I'll bear it in mind," I said flippantly. She gave me a sharp suspicious glance, but turned easily enough to go back to Bobbie.

Almost immediately outside the bar, we were stopped by Jack Roxford, who was hurrying toward us through the throng.

"Kelly," he said, half panting with the exertion. "I just wanted to catch you . . . to say how sorry I am that Grace went off the deep end like that. She's not herself, poor girl. . . . Miss Cranfield, I do apologize."

Roberta unbent a little. "That's all right, Mr. Roxford."

"I wouldn't like you to believe that what Grace said . . . all those things about your father . . . is what I think, too." He looked from her to me, and back again, the hesitant worry furrowing his forehead. A slight, unaggressive man of about forty-five: bald crown, nervous eyes, permanently worried expression. He was a reasonably good trainer but not enough of a man of the world to have achieved much personal stature. To me, though I had never ridden for him, he had always been friendly, but his restless anxiety state made him tiring to be with.

"Kelly," he said, "if it's really true that you were both framed, I do sincerely hope that you get your licenses back. I mean, I know there's a risk that Edwin will take his horses to your father, Miss Cranfield, but he did tell me this evening that he won't do so now, even if he could. . . . But, please believe me, I hold no dreadful grudge against either of you, like poor Grace. . . . I do hope you'll forgive her."

"Of course, Mr. Roxford," said Roberta, entirely placated. "Please don't give it another thought. And oh!" she added impulsively, "I think you've earned this!" and into the hands of the astonished man she thrust the bottle of vodka.

Chapter 9

When I went back toward the bar, I found Lord Gowery had come out of it. He was standing shoulder to shoulder with Lord Ferth, both of them watching me walk toward them with faces like thunder.

I stopped four feet away, and waited.

"Hughes," said Lord Gowery for openers, "you shouldn't be here."

"My lord," I said politely, "this isn't Newmarket Heath."

It went down badly. They were both affronted. They closed their ranks.

"Insolence will get you nowhere," Lord Ferth said, and Lord Gowery added, "You'll never get your license back if you behave like this."

I said without heat, "Does justice depend on good manners?"

They looked as if they couldn't believe their ears. From their point of view I was cutting my own throat, though I had always myself doubted that excessive meekness got licenses restored any quicker than they would have been without it. Meekness in the accused brought out leniency in some judges, but severity in others. To achieve a minimum sentence, the guilty should always bone up on the character of their judge, a sound maxim which I hadn't had the brains to see applied even more to the innocent.

"I would have thought some sense of shame would have kept you away," Lord Ferth said.

"It took a bit of an effort to come," I agreed.

His eyes narrowed and opened again quickly.

Gowery said, "As to spreading these rumors . . . I say categorically that you are not only not on the point of being given your license back, but that your suspension will be all the longer in consequence of your present behavior."

I gave him a level stare and Lord Ferth opened his mouth and shut it again.

"It is no rumor that Mr. Cranfield and I are not guilty," I said at length. "It is no rumor that two at least of the witnesses were lying. Those are facts."

"Nonsense," Gowery said vehemently.

"What you believe, sir," I said, "doesn't alter the truth."

"You are doing yourself no good, Hughes." Under his heavy authoritative exterior he was exceedingly angry. All I needed was a borehole and I'd get a gusher.

I said, "Would you be good enough to tell me who suggested to you or the other Stewards that you should seek out and question Mr. Newtonnards?"

There was the tiniest shift in his eyes. Enough for me to be certain.

"Certainly not."

"Then will you tell me upon whose instructions the enquiry agent David Oakley visited my flat?"

"I will not." His voice was loud, and for the first time alarmed.

Ferth looked in growing doubt from one of us to the other.

"What is all this about?" he said.

"Mr. Cranfield and I were indeed wrongly warned off," I said. "Someone sent David Oakley to my flat to fake that photograph. And I believe Lord Gowery knows who it was."

"I most certainly do not," he said furiously. "Do you want to be sued for slander?"

"I have not slandered you, sir."

"You said . . ."

"I said you knew who sent David Oakley. I did not say that you knew the photograph was a fake."

"And it wasn't," he insisted fiercely.

"Well," I said, "it was."

There was a loaded, glaring silence. Then Lord Gowery said heavily, "I'm not going to listen to this," and turned on his heel and dived back into the bar.

Lord Ferth, looking troubled, took a step after him.

I said, "My lord, may I talk to you?" And he stopped and turned back to me and said, "Yes, I think you'd better."

He gestured toward the supper room next door and we went through the archway into the brighter light. Nearly everyone had eaten and gone. The buffet table bore shambled remains and all but two of the small tables were unoccupied. He sat down at one and pointed to the chair opposite. I took it, facing him.

"Now," he said. "Explain."

I spoke in a flat calm voice, because emotion was going to repel him where reason might get through. "My lord, if you could look at the Enquiry from my point of view for a minute, it is quite simple. I know that I never had any five hundred pounds or any note from Mr. Cranfield; therefore I am obviously aware that David Oakley was lying. It's unbelievable that the Stewards should have sent him, since the evidence he produced was faked. So someone else did. I thought Lord Gowery might know who. So I asked him."

"He said he didn't know."

"I don't altogether believe him."

"Hughes, that's preposterous."

"Are you intending to say, sir, that men in power positions are infallibly truthful?"

He looked at me without expression in a lengthening silence. Finally he said, as Roberta had done, "Where did you go to school?"

In the usual course of things, I kept dead quiet about the type of education I'd had because it was not likely to endear me to either owners or trainers. Still, there was a time for everything, so I told him.

"Coedlant Primary, Tenby Grammar, and L.S.E."

"L.S.E. . . . you don't mean . . . the London School of Economics?" He looked astonished.

"Yes."

"My God . . ."

I watched while he thought it over. "What did you read there?"

"Politics, philosophy, and economics."

"Then what on earth made you become a jockey?"

"It was almost an accident," I said. "I didn't plan it. When I'd finished my final exams, I was mentally tired, so I thought I'd take a sort of paid holiday working on the land. . . . I knew how to do that, my father's a farmhand. I worked at harvesting for a farmer in Devon, and every morning I used to ride his chasers out at exercise, because I'd ridden most of my life, you see. He had a permit, and he was dead keen. And then his brother, who raced them for him, broke his shoulder at one of the early Devon meetings, and he put me up instead, and almost at once I started winning . . . and then it took hold of me . . . so I didn't get around to being a Civil Servant, as I'd always vaguely intended, and . . . well . . . I've never regretted it."

"Not even now?" he said with irony.

I shook my head. "Not even now."

"Hughes . . ." His face crinkled dubiously. "I don't know what to think. At first I was sure you were not the type to have stopped Squelch deliberately . . . and then there was all that damning evidence. Charlie West saying you had definitely pulled back . . ."

I looked down at the table. I didn't after all want an eye for an eye, when it came to the point.

"Charlie was mistaken," I said. "He got two races muddled up. I did pull back in another race at about that time . . . riding a novice chaser with no chance, well back in the field. I wanted to give it a good schooling race. That was what Charlie remembered."

He said doubtfully, "It didn't sound like it."

"No," I agreed. "I've had it out with Charlie since. He might be prepared to admit now that he was talking about the wrong race. If you will ask the Oxford Stewards, you'll find that Charlie said nothing to them directly after the Lemonfizz, when they made their first enquiries, about me not trying. He only said it later, at the Enquiry in Portman Square." Because in between some beguiling seducer had offered him five hundred pounds for the service.

"I see." He frowned. "And what was it that you asked Lord Gowery about Newtonnards?"

"Newtonnards didn't volunteer the information to the Stewards about Mr. Cranfield backing Cherry Pie, but he did tell several bookmaker colleagues. Someone told the Stewards. I wanted to know who."

"Are you suggesting that it was the same person who sent Oakley to your flat?"

"It might be. But not necessarily." I hesitated, looking at him doubtfully.

"What is it?" he said.

"Sir, I don't want to offend you, but would you mind telling me why you sat in at the Enquiry? Why there were four of you instead of three, when Lord Gowery, if you'll forgive me saying so, was obviously not too pleased at the arrangement."

His lips tightened. "You're being uncommonly tactful, all of a sudden."

"Yes, sir."

He looked at me steadily. A tall thin man with high cheekbones, strong black hair, hot fiery eyes. A man whose force of character reached out and hit you, so that you'd never forget meeting him. The best ally in the whole chasing setup, if I could only reach him.

"I cannot give you my reasons for attending," he said with some reproof.

"Then you had some . . . reservations . . . about how the Enquiry would be conducted?"

"I didn't say that," he protested. But he had meant it.

"Lord Gowery chose Andrew Tring to sit with him at the hearing, and Andrew Tring wants a very big concession from him just now. And he chose Lord Plimborne as the third Steward, and Lord Plimborne continually fell asleep."

"Do you realize what you're saying?" He was truly shocked.

"I want to know how Lord Gowery acquired all that evidence against us. I want to know why the Stewards' Secretaries sent for the wrong film. I want to know why Lord Gowery was so biased, so deaf to our denials, so determined too warn us off."

"That's slanderous. . . ."

"I want you to ask him," I finished flatly.

He simply stared.

I said, "He might tell you. He might just possibly tell you. But he'd never in a million years tell *me*."

"Hughes . . . You surely don't expect . . ."

"That wasn't a straight trial, and he knows it. I'm just asking you to tackle him with it, to see if he will explain."

"You are talking about a much-respected man," he said coldly.

"Yes, sir. He's a baron, a rich man, a Steward of long standing. I know all that."

"And you *still* maintain . . . ?"

"Yes."

His hot eyes brooded. "He'll have you in court for this."

"Only if I'm wrong."

"I can't possibly do it," he said with decision.

"And please, if you have one, use a tape recorder."

"I told you . . ."

"Yes, sir, I know you did."

He got up from the table, paused as if about to say something, changed his mind, and, as I stood up also, turned abruptly and walked sharply away. When he had gone, I found that my hands were trembling, and I followed him slowly out of the supper room feeling a battered wreck.

I had either resurrected our licenses or driven the nails into them, and only time would tell which.

Bobbie said, "Have a drink, my dear fellow. You look as though you've been clobbered by a steamroller."

I took a mouthful of champagne and thanked him, and watched Roberta swing her body to a compelling rhythm with someone else. The ringlets bounced against her neck. I wondered without disparagement how long it had taken her to pin them on.

"Not the best of evenings for you, old pal," Bobbie observed.

"You never know."

He raised his eyebrows, drawling down his nose, "Mission accomplished?"

"A fuse lit, rather."

He lifted his glass. "To a successful detonation."

"You are most kind," I said formally.

The music changed gear and Roberta's partner brought her back to the table.

I stood up. "I came to say goodbye," I said. "I'll be going now."

"Oh, not yet," she exclaimed. "The worst is over. No one's staring any more. Have some fun."

"Dance with the dear girl," Bobbie said, and Roberta put out a long arm and pulled mine, and so I went and danced with her.

"Lord Gowery didn't eat you, then?"

"He's scrunching the bones at this minute."

"Kelly! If you've done any damage . . ."

"No omelets without smashing eggs, love."

The chin went up. I grinned. She brought it down again. Getting quite human, Miss Cranfield.

After a while the hot rhythm changed to a slow smooch, and couples around us went into clinches. Bodies to bodies, heads to heads, eyes shut, swaying in the dimming light. Roberta eyed them coolly and prickled when I put my arms up to gather her in. She danced very straight, with four inches of air between us. Not human enough.

We ambled around in that frigid fashion through three separate wodges of glutinous music. She didn't come any closer, and I did nothing to persuade her, but equally she seemed to be in no hurry to break it up. Composed, cool, off-puttingly gracious, she looked as flawless in the small hours as she had when I'd arrived.

"I'm glad you were here," I said.

She moved her head in surprise. "It hasn't been exactly the best Jockeys' Fund dance of my life . . . but I'm glad I came."

"Next year this will be all over, and everyone will have forgotten."

"I'll dance with you again next year," she said.

"It's a pact."

She smiled, and just for a second a stray beam of light shimmered on some expression in her eyes which I didn't understand.

She was aware of it. She turned her head away, and then detached herself altogether, and gestured that she wanted to go back to the table. I delivered her to Bobbie, and she sat down immediately and began powdering a non-shiny nose.

"Good night," I said to Bobbie. "And thank you."

"My dear fellow. Any time."

"Good night, Roberta."

She looked up. Nothing in the eyes. Her voice was collected. "Good night, Kelly."

I lowered myself into the low-slung burnt-orange car in the park and drove away thinking about her. Roberta Cranfield. Not my idea of a cuddly bedmate. Too cold, too controlled, too proud. And it didn't go with that copper hair, all that rigidity. Or maybe she was only rigid to me because I was a farm laborer's son. Only that, and only a jockey . . . and her father had taught her that jockeys were the lower classes dear and don't get your fingers dirty. . . .

Kelly, I said to myself, you've a fair-sized chip on your shoulder, old son. Maybe she does think like that, but why should it bother you? And even if she does, she spent most of the evening with you . . . although she was really quite careful not to touch you too much. Well . . . maybe that was because so many people were watching

. . . and maybe it was simply that she didn't like the thought of it.

I was on the short cut home that led round the south of Reading, streaking down deserted back roads, going fast for no reason except that speed had become a habit. This car was easily the best I'd ever had, the only one I had felt proud of. Mechanically a masterpiece and with looks to match. Even thirty thousand miles in the past year hadn't dulled the pleasure I got from driving it. Its only fault was that, like so many other sports cars, it had a totally inefficient heater, which, in spite of coaxing and overhauls, stubbornly refused to do more than de-mist the windscreen and raise my toes one degree above frostbite. If kicked, it retaliated with a smell of exhaust.

I had gone to the dance without a coat, and the night was frosty. I shivered and switched on the heater to maximum. As usual, damn all.

There was a radio in the car, which I seldom listened to, and a spare crash helmet, and my five-pound racing saddle which I'd been going to take to Wetherby races.

Depression flooded back. Fierce though the evening had been, in many ways I had forgotten for a while the dreariness of being banned. It could be a long slog now, after what I had said to the Lords Gowery and Ferth. A very long slog indeed. Cranfield wouldn't like the gamble. I wasn't too sure that I could face telling him, if it didn't come off.

Lord Ferth . . . would he or wouldn't he? He'd be torn between loyalty to an equal and a concept of justice. I didn't know him well enough to be sure which would win. And maybe anyway he would shut everything I'd said clean out of his mind, as too far-fetched and preposterous to bother about.

Bobbie had been great, I thought. I wondered who he was. Maybe one day I'd ask Roberta.

Mrs. Roxford . . . poor dear Grace. What a life Jack must lead. . . . Hope he liked vodka . . .

I took an unexpectedly sharp bend far too fast. The wheels screeched when I wrenched the nose round and the car went weaving and skidding for a hundred yards before I had it in control again. I put my foot gingerly back on the accelerator and still had in my mind's eye the solid trunks of the row of trees I had just missed by centimeters.

God, I thought, how could I be so careless. It rocked me. I was a careful driver, even if fast, and I'd never had an accident. I could feel myself sweating. It was something to sweat about.

How stupid I was, thinking about the dance, not concentrating on driving, and going too fast for these small roads. I rubbed my forehead, which felt tense and tight, and kept my speed down to forty.

Roberta had looked beautiful . . . Keep your mind on the road, Kelly, for God's sake. . . . Usually I drove semiautomatically, without having to concentrate every yard of the way. I found myself going slower still, because both my reactions and my thoughts were growing sluggish. I'd drunk a total of about half a glass of champagne all evening, so it couldn't be that.

I was simply going to sleep.

I stopped the car, got out, and stamped about to wake myself up. People who went to sleep at the wheels of sports cars on the way home from dances were not a good risk.

Too many sleepless nights, grinding over my sorry state. Insulting the lions seemed to have released the worst of that. I felt I could now fall unconscious for a month.

I considered sleeping there and then, in the car. But the car was cold and couldn't be heated. I would drive on, I decided, and stop for good if I felt really dozy again. The fresh air had done the trick; I was wide awake and irritated with myself.

The beam of my headlights on the cats' eyes down the empty road was soon hypnotic. I switched on the radio to see if that would hold my attention, but it was all soft and sweet late-night music. Lullaby. I switched it off.

Pity I didn't smoke. That would have helped.

It was a star-clear night with a bright full moon. Ice crystals sparkled like diamond dust on the grass verges, now that I'd left the wooded part behind. Beautiful but unwelcome, because a hard frost would mean no racing tomorrow at Sundown. . . . With a jerk I realized that that didn't matter to me any more.

I glanced at the speedometer. Forty. It seemed very fast. I slowed down still further to thirty-five, and nodded owlishly to myself. Anyone would be safe at thirty-five.

The tightness across my forehead slowly developed into a headache. Never mind, only an hour to home, then sleep . . . sleep . . . sleep . . .

It's no good, I thought fuzzily. I'll have to stop and black out for a bit, even if I do wake up freezing, or I'll black out without stopping first, and that will be that.

The next lay-by, or something like that . . .

I began looking, forgot what I was looking for, took my foot still further off the accelerator, and reckoned that thirty miles an hour was quite safe. Maybe twenty-five . . . would be better.

A little further on, there were some sudden bumps in the road surface and my foot slipped off the accelerator altogether. The engine stalled. Car stopped.

Oh, well, I thought. That settles it. Ought to move over to the side, though. Couldn't see the side. Very odd.

The headache was pressing on my temples, and now that the engine had stopped I could hear a faint ringing in my ears.

Never mind. Never mind. Best to go to sleep. Leave the lights on . . . no one came along that road much . . . not at two in the morning . . . but have to leave the lights on just in case.

Ought to pull in to the side.

Ought to . . .

Too much trouble. Couldn't move my arms properly, anyway, so couldn't possibly do it.

Deep deep in my head, a tiny instinct switched itself to emergency.

Something was wrong. Something was indistinctly but appallingly wrong.

Sleep. Must sleep.

Get out, the flickering instinct said. Get out of the car.

Ridiculous.

Get out of the car.

Unwillingly, because it was such an effort, I struggled weakly with the handle. The door swung open. I put one leg out and tried to pull myself up, and was swept by a wave of dizziness. My head was throbbing. This wasn't . . . it couldn't be . . . just ordinary sleep.

Get out of the car . . .

My arms and legs belonged to someone else. They had me on my feet. . . . I was standing up . . . didn't remember how I got there. But I was out.

Out.

Now what?

I took three tottering steps toward the back of the car and leant against the rear fender. Funny, I thought, the moonlight wasn't so bright any more.

The earth was trembling.

Stupid. Quite stupid. The earth didn't tremble.

Trembling. And the air was wailing. And the moon was falling on me. Come down from the sky and rushing toward me . . .

Not the moon. A great roaring wailing monster with a blinding moon eye. A monster making the earth tremble. A monster racing to gobble me up, huge and dark and faster than the wind and unimaginably terrifying . . .

I didn't move. Couldn't.

The one-thirty mail express from Paddington to Plymouth plowed into my sturdy little car and carried its crumpled remains half a mile down the track.

Chapter 10

I didn't know what had happened. Didn't understand. There was a tremendous noise of tearing metal and a ninety-mile-an-hour whirl of hundred-and-twenty-ton diesel engine one foot away from me, and a thudding catapulting scrunch which lifted me up like a rag doll and toppled me somersaulting through the air in a kaleidoscopic black arc.

My head crashed against a concrete post. The rest of my body felt mangled beyond repair. There were rainbows in my brain, blue, purple, flaming pink, with diamond-bright pin stars. Interesting while it lasted. Didn't last very long. Dissolved into an embracing inferno in which colors got lost in pain.

Up the line, the train had screeched to a stop. Lights and voices were coming back that way.

The earth was cold, hard, and damp. A warm stream ran down my face. I knew it was blood. Didn't care much. Couldn't think properly, either. And didn't really want to.

More lights. Lots of lights. Lots of people. Voices.

A voice I knew.

"Roberta, my dear girl, don't look."

"It's Kelly!" she said. Shock. Wicked, unforgettable shock. "It's Kelly." The second time despair.

"Come away, my dear girl."

She didn't go. She was kneeling beside me. I could smell her scent, and feel her hand on my hair. I was lying on my side, face down. After a while I could see a segment of honey silk dress. There was blood on it.

I said, "You're ruining . . . your dress."

"It doesn't matter."

It helped somehow to have her there. I was grateful that she had stayed. I wanted to tell her that. I tried—and meant—to say "Roberta." What in fact I said was "Rosalind."

"Oh Kelly . . ." Her voice held a mixture of pity and distress.

I thought groggily that she would go away, now that I'd made such a silly mistake, but she stayed, saying small things like "You'll be all right soon," and sometimes not talking at all, but just being there. I didn't know why I wanted her to stay. I remembered that I didn't even like the girl.

All the people who arrive after accidents duly arrived. Police with blue flashing lights. Ambulance waking the neighborhood with its siren. Bobbie took Roberta away, telling her there was no more she could do. The ambulance men scooped me unceremoniously onto a stretcher, and if I thought them rough it was only because every movement brought a scream up as far as my teeth and heaven knows whether any of them got any further.

By the time I reached the hospital, the mists had cleared. I knew what had happened to my car. I knew that I wasn't dying. I knew that Bobbie and Roberta had taken the back-roads detour, as I had, and had reached the level crossing not long after me.

What I didn't understand was how I had come to stop on the railway. That crossing had drop-down fringe gates, and they hadn't been shut.

A young dark-haired doctor with tired dark-ringed eyes came to look at me, talking to the ambulance men.

"He'd just come from a dance," they said. "The police want a blood test."

"Drunk?" said the doctor.

The ambulance men shrugged. They thought it possible.

"No," I said. "It wasn't drink. At least . . ."

They didn't pay much attention. The young doctor stooped over my lower half, feeling the damage with slender gentle fingers. "That hurts? Yes." He parted my hair, looking at my head. "Nothing much up there. More blood than damage." He stood back. "We'll get your pelvis X-rayed. And that leg. Can't tell what's what until after that."

A nurse tried to take my shoes off. I said very loudly, "Don't!"

She jumped. The doctor signed to her to stop. "We'll do it under an anesthetic. Just leave him for now."

She came instead and wiped my forehead.

"Sorry," she said.

The doctor took my pulse. "Why ever did you stop on a level crossing?" he said conversationally. "Silly thing to do."

"I felt . . . sleepy. Had a headache." It didn't sound very sensible.

"Had a bit to drink?"

"Almost nothing."

"At a dance?" He sounded skeptical.

"Really," I said weakly. "I didn't."

He put my arm down. I was still wearing my dinner jacket, though someone had taken off my tie. There were bright scarlet blotches down my white shirt and an unmendable tear down the right side of my black trousers.

I shut my eyes. Didn't do much good. The screaming pain showed no signs of giving up. It had localized into my right side from armpit to toes, with repercussions up and down my spine. I'd broken a good many bones racing, but this was much worse. Much. It was impossible.

"It won't be long now," the doctor said comfortingly. "We'll have you under."

"The train didn't hit me," I said. "I got out of the car. . . . I was leaning against the back of it . . . the train hit the car . . . not me."

I felt sick. How long . . . ?

"If it had hit you, you wouldn't be here."

"I suppose not. . . . I had this thumping headache . . . needed air . . ." Why couldn't I pass out, I thought. People always passed out when it became unbearable. Or so I'd always believed.

"Have you still got the headache?" he asked clinically.

"It's gone off a bit. Just sore now." My mouth was dry. Always like that after injuries. The least of my troubles.

Two porters came to wheel me away, and I protested more than was stoical about the jolts. I felt gray. Looked at my hands. They were quite surprisingly red.

X-ray department. Very smooth, very quick. Didn't try to move me except for cutting the zipper out of my trousers. Quite enough.

"Sorry," they said.

"Do you work all night?" I asked.

They smiled. On duty if called.

"Thanks," I said.

Another journey. People in green uniforms and white masks, making soothing remarks. Could I face taking my coat off? No? Never mind, then. Needle into vein in back of hand. Marvelous. Oblivion rolled through me in gray and black, and I greeted it with a sob of welcome.

The world shuffled back in the usual way, bit by uncomfortable bit, with a middle-aged nurse patting my hand and telling me to wake up, dear, it was all over.

I had to admit that my wildest fears were not realized. I still had two legs. One I could move. The other had a plaster cast on. Inside the plaster it gently ached. The scream had died to a whisper. I sighed with relief.

What was the time? Five o'clock, dear.

Where was I? In the recovery ward, dear. Now go to sleep again and when you wake up you'll be feeling much better, you'll see.

I did as she said, and she was quite right.

Midmorning, a doctor came. Not the same one as the night before. Older, heavier, but just as tired-looking.

"You had a lucky escape," he said.

"Yes, I did."

"Luckier than you imagine. We took a blood test. Actually, we took two blood tests. The first one for alcohol. With practically negative results. Now, this interested us, because who except a drunk would stop a car on a level crossing and get out and lean against it? The casualty doctor told us you swore you hadn't been drinking and that anyway you seemed sober enough to him, but that you'd had a bad headache which was now better. We gave you a bit of thought, and we looked at those very bright scarlet stains on your shirt and tested your blood again, and there it was!" He paused triumphantly.

"What?"

"Carboxyhemoglobin."

"What?"

"Carbon monoxide, my dear chap. Carbon-monoxide poisoning. Explains everything, don't you see?"

"Oh . . . but I thought . . . with carbon monoxide . . . one simply blacked out."

"It depends. If you got a large dose all at once, that would happen, like it does to people who get stuck in snowdrifts and leave their engines running. But a trickle— that would affect you more slowly. But it would all be the same in the end, of course. The hemoglobin in the red corpuscles has a greater affinity for carbon monoxide than for oxygen, so it mops up any carbon monoxide you breathe in, and oxygen is disregarded. If the level of carbon monoxide in your blood builds up gradually, you get gradual symptoms. Very insidious they are, too. The trouble is, it seems that when people feel sleepy they light a cigarette to keep themselves awake, and tobacco smoke itself introduces significant quantities of carbon monoxide into the body, so the cigarette may be the final knockout. Er . . . do you smoke?"

"No." And to think I'd regretted it.

"Just as well. You obviously had quite a dangerous concentration of CO in any case."

"I must have been driving for half an hour . . . maybe forty minutes. I don't really know."

"It's a wonder you stopped safely at all. Much more likely to have crashed into something."

"I nearly did . . . on a corner."

He nodded. "Didn't you smell exhaust fumes?"

"I didn't notice. I had too much on my mind. And the

heater burps out exhaust smells sometimes. So I wouldn't take much heed if it wasn't strong." I looked down at myself under the sheets "What's the damage?"

"Not much now," he said cheerfully. "You were lucky there, too. You had multiple dislocations—hip, knee, and ankle. Never seen all three before. Very interesting. We reduced them all successfully. No crushing or fractures, no severed tendons. We don't even think there will be a recurring tendency to dislocate. One or two frayed ligaments round your knee, that's all."

"It's a miracle."

"Interesting case, yes. Unique sort of accident, of course. No direct force involved. We think it might have been air impact—that it sort of blew or stretched you apart. Like being on the rack, eh?" He chuckled. "We put plaster on your knee and ankle, to give them a chance to settle, but it can come off in three or four weeks. We don't want you to put weight on your hip yet, either. You can have some physiotherapy. But take it easy for a while when you leave here. There was a lot of spasm in the muscles, and all your ligaments and so on were badly stretched. Give everything time to subside properly before you run a mile." He smiled, which turned, halfway through, into a yawn. He smothered it apologetically. "It's been a long night."

"Yes," I said.

I went home on Tuesday afternoon in an ambulance, with a pair of crutches and instructions to spend most of my time horizontal.

Poppy was still sick. Tony followed my slow progress up the stairs apologizing that she couldn't manage to have me stay, the kids were exhausting her to distraction.

"I'm fine on my own."

He saw me into the bedroom, where I lay down in my clothes on top of the bedspread, as per instructions. Then he made for the whisky and refreshed himself after my labors.

"Do you want anything? I'll fetch you some food later."

"Thanks," I said. "Could you bring the telephone in here?"

He brought it in and plugged the lead into the socket beside my bed.

"O.K.?"

"Fine," I said.

"That's it, then." He tossed off his drink quickly and made for the door, showing far more haste than usual and edging away from me as though embarrassed.

"Is anything wrong?" I said.

He jumped. "No. Absolutely nothing. Got to get the kids their tea before evening stables. See you later, pal. With the odd crust." He smiled sketchily and disappeared.

I shrugged. Whatever it was that was wrong, he would tell me in time, if he wanted to.

I picked up the telephone and dialed the number of the local garage. Its best mechanic answered.

"Mr. Hughes . . . I heard . . . Your beautiful car." He commiserated genuinely for half a minute.

"Yes," I said. "Look, Derek, is there any way that exhaust gas could get into the car through the heater?"

He was affronted. "Not the way I looked after it. Certainly not."

"I apparently breathed in great dollops of carbon monoxide," I said.

"Not through the heater . . . I can't understand it." He paused, thinking. "They take special care not to let that happen, see? At the design stage. You could only get exhaust gas through the heater if there was a loose or worn gasket on the exhaust manifold *and* a crack or break in the heater tubing *and* a tube connecting the two together, and you can take it from me, Mr. Hughes, there was nothing at all like that on your car. Maintained perfect, it is."

"The heater does sometimes smell of exhaust. If you remember, I did mention it some time ago."

"I give the whole system a thorough check then, too. There wasn't a thing wrong. Only thing I could think of was the exhaust might have eddied forward from the back of the car when you slowed down, sort of, and got whirled in through the fresh-air intake, the one down beside the heater."

"Could you possibly go and look at my car? At what's left of it . . . ?"

"There's a good bit to do here," he said dubiously.

"The police have given me the name of the garage where it is now. Apparently all the bits have to stay there until the insurance people have seen them. But you know the car. . . . It would be easier for you to spot anything different with it from when you last serviced it. Could you go?"

"D'you mean." He paused. "You don't mean there might be something—well, *wrong* with it?"

"I don't know," I said. "But I'd like to find out."

"It would cost you," he said warningly. "It would be working hours."

"Never mind. If you can go, it will be worth it."

"Hang on, then." He departed to consult. Came back. "Yes, all right. The Guvnor says I can go first thing in the morning."

"That's great," I said. "Call me when you get back."

"It couldn't have been a gasket," he said suddenly.

"Why not?"

"You'd have heard it. Very noisy. Unless you had the radio on?"

"No."

"You'd have heard a blown gasket," he said positively. "But there again, if the exhaust was being somehow fed straight into the heater . . . perhaps not. The heater would damp the noise, same as a silencer . . . but I don't see how it could have happened. Well, all I can do is take a look."

I would have liked to go with him. I put down the receiver and looked gloomily at my right leg. The neat plaster casing stretched from well up my thigh down to the base of my toes, which were currently invisible inside a white hospital operating-room sock. A pair of Tony's slacks, though too long by six inches, had slid up easily enough over the plaster, decently hiding it, and as far as looks went, things were passable.

I sighed. The plaster was a bore. They'd designed it somehow so that I found sitting in a chair uncomfortable. Standing and lying down were both better. It wasn't going to stay on a minute longer than I could help, either. The muscles inside it were doing themselves no good in immobility. They would be getting flabby, unfit, wasting away. It would be just too ironic if I got my license back and was too feeble to ride.

Tony came back at eight with half a chicken. He didn't want to stay, not even for a drink.

"Can you manage?" he said.

"Sure. No trouble."

"Your leg doesn't hurt, does it?"

"Not a flicker," I said. "Can't feel a thing."

"That's all right, then." He was relieved: wouldn't look at me squarely: went away.

Next morning, Roberta Cranfield came.

"Kelly?" she called. "Are you in?"

"In the bedroom."

She walked across the sitting room and stopped in the doorway. Wearing the black and white striped fur coat, hanging open. Underneath it, black pants and stagnant-pond-colored sweater.

"Hullo," she said. "I've brought you some food. Shall I put it in the kitchen?"

"That's pretty good of you."

She looked me over. I was lying, dressed, on top of the bedspread, reading the morning paper. "You look comfortable enough."

"I am. Just bored. Er . . . not now you've come, of course."

"Of course," she agreed. "Shall I make some coffee?"

"Yes, do."

She brought it back in mugs, shed her fur, and sat loose-limbed in my bedroom armchair.

"You look a bit better today," she observed.

"Can you get that blood off your dress?"

She shrugged. "I chucked it at the cleaners. They're trying."

"I'm sorry about that. . . ."

"Think nothing of it." She sipped her coffee. "I rang the hospital on Saturday. They said you were O.K."

"Thanks."

"Why on earth did you stop on the railway?"

"I didn't know it was the railway until too late."

"But how did you get there, anyway, with the gates down?"

"The gates weren't down."

"They were when we came along," she said. "There were all those lights and people shouting and screaming and we got out of the car to see what it was all about, and someone said the train had hit a car . . . and then I saw you, lying spark out with your face all covered in blood, about ten feet up the line. Nasty. Very nasty. It was, really."

"I'm sorry. . . . I'd had a couple of lungfuls of carbon monoxide. What you might call diminished responsibility."

She grinned. "You're some moron."

The gates must have shut after I'd stopped on the line. I hadn't heard them or seen them. I must, I supposed, have been more affected by the gas than I remembered.

"I called you Rosalind," I said apologetically.

"I know." She made a face. "Did you think I was her?"

"No . . . It just came out. I meant to say Roberta."

She unrolled herself from the chair, took a few steps, and stood looking at Rosalind's picture. "She'd have been glad . . . knowing she still came first with you after all this time."

The telephone rang sharply beside me and interrupted my surprise. I picked up the receiver.

"Is that Kelly Hughes?" The voice was cultivated, authoritative, loaded indefinably with power. "This is Wykeham Ferth speaking. I read about your accident in the papers. . . . A report this morning says you are now home. I hope . . . you are well?"

"Yes, thank you, my lord."

It was ridiculous, the way my heart had bumped. Sweating palms, too.

"Are you in any shape to come to London?"

"I'm . . . I've got plaster on my leg. . . . I can't sit in a car very easily, I'm afraid."

"Hmm." A pause. "Very well. I will drive down to Corrie instead. It's Harringay's old place, isn't it?"

"That's right. I live in a flat over the yard. If you walk into the yard from the drive, you'll see a green door with a brass letter box in the far corner. It won't be locked. There are some stairs inside. I live up there."

"Right," he said briskly. "This afternoon? Good. Expect me at—er—four o'clock. Right?"

"Sir . . ." I began.

"Not now, Hughes. This afternoon."

I put the receiver down slowly. Six hours' suspense. Damn him.

"What an absolutely heartless letter," Roberta exclaimed.

I looked at her. She was holding the letter from my parents, which had been under Rosalind's photograph.

"I dare say I shouldn't have been so nosy as to read it," she said unrepentantly.

"I dare say not."

"How *can* they be so beastly?"

"They're not really."

"This sort of thing always happens when you get one bright son in a family of twits," she said disgustedly.

"Not always. Some bright sons handle things better than others."

"Stop clobbering yourself."

"Yes, ma'am."

"Are you going to stop sending them money?"

"No. All they can do about that is not spend it . . . or give it to the local cats' and dogs' home."

"At least they had the decency to see they couldn't take your money *and* call you names."

"Rigidly moral man, my father," I said. "Honest to the last farthing. Honest for its own sake. He taught me a lot that I'm grateful for."

"And that's why this business hurts him so much?"

"Yes."

"I've never . . . Well, I know you'll despise me for saying it . . . but I've never thought about people like your father before as—well—*people.*"

"If you're not careful," I said, "those chains will drop right off."

She turned away and put the letter back under Rosalind's picture.

"Which university did you go to?"

"London. Starved in a garret on a grant. Great stuff."

"I wish . . . how odd . . . I wish I'd trained for something. Learned a job."

"It's hardly too late," I said, smiling.

"I'm nearly twenty. I didn't bother much at school with exams. No one made us. Then I went to Switzerland for a year, to a finishing school . . . and since then I've just lived at home. . . . What a waste!"

"The daughters of the rich are always at a disadvantage," I said solemnly.

"Sarcastic beast."

She sat down again in the armchair and told me that her father really seemed to have snapped out of it at last, and had finally accepted a dinner invitation the night before. All the lads had stayed on. They spent most of their time playing cards and football, as the only horses left in the yard were four half-broken two-year-olds and three old chasers recovering from injuries. Most of the owners had promised to bring their horses back at once if Cranfield had his license restored in the next few weeks.

"What's really upsetting Father now is hope. With the big Cheltenham meeting only a fortnight away, he's biting his nails about whether he'll get Breadwinner back in time for him to run in his name in the Gold Cup."

"Pity Breadwinner isn't entered in the Grand National. That would give us a bit more leeway."

"Would your leg be right in time for the Gold Cup?"

"If I had my license, I'd saw the plaster off myself."

"Are you any nearer . . . with the licenses?"

"Don't know."

She sighed. "It was a great dream while it lasted. And you won't be able to do much about it now."

She stood up and came over and picked up the crutches which were lying beside the bed. They were black tubular metal, with elbow supports and handgrips.

"These are much better than those old-fashioned under-the-shoulder affairs," she said. She fitted the crutches round her arms and swung around the room a bit, with one foot off the floor. "Pretty hard on your hands, though."

She looked unself-conscious and intent. I watched her. I remembered the revelation it had been in my childhood when I first wondered what it was like to be someone else.

Into this calm sea Tony appeared with a wretched face and a folded paper in his hand.

"Hi," he said, seeing Roberta. A very gloomy greeting.

He sat down in the armchair and looked at Roberta standing balanced on the crutches with one knee bent. His thoughts were not where his eyes were.

"What is it, then?" I said. "Out with it."

"This letter . . . came yesterday," he said heavily.

"It was obvious last night that something was the matter."

"I couldn't show it to you then, not straight out of hospital. And I don't know what to do, Kelly pal, sure enough I don't."

"Let's see, then."

He handed me the paper worriedly. I opened it up. A brief letter from the racing authorities. Bang bang, both barrels.

Dear Sir,

It has been brought to our attention that a person warned off Newmarket Heath is living as a tenant in your stable yard. This is contrary to the regulations, and you should remedy the situation as soon as possible. It is perhaps not necessary to warn you that your own training license might have to be reviewed if you should fail to take the steps suggested.

"Sods," Tony said forcefully. "Bloody sods."

Chapter 11

Derek from the garage came while Roberta was clearing away the lunch she had stayed to cook. When he rang the doorbell, she went downstairs to let him in.

He walked hesitatingly across the sitting room looking behind him to see if his shoes were leaving dirty marks, and out of habit wiped his hands down his trousers before taking the one I held out to him.

"Sit down," I suggested. He looked doubtfully at the velvet armchair, but in the end lowered himself gingerly into it. He looked perfectly clean. No grease, no filthy overalls, just ordinary slacks and sports jacket. He wasn't used to it.

"You all right?" he said.

"Absolutely."

"If you'd been in that car . . ." He looked sick at what he was thinking; and his vivid imagination was one of the things which made him a reliable mechanic. He didn't want death on his conscience. Young, fair-haired, diffident, he kept most of his brains in his fingertips and, outside of cars, used the upstairs lot sparingly.

"You've never seen nothing like it," he said. "You wouldn't know it was a car, you wouldn't straight. It's all in little bits. . . . I mean, like, bits of metal that don't look as if they were ever part of anything. Honestly. It's like twisted shreds of stuff." He swallowed. "They've got it collected up in tin baths."

"The engine, too?"

"Yeah. Smashed into fragments. Still, I had a look. Took me a long time, though, because everything is all jumbled up, and honest you can't tell what anything used

139

to be. I mean, I didn't think it was a bit of exhaust manifold that I'd picked up, not at first, because it wasn't any shape that you'd think of."

"You found something?"

"Here." He fished in his trouser pocket. "This is what it was all like. This is a bit of the exhaust manifold. Cast iron, that is, you see, so of course it was brittle, sort of, and it had shattered into bits. I mean, it wasn't sort of crumpled up like all the aluminium and so on. It wasn't bent, see, it was just in bits."

"Yes, I do see," I said. The anxious lines on his forehead dissolved when he saw that he had managed to tell me what he meant. He came over and put the small black jagged-edged lump into my hands. Heavy for its size. About three inches long. Asymmetrically curved. Part of the side wall of a huge tube.

"As far as I can make out, see," Derek said, pointing, "it came from about where the manifold narrows down to the exhaust pipe, but really it might be anywhere. There were quite a few bits of manifold, when I looked, but I couldn't see the bit that fits into this, and I dare say it's still rusting away somewhere along the railway line. Anyway, see this bit here. . . ." He pointed a stubby finger at a round dent in part of one edge. "That's one side of a hole that was bored in the manifold wall. Now don't get me wrong, there's quite a few holes might have been drilled through the wall. I mean, some people have exhaust gas temperature gauges stuck into the manifold . . . and other gauges, too. Things like that. Only, see, there weren't no gauges in your manifold, now were there?"

"You tell me," I said.

"There weren't, then. Now you couldn't really say what the hole was for, not for certain you couldn't. But as far as I know, there weren't any holes in your manifold last time I did the service."

I fingered the little semicircular dent. No more than a quarter of an inch across.

"However did you spot something so small?" I asked.

"Dunno, really. Mind you, I was there a good couple of

hours, picking through those tubs. Did it methodical, like. Since you were paying for it and all."

"Is it a big job . . . drilling a hole this size through an exhaust manifold. Would it take long?"

"Half a minute, I should think."

"With an electric drill?" I asked.

"Oh, yeah, sure. If you did it with a hand drill, then it would take five minutes. Say nearer eight or ten, to be on the safe side."

"How many people carry drills around in their tool kits?"

"That, see, it depends on the chap. Now some of them carry all sorts of stuff in their cars. Proper workbenches, some of them. And then others, the tool kit stays strapped up fresh from the factory until the car's dropping to bits."

"People do carry drills, then?"

"Oh, yeah, sure. Quite a lot do. Hand drills, of course. You wouldn't have much call for an electric drill, not in a tool kit, not unless you did a lot of repairs, like, say on racing cars."

He went and sat down again. Carefully, as before.

"If someone drilled a hole this size through the manifold, what would happen?"

"Well, honestly, nothing much. You'd get exhaust gas out through the engine, and you'd hear a good lot of noise, and you might smell it in the car, but it would sort of blow away, see, it wouldn't come in through the heater. To do that, like I said before, you'd have to put some tubing into the hole there and then stick the other end of the tubing into the heater. Mind you, that would be pretty easy, you wouldn't need a drill. Some heater tubes are really only cardboard."

"Rubber tubing from one end to the other?" I suggested.

He shook his head. "No. Have to be metal. Exhaust gas, that's very hot. It'd melt anything but metal."

"Do you think anyone could do all that on the spur of the moment?"

He put his head on one side, considering. "Oh, sure,

yeah. If he'd got a drill. Like, say the first other thing he needs is some tubing. Well, he's only got to look around for that. Lots lying about, if you look. The other day, I used a bit of a kiddy's old cycle frame, just the job it was. Right, you get the tube ready first and then you fit a drill nearest the right size, to match. And Bob's your uncle."

"How long, from start to finish?"

"Fixing the manifold to the heater? Say, from scratch, including maybe having to cast around for a bit of tube, well, at the outside half an hour. A quarter, if you had something all ready handy. Only the drilling would take any time, see? The rest would be like stealing candy from a baby."

Roberta appeared in the doorway shrugging herself into the stripy coat. Derek stood up awkwardly and didn't know where to put his hands. She smiled at him sweetly and unseeingly and said to me, "Is there anything else you want, Kelly?"

"No. Thank you very much."

"Think nothing of it. I'll see . . . I might come over again tomorrow."

"Fine," I said.

"Right."

She nodded, smiled temperately, and made her usual poised exit. Derek's comment approached "Cor."

"I suppose you didn't see any likely pieces of tube in the wreckage?" I asked.

"Huh?" He tore his eyes away with an effort from the direction Roberta had gone. "No, like, it was real bad. Lots of bits, you couldn't have told what they were. I never seen anything like it. Sure, I seen crashes, stands to reason. Different, this was." He shivered.

"Did you have any difficulty with being allowed to search?"

"No, none. They didn't seem all that interested in what I did. Just said to help myself. Course, I told them it was my car, like. I mean, that I looked after it. Mind you, they were right casual about it anyway, because when I came away they were letting this other chap have a good look, too."

"Which other chap?"

"Some fellow. Said he was an insurance man, but he didn't have a notebook."

I felt like saying "Huh?" too. I said, "Notebook?"

"Yeah, sure, insurance men, they're always crawling round our place looking at wrecks and never one without a notebook. Write down every blessed detail, they do. But this other chap, looking at your car, he didn't have any notebook."

"What did he look like?"

He thought.

"That's difficult, see. He didn't look like anything, really. Medium, sort of. Not young and not old, really, either. A nobody sort of person, really."

"Did he wear sunglasses?"

"No. He had a hat on, but I don't know if he had ordinary glasses. I can't actually remember. I didn't notice that much."

"Was he looking through the wreckage as if he knew what he wanted?"

"Uh . . . don't know, really. Strikes me he was a bit flummoxed, like, finding it was all in such small bits."

"He didn't have a girl with him?"

"Nope." He brightened. "He came in a Volkswagen, an oldish gray one."

"Thousands of those about," I said.

"Oh, yeah, sure. Er . . . was this chap important?"

"Only if he was looking for what you found."

He worked it out.

"Cripes," he said.

Lord Ferth arrived twenty minutes after he'd said, which meant that I'd been hopping round the flat on my crutches for half an hour, unable to keep still.

He stood in the doorway into the sitting room holding a briefcase and bowler hat in one hand and unbuttoning his short fawn overcoat with the other.

"Well, Hughes," he said. "Good afternoon."

"Good afternoon, my lord."

He came right in, shut the door behind him, and put his hat and case on the oak chest beside him.

"How's the leg?"

"Stagnating," I said. "Can I get you some tea . . . coffee . . . or a drink?"

"Nothing just now . . ." He laid his coat on the chest and picked up the briefcase again, looking around him with the air of surprise I was used to in visitors. I offered him the green armchair with a small table beside it. He asked where I was going to sit.

"I'll stand," I said. "Sitting's difficult."

"But you don't stand all day!"

"No. Lie on my bed, mostly."

"Then we'll talk in your bedroom."

We went through the door at the end of the sitting room and this time he murmured aloud.

"Whose flat is this?" he asked.

"Mine."

He glanced at my face, hearing the dryness in my voice. "You resent surprise?"

"It amuses me."

"Hughes . . . it's a pity you didn't join the Civil Service. You'd have gone all the way."

I laughed. "There's still time. . . . Do they take in warned-off jockeys at the Administrative Grade?"

"So you can joke about it?"

"It's taken nine days. But, yes, just about."

He gave me a long straight assessing look, and there was a subtle shift somewhere both in his manner to me and in his basic approach, and when I shortly understood what it was I was shaken, because he was taking me on level terms, level in power and understanding and experience; and I wasn't level.

Few men in his position would have thought that this course was viable, let alone chosen it. I understood the compliment. He saw, too, that I did, and I knew later that had there not been this fundamental change of ground, this cancellation of the Steward-jockey relationship, he would not have said to me all that he did. It wouldn't have happened if he hadn't been in my flat.

He sat down in the armchair, putting the briefcase carefully on the floor beside him. I took the weight off my crutches and let the bedsprings have a go.

"I went to see Lord Gowery," he said neutrally. "And I can see no reason not to tell you straight away that you and Dexter Cranfield will have your warning off rescinded within the next few days."

"Do you mean it?" I exclaimed. I tried to sit up. The plaster intervened.

Lord Ferth smiled. "As I see it, there is no alternative. There will be a quiet notice to that effect in next week's *Calendar*."

"That is, of course," I said, "all you need to tell me."

He looked at me levelly. "True. But not all you want to know."

"No."

"No one has a better right . . . and yet you will have to use your discretion about whether you tell Dexter Cranfield."

"All right."

He sighed, reached down to open the briefcase, and pulled out a neat little tape recorder.

"I did try to ignore your suggestion. Succeeded, too, for a while. However . . ." He paused, his fingers hovering over the controls. "This conversation took place late on Monday afternoon, in the sitting room of Lord Gowery's flat near Sloane Square. We were alone . . . you will see that we were alone. He knew, though, that I was making a recording." He still hesitated. "Compassion. That's what you need. I believe you have it."

"Don't con me," I said.

He grimaced. "Very well."

The recording began with the self-conscious platitudes customary in front of the microphones, especially when no one wants to take the first dive into the deep end. Lord Ferth had leapt, eventually.

"Norman, I explained why we must take a good look at this Enquiry."

"Hughes is being ridiculous. Not only ridiculous, but

downright slanderous. I don't understand why you should take him seriously." Gowery sounded impatient.

"We have to, even if only to shut him up." Lord Ferth looked across the room, his hot eyes gleaming ironically. The recording plowed on, his voice like honey. "You know perfectly well, Norman, that it will be better all round if we can show there is nothing whatever in these allegations he is spreading around. Then we can emphatically confirm the suspension and squash all the rumors."

Subtle stuff. Lord Gowery's voice grew easier, assured now that Ferth was still an ally. As perhaps he was. "I do assure you, Wykeham, that if I had not sincerely believed that Hughes and Dexter Cranfield were guilty, I would not have warned them off."

There was something odd about that. Both Ferth and Gowery had thought so, too, as there were several seconds of silence on the tape.

"But you do still believe it?" Ferth said eventually.

"Of course." He was emphatic. "Of course I do." Much too emphatic.

"Then . . . er . . . taking one of Hughes's questions first . . . how did it come about that Newtonnards was called to the Enquiry?"

"I was informed that Cranfield had backed Cherry Pie with him."

"Yes . . . but who informed you?"

Gowery didn't reply.

Ferth's voice came next, with absolutely no pressure in it.

"Um . . . Have you any idea how we managed to show the wrong film of Hughes racing at Reading?"

Gowery was on much surer ground. "My fault, I'm afraid. I asked the Secretaries to write off for the film of the last race. Didn't realize there were seven races. Careless of me, I'll admit. But of course, as it was the wrong film, it was irrelevant to the case."

"Er . . ." said Lord Ferth. But he hadn't yet been ready to argue. He cleared his throat and said, "I suppose you thought it would be relevant to see how Hughes had ridden Squelch last time out."

After another long pause, Gowery said, "Yes."

"But in the event we didn't show it."

"No."

"Would we have shown it if, after having sent for it, we found that the Reading race bore out entirely Hughes's assertion that he rode Squelch in the Lemonfizz in exactly the same way as he always did?"

More silence. Then he said quietly, "Yes," and he sounded very troubled.

"Hughes asked at the Enquiry that we should show the right film," Ferth said.

"I'm sure he didn't."

"I've been reading the transcript. Norman, I've been reading and rereading that transcript all weekend, and frankly that is why I'm here. Hughes did in fact suggest that we should show the right film, presumably because he knew it would support his case—"

"Hughes was guilty!" Gowery broke in vehemently. "Hughes was guilty. I had no option but to warn him off."

Lord Ferth pressed the stop button on the tape recorder.

"Tell me," he said to me, "what you think of that last statement."

"I think," I said slowly, "that he did believe it. Both from that statement and from what I remember of the Enquiry. His certainty that day shook me. He believed me guilty so strongly that he was stone deaf to anything which looked even remotely likely to assault his opinion."

"That was your impression?"

"Overpowering," I said.

Lord Ferth took his lower lip between his teeth and shook his head, but I gathered it was at the general situation, not at me. He pressed the start button again. His voice came through, precise, carefully without emotion, gentle as vaseline.

"Norman, about the composition of the Enquiry . . . the members of the Disciplinary Committee who sat with you

. . . What guided you to choose Andrew Tring and old Plimborne?"

"What guided me?" He sounded astonished at the question. "I haven't any idea."

"I wish you'd cast back."

"I can't see that it has any relevance . . . but let's see. . . . I suppose I had Tring in my mind anyway, as I'm in the middle of some business negotiations with him. And Plimborne . . . well, I just saw him snoozing away in the Club. I was talking to him later in the lobby, and I asked him just on the spur of the moment to sit with me. I don't see the point of your asking."

"Never mind. It doesn't matter. Now . . . about Charlie West. I can see that of course you would call the rider of the third horse to give evidence. And it is clear from the transcript that you knew what the evidence would be. However, at the preliminary enquiry at Oxford, West said nothing at all about Hughes having pulled his horse back. I've consulted all three of the Oxford Stewards this morning. They confirm that West did not suggest it at the time. He asserted it, however, at the Enquiry, and you knew what he was going to say, so . . . er . . . how did you know?"

More silence.

Ferth's voice went on a shade anxiously, "Norman, if you instructed a Stipendiary Steward to interview West privately and question him further, for heaven's sake say so. These jockeys stick together. It is perfectly reasonable to believe that West wouldn't speak up against Hughes to begin with, but might do so if pressed with questions. Did you send a Stipendiary?"

Gowery said faintly, "No."

"Then how did you know what West was going to say?"

Gowery didn't answer. He said instead, "I did instruct a Stipendiary to look up all the races in which Cranfield had run two horses and compile me a list of all the occasions when the lesser-backed had won. And, as you know, it is the accepted practice to bring up everything in

a jockey's past history at an Enquiry. It was a perfectly
normal procedure."

"I'm not saying it wasn't," Ferth's voice said, puzzled.

Ferth stopped the recorder and raised his eyebrows at
me.

"What d'you make of *that?*"

"He's grabbing for a rock in a quicksand."

He sighed, pressed the starter again, and Gowery's
voice came back.

"It was all there in black and white. . . . It was quite
true . . . they'd been doing it again and again."

"What do you mean, it was quite true? Did someone
tell you they'd been doing it again and again?"

More silence. Gowery's rock was crumbling.

Again Ferth didn't press him. Instead, he said in the
same unaccusing way, "How about David Oakley?"

"Who?"

"David Oakley. The enquiry agent who photographed
the money in Hughes's flat. Who suggested that he should
go there?"

No answer.

Ferth said with the first faint note of insistence, "Norman, you really must give some explanation. Can't you
see that all this silence just won't do? We *have* to have
some answers if we are going to squash Hughes's rumors."

Gowery reacted with defense in his voice. "The evidence against Cranfield and Hughes was collected. What
does it matter who collected it?"

"It matters because Hughes asserts that much of it was
false."

"No," he said fiercely. "It was not false."

"Norman," Ferth said, "is that what you believe . . . or
what you *want* to believe?"

"Oh . . ." Gowery's exclamation was more of anguish
than surprise. I looked sharply across at Ferth. His dark
eyes were steady on my face. His voice went on, softer
again. Persuasive.

"Norman, was there any reason why you—*wanted*
Cranfield and Hughes warned off?"

"No." Half a shout. Definitely a lie.

"Any reason why you should go so far as to manufacture evidence against them, if none existed?"

"Wykeham!" He was outraged. "How can you say that! You are suggesting— You are suggesting—something so dishonorable . . ."

Ferth pressed the stop button. "Well?" he said challengingly.

"That was genuine," I said. "He didn't manufacture it himself. But then I never thought he did. I just wanted to know where he got it from."

Ferth nodded. Pressed the start again.

His voice. "My dear Norman, you lay yourself open to such suggestions if you will not say how you came by all the evidence. Do you not see? If you will not explain how you came by it, you cannot be too surprised if you are thought to have procured it yourself."

"The evidence was genuine!" he asserted. A rear-guard action.

"You are still trying to convince yourself that it was."

"No! It was."

"Then where did it come from?"

Gowery's back was against the wall. I could see from the remembered emotion twisting Ferth's face that this had been a saddening and perhaps embarrassing moment.

"I was sent," said Gowery with difficulty, "a package. It contained . . . various statements . . . and six copies of the photograph taken in Hughes's flat."

"Who sent it to you?"

Gowery's voice was very low. "I don't know."

"You don't know?" Ferth was incredulous. "You warned two men off on the strength of it, and you don't know where it came from?"

A miserable assenting silence.

"You just accepted all that so-called evidence on its face value?"

"It was all true." He clung to it.

"Have you still got that package?"

"Yes."

"I'd like to see it." A touch of iron in Ferth's voice.

Gowery hadn't argued. There were sounds of moving about, a drawer opening and closing, a rustling of papers.

"I see," Ferth said slowly. "These papers do, in fact, look very convincing."

"Then you see why I acted on them," Gowery said eagerly, with a little too much relief.

"I can see why you should consider doing so . . . after making a careful check."

"I did check."

"To what extent?"

"Well . . . the package only came four days before the Enquiry. On the Thursday before. I had the Secretaries send out the summonses to Newtonnards, Oakley, and West immediately. They were asked to confirm by telegram that they would be attending, and they all did so. Newtonnards was asked to bring his records for the Lemonfizz Cup. And then, of course, I asked a Stipendiary to ask the Totalisator people if anyone had backed Cherry Pie substantially, and he collected those affidavits . . . the ones we produced at the Enquiry. There was absolutely no doubt whatsoever that Cranfield had backed Cherry Pie. He lied about it at the Enquiry. That made it quite conclusive. He was entirely guilty, and there was no reason why I should not warn him off."

Ferth stopped the recorder. "What do you say to that?" he asked.

I shrugged. "Cranfield did back Cherry Pie. He was stupid to deny it, but admitted it was, as he saw it, cutting his own throat. He told me that he backed him—through this unidentified friend—with Newtonnards and on the Tote, and not with his normal bookmaker, because he didn't want Jessel to know, as Jessel and the bookmaker are tattle-swapping buddies. He in fact put a hundred pounds on Cherry Pie because he thought the horse might be warming up to give everyone a surprise. He also put two hundred pounds on Squelch, because reason suggested that *he* would win. And where is the villainy in that?"

Ferth looked at me levelly. "You didn't know he had backed Cherry Pie, not at the Enquiry."

"I tackled him with it afterward. It had struck me by then that that had to be true, however hard he had denied it. Newtonnards might have lied or altered his books, but no one can argue against Tote tickets."

"That was one of the things which convinced me, too," he admitted.

He started the recorder. He himself was speaking, and now there was a distinct flavor in his voice of cross-examination. The whole interview moved suddenly into the shape of an Enquiry of its own. "This photograph . . . didn't it seem at all odd to you?"

"Why should it?" Gowery said sharply.

"Didn't you ask yourself how it came to be taken?"

"No."

"Hughes says Oakley took the money and the note with him and simply photographed them in his flat."

"No."

"How can you be sure?" Ferth pounced on him.

"No!" Gowery said again. There was a rising note in his voice, the sound of pressure approaching blowup.

"Who sent Oakley to Hughes's flat?"

"I've told you, I don't know."

"But you're sure that is a genuine photograph?"

"Yes. Yes, it is."

"You are sure beyond doubt?" Ferth insisted.

"Yes!" The voice was high, the anxiety plain, the panic growing. Into this screwed-up moment Ferth dropped one intense word, like a bomb.

"Why?"

Chapter 12

The tape ran on for nearly a minute. When Gowery finally answered, his voice was quite different. Low, broken up, distressed to the soul.

"It had . . . to be true. I said at first . . . I couldn't warn them off if they weren't guilty . . . and then the package came . . . and it was such a relief . . . they really were guilty. . . . I could warn them off . . . and everything would be all right."

My mouth opened. Ferth watched me steadily, his eyes narrowed with pity.

Gowery went on compulsively. Once started, he needed to confess.

"If I tell you . . . from the beginning . . . perhaps you will understand. It began the day after I was appointed to substitute for the Disciplinary Steward at the Cranfield-Hughes Enquiry. It's ironic to think of it now, but I was quite pleased to be going to do it . . . and then . . . and then . . ." He paused and took an effortful control of his voice. "Then I had a telephone call." Another pause. "This man said . . . said . . . I must warn Cranfield off." He cleared his throat. "I told him I would do no such thing, unless Cranfield was guilty. Then he said . . . then he said . . . that he knew things about me . . . and he would tell everyone . . . if I didn't warn Cranfield off. I told him I couldn't warn him off if he wasn't guilty . . . and you see I didn't think he *was* guilty. I mean, race horses are so unpredictable, and I saw the Lemonfizz myself, and although after that crowd demonstration it was obvious the Stewards would have Cranfield and Hughes in, I was surprised when they referred it to the

Disciplinary Committee. . . . I thought that there must have been circumstances that I didn't know of . . . and then I was asked to take the Enquiry . . . and I had an open mind. . . . I told the man on the telephone that no threats could move me from giving Cranfield a fair judgment."

Less jelly in his voice while he remembered that first strength. It didn't last.

"He said . . . in that case . . . I could expect . . . after the Enquiry . . . if Cranfield got off . . . that my life wouldn't be worth living. . . . I would have to resign from the Jockey Club . . . and everyone would know. . . . And I said again that I would not warn Cranfield off unless I was convinced of his guilt, and that I would not be blackmailed, and I put down the receiver and cut him off."

"And then," Ferth suggested, "you began to worry?"

"Yes." Little more than a whisper.

"What exactly did he threaten to publish?"

"I can't . . . can't tell you. Not criminal . . . not a matter for the police . . . but . . ."

"But enough to ruin you socially?"

"Yes . . . I'm afraid so . . . yes, completely."

"But you stuck to your guns?"

"I was desperately worried. . . . I couldn't . . . how could I? . . . take away Cranfield's livelihood just to save myself. . . . It would have been dishonorable . . . and I couldn't see myself living with it . . . and in any case I couldn't just warn him off, just like that, if there was no proof he was guilty. . . . So I did worry . . . couldn't sleep . . . or eat. . . ."

"Why didn't you ask to be relieved of the Enquiry?"

"Because he told me . . . if I backed out . . . it would count the same with him as letting Cranfield off . . . so I had to go on, just in case some proof turned up."

"Which it did," Ferth said dryly. "Conveniently."

"Oh . . ." Again the anguish. "I didn't realize . . . I didn't indeed . . . that it might have been the blackmailer who had sent the package. I didn't wonder very much who had sent it. It was release . . . that's all I could

see . . . it was a heaven-sent release from the most unbearable . . . I didn't question . . . I just believed it . . .
believed it absolutely . . . and I was so grateful . . . so
grateful . . ."

Four days before the Enquiry, that package had come.
He must have been sweating for a whole week, taking a
long bleak look at the wilderness. Send a St. Bernard to a
dying mountaineer and he's unlikely to ask for the dog
license.

"When did you begin to doubt?" Ferth said calmly.

"Not until afterward. Not for days. It was Hughes . . .
at the dance. You told me he was insisting he'd been
framed and was going to find out who . . . and then he
asked me directly who had sent Oakley to his flat . . . and
it . . . Wykeham, it was *terrible*. I realized . . . what I'd
done. Inside, I did know . . . but I couldn't admit to it
myself. . . . I shut it away . . . they *had* to be guilty. . . ."

There was another long silence. Then Gowery said,
"You'll see to it . . . that they get their licenses back?"

"Yes," Ferth said.

"I'll resign." He sounded desolate.

"From the Disciplinary Committee, I agree," Ferth said
reasonably. "As to the rest . . . we will see."

"Do you think the . . . the blackmailer . . . will tell . . .
everyone . . . anyway, when Cranfield has his license
back?"

"He would have nothing to gain."

"No, but . . ."

"There are laws to protect you."

"They couldn't."

"What does he in fact have over you?"

"I . . . I . . . Oh God." The tape stopped abruptly,
cutting off words that were disintegrating into gulps.

Ferth said, "I switched it off. He was breaking down.
One couldn't record that."

"No."

"He told me what it was he was being blackmailed
about. I think I am prepared to tell you also, although he
would hate it if he knew. But you only."

"Only," I said. "I won't repeat it."

"He told me . . ." His nose wrinkled in distaste. "He told me that he has . . . he suffers from . . . unacceptable sexual appetites. Not homosexual. Perhaps that would have been better . . . simpler . . . he wouldn't nowadays have been much reviled for that. No. He says he belongs to a sort of club where people like him can gratify themselves fairly harmlessly, as they are all there because they enjoy . . . in varying forms . . . the same thing." He stopped. He was embarrassed.

"Which is what?" I said matter-of-factly.

He said, as if putting a good yard of clean air between himself and the word, "Flagellation."

"That old thing!" I said.

"What?"

"The English disease. Shades of Fanny Hill. Sex tangled up with self-inflicted pain, like nuns with their little disciplines and sober citizens paying a pound a lash to be whipped."

"Kelly!"

"You must have read their coy little advertisements? 'Correction given.' That's what it's all about. More widespread than most people imagine. Starts with husbands spanking their wives regularly before they bed them, and carries right on up to the parties where they all dress up in leather and have a right old orgy. I don't actually understand why anyone should get fixated on leather or rubber or hair, or on those instead of anything else. Why not coal, for instance—or silk? But they do, apparently."

"In this case . . . leather."

"Boots and whips and naked bosoms?"

Ferth shook his head in disbelief. "You take it so coolly."

"Live and let live," I said. "If that's what they feel compelled to do, why stop them? As he said, they're not harming anyone, if they're in a club where everyone else is the same."

"But for a Steward," he protested. "A member of the Disciplinary Committee!"

"Gives you pause," I agreed.

He looked horrified. "But there would be nothing sexual in his judgment on racing matters."

"Of course not. Nothing on earth as unsexual as racing."

"But one can see . . . he would be finished in the racing world if this got out. Even I—I cannot think of him now without this—this perversion coming into my mind. It would be the same with everyone. One can't respect him any more. One can't like him."

"Difficult," I agreed.

"It's . . . horrible." In his voice, all the revulsion of the normal for the deviate. Most racing men were normal. The deviate would be cast out. Ferth felt it. Gowery knew it. And so did someone else. . . .

"Don't they wear masks at this club?" I asked.

Ferth looked surprised. "Why, yes, they do. I asked him who could know about him—in order to blackmail him—and he said he didn't know, they all wore masks. Hoods, actually, was the word he used. Hoods . . . and aprons . . ." He was revolted.

"All leather?"

He nodded. "How can they?"

"They do less harm than the ones who go out and rape small children."

"I'm glad I . . ." He said passionately.

"Me, too," I said. "But it's just luck." Gowery had been unlucky, in more ways than one. "Someone may have seen him going in, or leaving afterward."

"That's what he thinks. But he says he doesn't know the real names of any of his fellow members. They all call each other by fanciful made-up names, apparently."

"There must be a secretary . . . with a list of members?"

Ferth shook his head. "I asked him that. He said he'd never given his own name to anyone there. It wasn't expected. There's no annual subscription, just ten pounds in cash every time he attends. He says he goes about once a month, on average."

"How many other members are there?"

"He didn't know the total number. He says there are

never fewer than ten, and sometimes thirty or thirty-five. More men than women, usually. The club isn't open every day; only Mondays and Thursdays."

"Where is it?"

"In London. He wouldn't tell me exactly where."

"He wants—needs—to keep on going," I said.

"You don't think he will!"

"After a while. Yes."

"Oh, no . . ."

"Who introduced him to the club, do you know?"

"He said it couldn't be the person who introduced him to the club. She was a prostitute. . . He'd never told her his real name."

"But she understood his needs."

He sighed. "It would seem so."

"Some of these girls make more money out of whipping men than sleeping with them."

"How on earth do you know?"

"I had digs once in the next room to one. She told me."

"Good Lord." He looked as if he'd turned over a stone and found creepy-crawlies underneath. He had plainly no inkling of what it was like to *be* a creepy-crawly. His loss.

"Anyway," he said slowly, "you will understand why he accepted that package at its face value."

"And why he chose Lord Plimborne and Andy Tring."

Lord Ferth nodded. "At the end, when he'd recovered a little, he understood that he'd chosen them for the reasons you said, but he believed at the time that they were impulsive choices. And he is now, as you would expect, a very worried and troubled man."

"Was he," I asked, "responsible for this?"

I held out to him the letter Tony had received from the Stewards' Secretaries. He stood up, came to take it, and read its brief contents with exasperation.

"I don't know," he said explosively. "I really don't know. When did this arrive?"

"Tuesday. Postmarked noon on Monday."

"Before I saw him. . . . He didn't mention it."

"Could you find out if it was his doing?"

"Do you mean . . . it will be all the more impossible to forgive him?"

"No. Nothing like that. I was just wondering if it was our little framer-blackmailer at work again. See those words 'It has been brought to our attention'? What I'd like to know is who brought it."

"I'll find out," he said positively. "That shouldn't be difficult. And, of course, disregard the letter. There won't be any question now of your having to move."

"How are you going to work it? Giving our licenses back. How are you going to explain it?"

He raised his eyebrows. "We never have to give reasons for our decisions."

I smothered a laugh. The system had its uses.

Lord Ferth sat down in the chair again and put the letter in his briefcase. Then he packed up the tape recorder and tucked that away, too. Then, with an air of delicately choosing his words, he said, "A scandal of this sort would do racing a great deal of harm."

"So you want me to take my license back and shut up?"

"Er . . . yes."

"And not chase after the blackmailer, in case he blows the gaff?"

"Exactly." He was relieved that I understood.

"No," I said.

"Why not?" Persuasion in his voice.

"Because he tried to kill me."

"What?"

I showed him the chunk of exhaust manifold, and explained. "Someone at the dance," I said. "That means that our blackmailer is one of about six hundred people, and from there it shouldn't be too hard. You can more or less rule out the women, because few of them would drill through cast iron wearing an evening dress. Much too conspicuous, if anyone saw them. That leaves three hundred men."

"Someone who knew your car," he said. "Surely that would narrow it down considerably."

"It might not. Anyone could have seen me getting out of it at the races. It was a noticeable car, I'm afraid. But I arrived late at the dance. The car was parked right at the back."

"Have you . . ." He cleared his throat. "Are the police involved in this?"

"If you mean are they at present investigating an attempted murder, then, no, they are not. If you mean, am I going to ask them to investigate etcetera, then I haven't decided."

"Once you start the police on something, you can't stop them."

"On the other hand, if I don't start them the blackmailer might have another go at me, with just a fraction of an inch more success. Which would be quite enough."

"Um." He thought it over. "But if you made it clear to everyone now that you are not any longer trying to find out who framed you . . . he might not try again."

I said curiously, "Do you really think it would be best for racing if we just leave this blackmailing murderer romping around free?"

"Better than a full-blown scandal."

The voice of Establishment diplomacy.

"And if he doesn't follow your line of reasoning . . . and he does kill me . . . how would that do for a scandal?"

He didn't answer. Just looked at me levelly with the hot eyes.

"All right, then," I said. "No police."

"Thank you."

"Us, though. We'll have to do it ourselves. Find him and deal with him."

"How do you mean?"

"I'll find him. You deal with him."

"To your satisfaction, I suppose," he said ironically.

"Absolutely."

"And Lord Gowery?"

"He's yours entirely. I shan't tell Dexter Cranfield anything at all."

"Very well." He stood up, and I struggled off the bed onto the crutches.

"Just one thing," I said. "Could you arrange to have that package of Lord Gowery's sent to me here?"

"I have it with me." Without hesitation he took a large manila envelope out of the briefcase and put it on the bed. "You'll understand how he fell on it with relief."

"Things being as they were," I agreed. He walked across the sitting room to the way out, stopping by the chest to put on his coat.

"Can Cranfield tell his owners to shovel their horses back?" I said. "The sooner the better, you see, if they're to come back in time for Cheltenham."

"Give me until tomorrow morning. There are several other people who must know first."

"All right."

He held out his hand. I transferred the right crutch to the left, and shook it.

He said, "Perhaps one day soon—when this is over—you will dine with me?"

"I'd like to," I said.

"Good." He picked up his bowler and his briefcase, swept a last considering glance round my flat, nodded to me as if finalizing a decision, and quietly went away.

I telephoned to the orthopedist who regularly patched me up after falls.

"I want this plaster off."

He went into a long spiel of which the gist was two or three more weeks.

"Monday," I said.

"I'll give you up."

"Tuesday I start getting it off with a chisel."

I always slept in shirt-and-shorts pajamas, which had come in very handy in the present circs. Bedtime that night I struggled into a lime-green and white checked lot I had bought in an off moment at Liverpool the year before with my mind more on the imminent Grand National than on what they would do to my yellow complexion at six on a winter's morning.

Tony had gloomily brought me some casseroled beef and had stayed to celebrate when I told him I wouldn't

have to leave. I was out of whisky again in consequence.

When he'd gone, I went to bed and read the pages
which had sent me to limbo. And they were, indeed,
convincing. Neatly typed, well set out, written in authoritative language. Not at first, second, or even third sight
the product of malevolence. Emotionless. Cool. Damaging.

"Charles Richard West is prepared to testify that during the course of the race, and in particular at a spot six
furlongs from the winning post on the second circuit, he
heard Hughes say that he (Hughes) was about to ease his
horse so that it should be in no subsequent position to
win. Hughes's precise words were, 'O.K. Brakes on,
chaps.'"

The four other sheets were equally brief, equally to the
point. One said that through an intermediary Dexter
Cranfield had backed Cherry Pie with Newtonnards. The
second pointed out that an investigation of past form
would show that on several other occasions Cranfield's
second string had beaten his favorite. The third suggested
watching the discrepancies in Hughes's riding in the Lemonfizz and in the last race at Reading . . . and there it was
in black and white, "the last race at Reading." Gowery
hadn't questioned it or checked; had simply sent for the
last race at Reading. If he had shown it privately to
Plimborne and Tring only, and not to me as well, no one
might ever have realized it was the wrong race. This
deliberate piece of misleading had in fact gone astray, but
only just. And the rest hadn't. Page 4 stated categorically
that Cranfield had bribed Hughes not to win, and photographic evidence to prove it was hereby attached.

There was also a short covering note of explanation.

"These few facts have come to my notice. They should
clearly be laid before the appropriate authorities, and I
am therefore sending them to you, sir, as Steward in
command of the forthcoming Enquiry."

The typewriting itself was unremarkable, the paper
medium-quality quarto. The paper clip holding the sheets
together was sold by the hundred million, and the buff

envelope in which they'd been sent cost a penny or two in any stationer's in the country.

There were two copies only of the photograph. On the back, no identifications.

I slid them all back into the envelope, and put it in the drawer of the table beside my bed. Switched out the light. Lay thinking of riding races again with a swelling feeling of relief and excitement. Wondered how poor old Gowery was making out, going fifteen rounds with his conscience. Thought of Archie and his mortgage . . . Jessel having to admit he'd been wrong . . . Roberta stepping off her dignity . . . the blackmailer biting his nails in apprehension . . . sweet dreams every one . . . slid into the first easy sleep since the Enquiry.

I woke with a jolt, knowing I'd heard a sound which had no business to be there.

A pen-sized flashlight was flickering round the inside of one of the top drawers of the dressing chest. A dark shape blocked off half of its beam as an arm went into the drawer to feel around. Cautious. Very quiet, now.

I lay watching through slit-shut eyes, wondering how close I was this time to the Pearly Gates. Inconveniently my pulse started bashing against my eardrums as fear stirred up the adrenals, and inside the plaster all the hairs on my leg fought to stand on end.

Trying to keep my breathing even and make no rustle with the sheets, I very cautiously slid one arm over the side of the bed and reached down to the floor for a crutch. Any weapon handy was better than none.

No crutches.

I felt around, knowing exactly where I'd laid them beside me, feeling nothing but carpet under my fingers.

The flashlight moved out of the drawer and swung in a small arc while the second top drawer was opened, making the same tiny crack as it loosened which had waked me with the other. The scrap of light shone fractionally on my two crutches propped up against the wall by the door.

I drew the arm very slowly back into bed and lay still. If he'd meant just to kill me, he would have done it by now; and whatever he intended I had little chance of avoiding. The plaster felt like a ton, chaining me immobile.

A clammy crawling feeling all over my skin. Jaw tight-clenched with tension. Dryness in the mouth. Head feeling as if it were swelling. I lay and tried to beat the physical sensations, tried to will them away.

No noticeable success.

He finished with the drawers. The flashlight swung over the khaki chair and steadied on the polished oak chest behind it, against the wall. He moved over soundlessly and lifted the lid. I almost cried out to him not to; it would wake me. The lid always creaked loudly. I really didn't want him to wake me; it was much too dangerous.

The lid creaked sharply. He stopped dead with it six inches up. Lowered it back into place. It creaked even louder.

He stood there, considering. Then there were quick soft steps on the carpet, a hand fastening in my hair and yanking my head back and the flashlight beam full in my eyes.

"Right, mate. You're awake. So you'll answer some questions."

I knew the voice. I shut my eyes against the light and spoke in as bored a drawl as I could manage.

"Mr. Oakley, I presume?"

"Clever Mr. Hughes."

He let go of my hair and stripped the bedclothes off with one flick. The flashlight swung away and fell on top of them. I felt his grip on my neck and the front of my shirt as he wrenched me off the bed and onto the floor. I fell with a crash.

"That's for starters," he said.

Chapter 13

He was fast, to give him his due. Also strong and ruthless, and used to this sort of thing.

"Where is it?" he said.

"What?"

"A chunk of metal with a hole in it."

"I don't know what you're talking about."

He swung his arm and hit me with something hard and knobby. When it followed through to the tiny light, I could see what it was. One of my own crutches. Delightful.

I tried to disentangle my legs and roll over and stand up. He shone the light on me to watch. When I was half up, he knocked me down again.

"Where is it?"

"I told you . . ."

"We both know, chum, that you have this chunk of metal. I want it. I have a customer for it. And you're going to hand it over like a good little warned-off crook."

"Go scratch yourself."

I rolled fast and almost missed the next swipe. It landed on the plaster. Some flakes came off. Less work for Tuesday.

"You haven't a hope," he said. "Face facts."

The facts were that if I yelled for help only the horses would hear.

Pity.

I considered giving him the chunk of metal with the hole in it. Correction, half a hole. He didn't know it was only half a hole. I wondered whether I should tell him. Perhaps he'd be only half as savage.

"Who wants it?" I said.

"Be your age." He swung the crutch.

Contact.

I cursed.

"Save yourself, chum. Don't be stupid."

"What is this chunk of metal?"

"Just hand it over."

"I don't know what you're looking for."

"Chunk of metal with a hole in it."

"What chunk of metal?"

"Look, chum, what does it matter what chunk of metal? The one you've got."

"I haven't."

"Stop playing games." He swung the crutch. I grunted. "Hand it over."

"I haven't . . . got . . . any chunk of metal."

"Look, chum, my instructions are as clear as glass. You've got some lump of metal and I've come to fetch it. Understand? Simple. So save yourself, you stupid crumb."

"What is he paying for it?"

"You still offering more?"

"Worth a try."

"So you said before. But nothing doing."

"Pity."

"Where's the chunk?"

I didn't answer, heard the crutch coming, rolled at the right instant, and heard it thud on the carpet roughly where my nose had been.

The little flashlight sought me out. He didn't miss the second time, but it was only my arm, not my face.

"Didn't you ask what it was?" I said.

"None of your bloody business. You just tell me"—bash—"where"—bash—"it is."

I'd had about enough. Too much, in fact. And I'd found out all I was likely to, except how far he was prepared to go, which was information I could do without.

I'd been trying to roll toward the door. Finally made it

near enough. Stretched backward over my head and felt my fingers curl round the bottom of the other crutch still propped against the wall.

The rubber knob came into my hand, and with one scything movement I swept the business end round viciously at knee level.

It caught him square and unexpected on the back of his legs just as he himself was in mid-swing, and he overbalanced and crashed down half on top of me. I reached out and caught something, part of his coat, and gripped and pulled, and tried to swing my plaster leg over his body to hold him down.

He wasn't having any. We scrambled around on the floor, him trying to get up and me trying to stop him, both of us scratching and punching and gouging in a thoroughly unsportsmanlike manner. The flashlight had fallen away across the far side of the room and shone only on the wall. Not enough light to be much good. Too much for total evasion of his efficient fists.

The bedside table fell over with a crash and the lamp smashed. Oakley somehow reached into the ruins and picked up a piece of glass, and I just saw the light shimmer on it as he slashed it toward my eyes. I dodged it by a millimeter in the last half second.

"You bugger," I said bitterly.

We were both gasping for breath. I loosed the grip I had on his coat in order to have both hands free to deal with the glass, and as soon as he felt me let go he was heaving himself back onto his feet.

"Now," he said, panting heavily, "where bloody is it?"

I didn't answer. He'd got hold of a crutch again. Back to square one. On the thigh, that time.

I was lying on the other crutch. The elbow supports were digging into my back. I twisted my arm underneath me and pulled out the crutch, and swung it at him just as he was having a second go. The crutches met and crashed together in the air. I held on to mine for dear life and rolled toward the bed.

"Give . . . up," he said.

"Get . . . stuffed."

I made it to the bed and lay in the angle between it and the floor. He couldn't get a good swing at me there. I turned the crutch round, and held it by the elbow and the handgrip with both of my hands. To hit me where I was lying he had to come nearer.

He came. His dark shadow was above me, exaggerated by the dim flashlight. He leant over, swinging. I shoved the stick end of the crutch hard upward. It went into him solidly and he screeched sharply. The crutch he had been swinging dropped harmlessly on top of me as he reeled away clutching at his groin.

"I'll . . . kill you . . . for that. . . ." His voice was high with pain. He groaned, hugging himself.

"Serves . . . you . . . right," I said breathlessly.

I pulled myself across the floor, dragging the plaster, aiming for the telephone which had crashed onto the floor with the little table. Found the receiver. Pulled the cord. The telephone bumped over the carpet into my hand.

Put my finger on the button. Small ting. Dialing tone. Found the numbers. Three . . . nine . . . one . . .

"Yeah?" Tony's voice, thick with sleep.

Dead careless, I was. Didn't hear a thing. The crutch swung wickedly down on the back of my head and I fell over the telephone and never told him to gallop to the rescue.

I woke where Oakley had left me, still lying on the floor over the telephone, the receiver half in and half out of my hand.

It was daylight, just. Gray and raw and raining. I was stiff. Cold. Had a headache.

Remembered bit by bit what had happened. Set about scraping myself off the carpet.

First stop, back onto the bed, accompanied by bed-clothes. Lay there feeling terrible and looking at the mess he had made of my room.

After he'd knocked me out, he had nothing to be quiet about. Everything had been pulled out of the closet and drawers and flung on the floor. Everything smashable was smashed. The sleeves of some of my suits were ripped and lying in tatters. Rosalind's picture had been torn into four pieces and the silver frame twisted and snapped. It had been revenge more than a search. A bad loser, David Oakley.

What I could see of the sitting room through the open door seemed to have received the same treatment.

I lay and ached in most places you could think of.

Didn't look to see if Oakley had found the piece of manifold, because I knew he wouldn't have. Thought about him coming, and about what he'd said.

Thought about Cranfield.

Thought about Gowery.

Once I got the plaster off and could move about again, it shouldn't take me too long now to dig out the enemy. A bit of legwork. Needed two legs.

Oakley would shortly be reporting no success from the night's work. I wondered if he would be sent to try again. Didn't like that idea particularly.

I shifted on the bed, trying to get comfortable. I'd been concussed twice in five days once before, and got over it. I'd been kicked along the ground by a large field of hurdlers, which had been a lot worse than the crutches. I'd broken enough bones to stock a cemetery and this time they were all whole. But all the same I felt sicker than after racing falls, and in the end realized my unease was revulsion against being hurt by another man. Horses, hard ground, even express trains, were impersonal. Oakley had been a different type of invasion. The amount you were mentally affected by a pain always depended on how you got it.

I felt terrible. Had no energy at all to get up and tidy the mess.

Shut my eyes to blot it out. Blotted myself out, too. Went to sleep.

A voice said above my head, "Won't you ever learn to keep your door shut?"

I smiled feebly. "Not if you're coming through it."

"Finding you flat out is becoming a habit."

"Try to break it."

I opened my eyes. Broad daylight. Still raining.

Roberta was standing a foot from the bed wearing a blinding yellow raincoat covered in trickling drops. The copper hair was tied up in a ponytail and she was looking around her with disgust.

"Do you realize it's half past ten?" she said.

"No."

"Do you always drop your clothes all over the place when you go to bed?"

"Only on Wednesdays."

"Coffee?" she said abruptly, looking down at me.

"Yes, please."

She picked her way through the mess to the door, and then across the sitting room until she was out of sight. I rubbed my hand over my chin. Bristly. And there was a tender lump on the back of my skull and a sore patch all down one side of my jaw, where I hadn't dodged fast enough. Bruises in other places set up a morning chorus. I didn't listen.

She came back minus the raincoat and carrying two steaming mugs, which she put carefully on the floor. Then she picked up the bedside table and transferred the mugs to its top.

The drawer had fallen out of the table, and the envelope had fallen out of the drawer. But Oakley hadn't apparently looked into it, hadn't known it was there to find.

Roberta picked up the scattered crutches and brought them over to the bed.

"Thanks," I said.

"You take it very calmly."

"I've seen it before," I pointed out.

"And you just went to sleep?"

"Opted out," I agreed.

She looked more closely at my face and rolled my head over on the pillow. I winced. She took her hand away.

"Did you get the same treatment as the flat?"

"More or less."

"What for?"

"For being stubborn."

"Do you mean," she said incredulously, "that you could have avoided all this . . . and didn't?"

"If there's a good reason for backing down, you back down. If there isn't, you don't."

"And all this . . . isn't a good enough reason?"

"No."

"You're crazy," she said.

"You're so right." I sighed, pushed myself up a bit, and reached for the coffee.

"Have you called the police?" she asked.

I shook my head. "Not their quarrel."

"Who did it, then?"

I smiled at her. "Your father and I have got our licenses back."

"*What?*"

"It'll be official sometime today."

"Does Father know? How did it happen? Did you do it?"

"No, he doesn't know yet. Ring him up. Tell him to get on to all the owners. It'll be confirmed in the papers soon, either today's evening editions or tomorrow's dailies."

She picked the telephone off the floor and sat on the edge of my bed, and telephoned to her father with real joy and sparkling eyes. He wouldn't believe it at first.

"Kelly says it's true," she said.

He argued again, and she handed the telephone to me.

"You tell him."

Cranfield said, "Who told you?"

"Lord Ferth."

"Did he say why?"

"No," I lied. "Just that the sentences had been reviewed . . . and reversed. We're back, as from today. The official notice will be in next week's *Calendar.*"

"No explanation at all?" he insisted.

"They don't have to give one," I pointed out.

"All the same . . ."

"Who cares why?" I said. "The fact that we're back—that's all that matters."

"Did you find out who framed us?"

"No."

"Will you go on trying?"

"I might do," I said. "We'll see."

He had lost interest in that. He bounded into a stream of plans for the horses, once they were back. "And it will give me great pleasure to tell Henry Jessel . . ."

"I'd like to see his face," I agreed. But Pat Nikita would never part with Squelch, nor with Jessel, now. If Cranfield thought Jessel would come crawling apologetically back, he didn't know his man. "Concentrate on getting Breadwinner back," I suggested. "I'll be fit to ride him in the Gold Cup."

"Old Strepson promised Breadwinner would come back at once . . . and Pound Postage of his . . . that's entered in the National, don't forget."

"I haven't forgotten," I assured him.

He ran down eventually and disconnected, and I could imagine him sitting at the other end still wondering whether to trust me.

Roberta stood up with a spring, as if the news had filled her with energy.

"Shall I tidy up for you?"

"I'd love some help."

She bent down and picked up Rosalind's torn picture.

"They didn't have to do that," she said in disgust.

"I'll get the bits stuck together and rephotographed."

"You'd hate to lose her. . . ."

I didn't answer at once. She looked at me curiously, her eyes dark with some unreadable expression.

"I lost her," I said slowly. "Rosalind . . . Roberta . . . you are so unalike."

She turned away abruptly and put the pieces on the chest of drawers where they had always stood.

"Who wants to be a carbon copy?" she said, and her voice was high and cracking. "Get dressed . . . while I start on the sitting room." She disappeared fast and shut the door behind her.

I lay there looking at it.

Roberta Cranfield. I'd never liked her.

Roberta Cranfield. I couldn't bear it . . . I was beginning to love her.

She stayed most of the day, helping clear up the mess.

Oakley had left little to chance: the bathroom and the kitchen both looked as if they'd been gutted by a whirlwind. He'd searched everywhere a good enquiry agent could think of, including in the lavatory cistern and the refrigerator; and everywhere he'd searched he'd left his trail of damage.

After midday, which was punctuated by some scrambled eggs, the telephone started ringing. Was it true, asked the *Daily Witness* in the shape of Daddy Leeman, that Cranfield and I . . . ? "Check with the Jockey Club," I said.

The other papers had checked first. "May we have your comments?" they asked.

"Thrilled to bits," I said gravely. "You can quote me."

A lot of real chums rang to congratulate, and a lot of pseudo-chums rang to say they'd never believed me guilty anyway.

For most of the afternoon, I lay flat on the sitting-room floor with my head on a cushion, talking down the telephone while Roberta stepped around and over me nonchalantly, putting things back into place.

Finally she dusted her hands off on the seat of her black pants and said she thought that that would do. The flat looked almost as good as ever. I agreed gratefully that it would do very well.

"Would you consider coming down to my level?" I asked.

She said calmly, "Are you speaking literally, metaphorically, intellectually, financially, or socially?"

"I was suggesting you might sit on the floor."

"In that case," she said serenely, "yes." And she sank gracefully into a cross-legged sprawl.

I couldn't help grinning. She grinned companionably back.

"I was scared stiff of you when I came here last week," she said.

"You were *what?*"

"You always seemed so aloof. Unapproachable."

"Are we talking about me . . . or you?"

"You, of course," she said in surprise. "You always made me nervous. I always get sort of . . . strung up . . . when I'm nervous. Put on a bit of an act, to hide it, I suppose."

"I see," I said slowly.

"You're still a pretty good cactus, if you want to know . . . but . . . well, you see people differently when they've been bleeding all over your best dress."

I began to say that in that case I would be prepared to bleed on her any time she liked, but the telephone interrupted me at half way. And it was old Strepson, settling down for a long cozy chat about Breadwinner and Pound Postage.

Roberta wrinkled her nose and got to her feet.

"Don't go," I said with my hand over the mouthpiece.

"Must. I'm late already."

"Wait," I said. But she shook her head, fetched the yellow raincoat from the bath, where she'd put it, and edged herself into it.

" 'Bye," she said.

"Wait . . ."

She waved briefly and let herself out the door. I struggled up onto my feet, and "Sir . . . could you hold on a minute?" into the telephone, and hopped without the crutches over to the window. She looked up when I opened it. She was standing in the yard, tying on a headscarf. The rain had eased to drizzle.

"Will you come tomorrow?" I shouted down.

"Can't tomorrow. Got to go to London."

"Saturday?"

"Do you want me to?"

"Yes."

"I'll try, then."

"Please come."

"Oh . . ." She suddenly smiled in a way I'd never seen before. "All right."

Careless I might be about locking my front door, but in truth I left little about worth stealing. Five hundred pounds would never have been lying around on my chest of drawers for enquiry agents to photograph.

When I'd converted the flat from an old hayloft, I'd built in more than mod cons. Behind the cabinet in the kitchen which housed things like fly killer and soap powder, and tucked into a crafty piece of brickwork, lay a maximum security safe. It was operated not by keys or combinations but by electronics. The manufacturers had handed over the safe itself and also the tiny ultrasonic transmitter that sent out the special series of radio waves which alone would release the lock mechanism, and I'd installed them myself: the safe in the wall and the transmitter in a false bottom to the cabinet. Even if anyone found the transmitter, they had still to find the safe and to know the sequence of frequencies which unlocked it.

A right touch of the Open Sesame. I'd always liked gadgets.

Inside the safe there were, besides money and some racing trophies, several pieces of antique silver, three paintings by Houthuesen, two Chelsea figures, a Meissen cup and saucer, a Louis XIV snuffbox, and four uncut diamonds totaling twenty-eight carats. My retirement pension, all wrapped in green baize and appreciating nicely. Retirement for a steeplechase jockey could lurk in the very next fall; and the ripe age of forty, if one lasted that long, was about the limit.

There was also a valueless lump of cast iron, with a semicircular dent in it. To these various treasures I added the envelope which Ferth had given me, because it wouldn't help if I lost that either.

Bolting my front door meant a hazardous trip down the stairs, and another in the morning to open it. I decided it could stay unlocked as usual. Wedged a chair under the door into my sitting room instead.

During the evening, I telephoned to Newtonnards in his pink-washed house in Mill Hill.

"Hallo," he said. "You've got your license back, then. Talk of the meeting it was at Wincanton today, soon as the Press Association chaps heard about it."

"Yes, it's great news."

"What made their lordships change their minds?"

"I've no idea. . . . Look, I wondered if you'd seen that man again yet, the one who backed Cherry Pie with you."

"Funny thing," he said, "but I saw him today. Just after I'd heard you were back in favor, though, so I didn't think you'd be interested any more."

"Did you by any chance find out who he is?"

"I did, as a matter of fact. More to satisfy my own curiosity, really. He's the Honourable Peter Foxcroft. Mean anything to you?"

"He's a brother of Lord Middleburg."

"Yeah. So I'm told."

I laughed inwardly. Nothing sinister about Cranfield refusing to name his mysterious pal. Just another bit of ladder climbing. He might be one rung up being in a position to use the Honourable P. Foxcroft as a runner, but he would certainly be five rungs down involving him in a messy Enquiry.

"There's one other thing. . . ." I hesitated. "Would you—could you—do me a considerable favor?"

"Depends what it is." He sounded cautious but not truculent. A smooth, experienced character.

"I can't offer much in return."

He chuckled. "Warning me not to expect tip-offs when you're on a hot number?"

"Something like that," I admitted.

"O.K., then. You want something for strictly nothing. Just as well to know where we are. So shoot."

"Can you remember who you told about Cranfield backing Cherry Pie?"

"Before the Enquiry, you mean?"

"Yes. Those bookmaker colleagues you mentioned."

"Well . . ." He sounded doubtful.

"If you can," I said, "could you ask *them* who *they* told?"

"Phew." He half breathed, half whistled down the receiver. "That's some favor."

"I'm sorry. Just forget it."

"Hang on, hang on, I didn't say I wouldn't do it. It's a bit of a tall order, though, expecting them to remember."

"I know. Very long shot. But I still want to know who told the Stewards about the bet with you."

"You've got your license back. Why don't you let it rest?"

"Would you?"

He sighed. "I don't know. All right, then, I'll see what I can do. No promises, mind. Oh, and by the way, it can be just as useful to know when one of your mounts is *not* fit or likely to win. If you take my meaning."

"I take it," I said, smiling. "It's a deal."

I put down the receiver reflecting that only a minority of bookmakers were villains, and that most of them were more generous than they got credit for. The whole tribe were reviled for the image of the few. Like students.

Chapter 14

Oakley didn't come. No one came. I took the chair from under the doorknob to let the world in with the morning. Not much of the world accepted the invitation.

Made some coffee. Tony came while I was standing in the kitchen drinking it and put whisky into a mug of it for himself by way of breakfast. He'd been out with one lot of horses at exercise and was waiting to go out with the other, and spent the interval discussing their prospects as if nothing had ever happened. For him the warning off was past history, forgotten. His creed was that of newspapers: today is important, tomorrow more so, but yesterday is nothing.

He finished the coffee and left, clapping me cheerfully on the shoulder and setting up a protest from an Oakley bruise. I spent most of the rest of the day lying flat on my bed, answering the telephone, staring at the ceiling, letting nature get on with repairing a few ravages, and thinking.

Another quiet night. I had two names in my mind, juggling them. Two to work on. Better than three hundred. But both could be wrong.

Saturday morning the postman brought the letters right upstairs, as he'd been doing since the era of plaster. I thanked him, sorted through them, dropped a crutch, and had the usual awkward fumble picking it up. When I opened one of the letters, I dropped both the crutches in surprise.

Left the crutches on the floor, leaned against the wall and read.

Dear Kelly Hughes,

I have seen in the papers that you have had your license restored, so perhaps this information will be too late to be of any use to you. I am sending it anyway, because the friend who collected it is considerably out of pocket over it, and would be glad if you could reimburse him. I append also his list of expenses.

As you will see, he went to a good deal of trouble over this, though to be fair he also told me that he had enjoyed doing it. I hope it is what you wanted.

> Sincerely,
> Teddy Dewar
> Great Stag Hotel, Birmingham

Clipped behind the letter were several other sheets of varying sizes. The top one was a schematic presentation of names which looked at first glance like an inverted family tree. There were clumps of three or four names inside two-inch circles. The circles led via arrows to other circles below and sometimes beside them, but the eye was led downward continually until all the arrows had converged to three circles, and then to two, and finally to one. And the single name in the bottom circle was David Oakley.

Behind the page was an explanatory note.

I knew one contact, the J. L. Jones underlined in the third row of circles. From him I worked in all directions, checking people who knew of David Oakley. Each clump of people heard about him from one of the people in the next clump. Everyone on the page, I guarantee, has heard either directly or indirectly that Oakley is the man to go to if one is in trouble. I posed as a man in trouble, as you suggested, and nearly all that I talked to either mentioned him of their own accord or agreed when I brought him up as a possibility.

I only hope that one at least of these names has

some significance for you, as I'm afraid the expenses were rather high. Most of the investigation was conducted in pubs or hotels, and it was sometimes necessary to get the contact tight before he would divulge.

Faithfully,
B.R.S. Timieson

The expense list was high enough to make me whistle. I turned back to the circled names and read them carefully through.

Looking for one of two.

One was there.

Perhaps I should have rejoiced. Perhaps I should have been angry. Instead, I felt sad.

I doubled the expenses and wrote out a check with an accompanying note:

"This is really magnificent. Cannot thank you enough. One of the names has great significance, well worth all your perseverance. My eternal thanks."

I also wrote a grateful letter to Teddy Dewar, saying the information couldn't have been better timed and enclosing the envelope for his friend Timieson.

As I was sticking on the stamp, the telephone rang. I hopped over to it and lifted the receiver.

George Newtonnards.

"Spent all last evening on the blower. Astronomical phone bill I'm going to have."

"Send me the account," I said resignedly.

"Better wait to see if I've got results," he suggested. "Got a pencil handy?"

"Just a sec." I fetched a writing pad and ballpoint. "O.K. Go ahead."

"Right, then. First, here are the chaps *I* told." He dictated five names. "The last one, Pelican Jobberson, is the one who holds a fierce grudge against you for that bum steer you gave him, but as it happens, he didn't tell the Stewards or anyone else because he went off to Casablanca the next day for a holiday. Well . . . here are the people Harry Ingram told . . ." He read out three names. "And these are the people Herbie Subbing told . . ." Four names. "These are the people Dimmie Ovens told . . ." Five names. "And Clobber Mackintosh, he really spread it around . . ." Eight names. "That's all they can remember. They wouldn't swear there was no one else. And, of course, all those people they've mentioned could have passed the info on to someone else. . . . I mean, things like this spread out in ripples."

"Thanks anyway," I said sincerely. "Thank you very much indeed for taking so much trouble."

"Has it been any help?"

"Oh, yes, I think so. I'll let you know sometime."

"And don't forget. The obvious non-winner . . . give me the wink."

"I'll do that," I promised. "If you'll risk it, after Pelican Jobberson's experience."

"He's got no sense," he said. "But I have."

He rang off, and I studied his list of names. Several were familiar and belonged to well-known racing people: the bookmakers' clients, I supposed. None of the names were the same as those on Timieson's list of Oakley contacts, but there was something. . . .

For ten minutes I stood looking at the paper wondering what was hovering around the edge of consciousness, and finally, with a thud, the association clicked.

One of the men Herbie Subbing had told was the brother-in-law of the person I had found among the Oakley contacts.

I thought for a while, and then opened the newspaper and studied the program for the day's racing, which was at Reading. Then I telephoned to Lord Ferth at his London house, and reached him via a plummy-voiced manservant.

"Well, Kelly?" There was something left of Wednesday's relationship. Not all, but something.

"Sir," I said, "are you going to Reading races?"

"Yes, I am."

"I haven't yet had any official notice of my license

being restored. . . . Will it be all right for me to turn up there? I would particularly like to talk to you."

"I'll make sure you have no difficulty, if it's important." There was a faint question in his tone, which I answered.

"I know," I said, "who engineered things."

"Ah . . . yes. Then come. Unless the journey would be too uncomfortable for you? I have no engagements to-night."

"You're very thoughtful. But I think our engineer will be at the races, too . . . or at least there's a very good chance of it."

"As you like," he agreed. "I'll look out for you."

Tony had two runners at the meeting and I could ask him to take me. But there was also Roberta. . . . She was coming over, probably, and she, too, might take me. I smiled wryly to myself. She might take me anywhere. Roberta Cranfield. Of all people.

As if by telepathy, the telephone rang and it was Roberta herself on the other end. She sounded breathless and worried.

"Kelly! I can't come just yet. In fact . . ." The words came in a rush. "Can you come over here?"

"What's the matter?"

"Well . . . I don't really know if *anything's* the matter . . . seriously, that is. But Grace Roxford has turned up here."

"Dear Grace?"

"Yes. . . . Look, Kelly, she's just sitting in her car outside the house sort of glaring at it. Honestly, she looks a bit mad. We don't know quite what to do. Mother wants to call the police, but, I mean, one *can't*. . . . Supposing the poor woman has come to apologize or something, and is just screwing her courage up?"

"She's still sitting in the car?"

"Yes. I can see her from here. Can you come? I mean . . . Mother's useless and you know how dear Grace feels about *me*. . . . She looks pretty odd, Kelly." Definite alarm in her voice.

"Where's your father?"

"Out on the gallops with Breadwinner. He won't be back for about an hour."

"All right, then. I'll get Tony or someone to drive me over. As soon as I can."

"That's great," she said with relief. "I'll try and stall her till you come."

It would take half an hour to get there. More, probably. By then dear Grace might not still be sitting in her car. . . .

I dialed three nine one.

"Tony," I said urgently, "can you drop everything instantly and drive me to Cranfield's? Grace Roxford has turned up there and I don't like the sound of it."

"I've got to go to Reading," he protested.

"You can go on from Cranfield's when we've sorted Grace out . . . and anyway, I want to go to Reading, too, to talk to Lord Ferth. So be a pal, Tony. Please."

"Oh, all right. If you want it that much. Give me five minutes."

He took ten. I spent some of them telephoning to Jack Roxford. He was surprised I should be calling him.

"Look, Jack," I said, "I'm sorry to be upsetting you like this, but have you any idea where your wife has gone?"

"Grace?" More surprise, but also anxiety. "Down to the village, she said."

The village in question was roughly forty miles from Cranfield's house.

"She must have gone some time ago," I said.

"I suppose so. . . . What's all this about?" The worry was sharp in his voice.

"Roberta Cranfield has just telephoned to say that your wife is outside their house, just sitting in her car."

"Oh God," he said. "She can't be."

"I'm afraid she is."

"Oh, *no* . . ." he wailed. "She seemed better this morning . . . quite her old self . . . it seemed safe to let her go and do the shopping . . . she's been so upset, you see . . . and then you and Dexter got your licenses back . . . it's affected her . . . it's all been so awful for her."

"I'm just going over there to see if I can help," I said. "But . . . can you come down and collect her?"

"Oh, *yes,*" he said. "I'll start at once. Oh, poor dear Grace . . . Take care of her till I come."

"Yes," I said reassuringly, and disconnected.

I made it without mishap down the stairs and found Tony had commandeered Poppy's station wagon for the journey. The back seat lay flat so that I could lie instead of sit, and there were even cushions for my shoulders and head.

"Poppy's idea," Tony said briefly, helping me climb in through the rear door. "Great girl."

"She sure is," I said gratefully, hauling in the crutches behind me. "Lose no time, now, friend."

"You sound worried." He shut the doors, switched on, and drove away with minimum waste of time.

"I am, rather. Grace Roxford is unbalanced."

"But surely not dangerous?"

"I hope not."

I must have sounded doubtful, because Tony's foot went heavily down on the accelerator. "Hold on to something," he said. We rocked round corners. I couldn't find any good anchorage, had to wedge my useful foot against the rear door and push myself off the swaying walls with my hands.

"O.K.?" he shouted.

"Uh . . . yes," I said breathlessly.

"Good bit of road just coming up." We left all the other traffic at a standstill. "Tell me if you see any cops."

We saw no cops. Tony covered the eighteen miles through Berkshire in twenty-three minutes. We jerked to a stop outside Cranfield's house, and the first thing I saw was that there was no one in the small gray Volkswagen standing near the front door.

Tony opened the back of the car with a crash and unceremoniously tugged me out.

"She's probably sitting down cozily having a quiet cup of tea," he said.

She wasn't.

Tony rang the front doorbell and after a lengthy interval Mrs. Cranfield herself opened it.

Not her usual swift wide-opening fling. She looked at us through a nervous six inches.

"Hughes. What are you doing here? Go away."

"Roberta asked me to come. To see Grace Roxford."

"Mrs. Roxford is no longer here." Mrs. Cranfield's voice was as strung up as her behavior.

"Isn't that her car?" I pointed to the Volkswagen.

"No," she said sharply.

"Whose is it, then?"

"The gardener's. Now, Hughes, go away at once. Go away."

"Very well," I said, shrugging. And she instantly shut the door.

"Help me back into the car," I said to Tony.

"Surely you're not just *going?*"

"Don't argue," I said. "Get me into the car, drive away out through the gates, then go round and come back in through the stable entrance."

"That's better." He shuffled me in, threw in the crutches, slammed the door, and hustled round to the driving seat.

"Don't rush so," I said. "Scratch your head a bit. Look disgusted."

"You think she's watching?" He didn't start the car: looked at me over his shoulder.

"I think Mrs. Cranfield would never this side of doomsday allow her gardener to park outside her front door. Mrs. Cranfield would know I would know that. Mrs. Cranfield was doing her best to ask for help."

"Which means," he added slowly, "that Grace Roxford is very dangerous indeed."

I nodded with a dry mouth. "Drive away, now."

He went slowly. Rolled round into the back drive, accelerated along that, and stopped with a jerk beside the stables. Yet again he helped me out.

"There's a telephone in the small office in the yard," I said. "Next to the tack room. Look up in the classified directory and find a local doctor. Tell him to come smartish. Then wait here until Dexter Cranfield comes back with the horses, and stop him going into the house."

"Kelly, couldn't you be exaggerating?"

"I could. Better to be on the safe side, though."

"I'll never be able to stop Cranfield."

"Tell him no one ever believes anything tragic will happen until it has."

He looked at me for two seconds, then wheeled away into the yard.

I peglegged up the back drive and tried the back door. Open. It would be. For Cranfield to walk easily through it. And to what?

I went silently along into the main hall, and listened. There was no sound in the house.

Tried the library first, juggling the crutches to get a good grip on the door handle, sweating lest I should drop one with a crash. Turned the handle, pressed the door quietly inward.

The library was uninhabited. A large clock on the mantel ticked loudly. Out of time with my heart.

I left the door open. Went slowly, silently, toward the small sitting room beside the front door. Again the meticulously careful drill with the handle. If they'd seen me come, they would most probably be in this room.

The door swung inward. Well oiled. No creaks. I saw the worn chintz covers on the armchairs, the elderly rugs, the debris of living: scattered newspapers, a pair of spectacles on some letters, a headscarf, and a flower basket. No people.

On the other side of the hall there were the double doors into the large formal drawing room, and at the back, beyond the staircase, the doors to the dining room and to Dexter Cranfield's own study, where he kept his racing books and did all his paperwork.

I swung across to the study, and opened the door. It was quiet in there. Dust slowly gravitated. Nothing else moved.

That left only the two large rooms downstairs, and the whole of upstairs. I looked at the long broad flight uneasily. Wished it were an escalator.

The dining room was empty. I shifted back through the hall to the double doors of the drawing room. Went through the crutch routine with more difficulty, because if I was going in there I would need both doors open, and to open both doors took both hands. I managed it in the end by hooking both crutches over my left arm like walking sticks, and standing on one leg.

The doors parted and I pushed them wide. The quarter acre of drawing room contained chairs of gold brocade upholstery, a pale cream Chinese carpet, and long soft blue curtains. A delicate, elegant, class-conscious room designed for Cranfield's glossiest aspirations.

Everything in there was motionless. A tableau.

I hitched the crutches into place, and walked forward. Stopped after a very few paces. Stopped because I had to.

Mrs. Cranfield was there. And Roberta. And Grace Roxford. Mrs. Cranfield was standing by the fireplace, hanging on to the shoulder-high mantel as if needing support. Roberta sat upright in an armless wooden chair set out of its usual place in a large clear area of carpet. Behind her and slightly to one side, and with one hand firmly grasping Roberta's shoulder, stood Grace Roxford.

Grace Roxford held the sort of knife used by fishmongers. Nearly a foot long, razor sharp, with a point like a needle. She was resting the lethal end of it against Roberta's neck.

"Kelly!" Roberta said. Her voice was high and a trifle wavery, but the relief in it was overwhelming. I feared it might be misplaced.

Grace Roxford had a bright color over her taut cheekbones and a piercing glitter in her eyes. Her body was rigid with tension. The hand holding the knife trembled in uneven spasms. She was as unstable as wet gelignite; but she still knew what she was doing.

"You went away, Kelly Hughes," she said. "You went away."

"Yes, Grace," I agreed. "But I came back to talk to Roberta."

"You come another step," she said, "and I'll cut her throat."

Mrs. Cranfield drew a breath like a sob, but Roberta's expression didn't change. Grace had made that threat already. Several times, probably. Especially when Tony and I had arrived at the front door.

She was desperately determined. Neither I nor the Cranfields had room to doubt that she wouldn't do as she said. And I was twenty feet away from her and a cripple besides.

"What do you want, Grace?" I said, as calmly as possible.

"Want? Want?" Her eyes flickered. She seemed to be trying to remember what she wanted. Then her rage sharpened on me like twin darts, and her purpose came flooding back.

"Dexter Cranfield . . . bloody snob . . . I'll see he doesn't get those horses . . . I'm going to kill him, see, kill him . . . then he can't get them, can he? No . . . he can't."

Again there was no surprise either in Roberta or her mother. Grace had told them already what she'd come for.

"Grace, killing Mr. Cranfield won't help your husband."

"Yes. Yes. Yes. Yes." She nodded sharply between each yes, and the knife jumped against Roberta's neck. Roberta shut her eyes for a while and swayed on the chair.

I said, "How do you hope to kill him, Grace?"

She laughed. It got out of control at halfway and ended in a maniacal high-pitched giggle. "He'll come here, won't he? He'll come here and stand beside me, because he'll do just what I say, won't he? Won't he?"

I looked at the steel blade beside Roberta's pearly skin and knew that he would indeed do as she said. As I would.

"And then, see," she said, "I'll just stick the knife into him, not into her. See? See?"

"I see," I said.

She nodded extravagantly and her hand shook.

"And then what?" I asked.

"Then what?" She looked puzzled. She hadn't got any further than killing Cranfield. Beyond that lay only darkness and confusion. Her vision didn't extend to consequences.

"Edwin Byler could send his horses away to someone else," I said.

"No. No. Only Dexter Cranfield. Only him. Telling him he ought to have a more snobbish trainer, taking him away from us. I'm going to kill him. Then he can't have those horses." The words tumbled out in a vehement monotone, all the more frightening for being clearly automatic. These were thoughts she'd had in her head for a very long time.

"It would have been all right, of course," I said slowly. "If Mr. Cranfield hadn't got his license back."

"Yes!" It was a bitterly angry shriek.

"I got it back for him," I said.

"They just gave it back. They just gave it back. They shouldn't have done that. They shouldn't."

"They didn't just give it back," I said. "They gave it back because I made them."

"You couldn't. . . ."

"I told everyone I was going to. And I did."

"No. No. No."

"Yes," I said flatly.

Her expression slowly changed, and highly frightening it was too. I waited while it sank into her disorganized brain that if Byler sent his horses to Cranfield after all it was me alone she had to thank for it. I watched the intention to kill widen to embrace me too. The semi-cautious restraint in her manner toward me was transforming itself into a vicious glare of hate.

I swallowed. I said again, "If I hadn't made the Stewards give Mr. Cranfield's license back, he would still be warned off."

Roberta said in horror, "No, Kelly. Don't. Don't do it."

"Shut up," I said. "Me or your father . . . which has more chance? And run, when you can."

Grace wasn't listening. Grace was grasping the essentials and deciding on a course of action.

There was a lot of white showing round her eyes.

"I'll kill you," she said. "I'll kill you."

I stood still. I waited. The seconds stretched like centuries.

"Come here," she said. "Come here, or I'll cut her throat."

Chapter 15

I took myself, crutch by crutch, toward her. When I was halfway there, Mrs. Cranfield gave a moaning sigh and fainted, falling awkwardly on the rug and scattering the brass fire irons with a nerve-shattering crash.

Grace jumped. The knife snicked into Roberta's skin and she cried out. I stood half unbalanced, freezing into immobility, trying to will Grace not to disintegrate into panic, not to go over the edge, not to lose the last tiny grip she had on her reason. She wasn't far from stabbing everything in sight.

"Sit still," I said to Roberta with dreadful urgency, and she gave me a terrified look and did her best not to move. She was trembling violently. I had never thought I could pray. I prayed.

Grace was moving her head in sharp birdlike jerks. The knife was still against Roberta's neck. Grace's other hand still grasped Roberta's shoulder. A thread of blood trickled down Roberta's skin and was blotted up in a scarlet patch by her white jersey.

No one went to help Roberta's mother. I didn't even dare to look at her, because it meant turning my eyes away from Grace.

"Come here," Grace said. "Come here."

Her voice was husky, little more than a loud whisper. And although she was watching me come with unswerving murder in her eyes, I was inexpressibly thankful that she could still speak at all, still think, still hold a purpose.

During the last few steps, I wondered how I was going to dodge, since I couldn't jump, couldn't bend my knees, and hadn't even my hands free. A bit late to start worrying. I took the last step short, so that she would have to move to reach me, and at the same time eased my elbow out of the right-hand crutch.

She was almost too fast. She struck at me instantly, in a flashing thrust directed at my throat, and although I managed to twist the two inches needed to avoid it, the hissing knife came close enough, through the collar of my coat. I brought my right arm up and across, crashing the crutch against her as she prepared to try again.

Out of the corner of my eye I saw Roberta wrench herself out of Grace's clutching grasp, and half stumble, half fall as she got away from the chair.

"Kill you," Grace said. The words were distorted. The meaning clear. She had no thought of self-defense. No thought at all, as far as I could see. Just one single burning obsessive intention.

I brought up the left-hand crutch like a pole to push her away. She dived round it and tried to plunge her knife through my ribs, and in throwing myself away from that I overbalanced and half fell down, and she was standing over me with her arm raised like a priest at a human sacrifice.

I dropped one crutch altogether. Useless warding off a knife with a bare hand. I tried to shove the other crutch round into her face, but got it tangled up against an armchair.

Grace brought her arm down. I fell right to the floor as soon as I saw her move and the knife followed me harmlessly, all the impetus gone by the time it reached me. Another tear in my coat.

She came down on her knees beside me, her arm going up again.

From nowhere my lost crutch whistled through the air and smashed into the hand which held the knife. Grace hissed like a snake and dropped it, and it fell point down onto my plaster. She twisted round to see who had hit her and spread out her hands toward the crutch that Roberta was aiming at her again.

She caught hold of it and tugged. I wriggled round on the floor, stretched until I had my fingers on the handle of the knife, and threw it as hard as I could toward the open door into the hall.

Grace was too much for Roberta. Too much for me. She was appallingly, insanely strong. I heaved myself up onto my left knee and clasped my arms tight round her chest from behind, trying to pin her arms down to her sides. She shook me around like a sack of feathers, struggling to get to her feet.

She managed it, lifting me with her, plaster and all. She knew where I'd thrown the knife. She started to go that way, dragging me with her still fastened to her back like a leech.

"Get that knife and run to the stables," I gasped to Roberta. A girl in a million. She simply ran and picked up the knife and went on running, out into the hall and out of the house.

Grace started yelling unintelligibly and trying to unclamp the fingers I had laced together over her thin breastbone. I hung on for everyone's dear life, and when she couldn't dislodge them she began pinching wherever she would reach with fierce hurting spite.

The hair which she usually wore twisted into a fold up the back of her neck had come undone and was falling into my face. I could see less and less of what was going on. I knew only that she was still headed toward the doorway, still unimaginably violent, and mumbling now in a continuous flow of senseless words interspersed with sudden shrieks.

She reached the doorway and started trying to get free of me by crashing me against the jamb. She had a hard job of it, but she managed it in the end, and when she felt my weight fall off her she turned in a flash, sticking out her hands with rigid fingers toward my neck.

Her face was a dark congested crimson. Her eyes were stretched wide in a stark screaming stare. Her lips were drawn back in a tight line from her teeth.

I had never in all my life seen anything so terrifying. Hadn't imagined a human could look like that, had never visualized homicidal madness.

She would certainly have killed me if it hadn't been for

Tony, because her strength made a joke of mine. He came tearing into the hall from the kitchen and brought her down with a rugger tackle about the knees, and I fell, too, on top of her, because she was trying to tear my throat out in handfuls, and she didn't let go.

It took all Tony could do, all Archie could do, all three other lads could do to unlatch her from me and hold her down on the floor. They sat on her arms and legs and chest and head, and she thrashed about convulsively underneath them.

Roberta had tears streaming down her face and I hadn't any breath left to tell her to cheer up, there was no more danger, no more . . . no more . . . I leant weakly against the wall and thought it would be too damned silly to pass out now. Took three deep breaths instead. Everything steadied again, reluctantly.

Tony said, "There's a doctor on the way. Don't think he's expecting this, though."

"He'll know what to do."

"Mother!" exclaimed Roberta suddenly. "I'd forgotten about her." She hurried past me into the drawing room and I heard her mother's voice rising in a disturbed, disorientated question.

Grace was crying out, but her voice sounded like sea gulls and nothing she said made sense. One of the lads said sympathetically, "Poor thing, oughtn't we let her get up?" and Tony answered fiercely, "Only under a tiger net."

"She doesn't know what's happening," I said wearily. "She can't control what she does. So don't for God's sake let go of her."

Except for Tony's resolute six feet, they all sat on her gingerly and twice she nearly had them off. Finally and at long last, the front doorbell rang, and I hopped across the hall to answer it.

It was the local doctor, looking tentative, wondering no doubt if it was a hoax. But he took one look at Grace and was opening his case while he came across the hall. Into her arm he pushed a hypodermic needle, and soon the

convulsive thrashing slackened, and the high-pitched crying dulled to murmurs and in the end to silence.

The men slowly stood up and stepped away from her,
and she lay there looking shrunk and crumpled, her graying hair falling in streaks away from her flaccidly relax-
ing face. It seemed incredible that such thin limbs, such a
meager body, could have put out such strength. We all
stood looking down at her with more awe than pity,
watching while the last twitches shook her and she sank
into unconscious peace.

Half an hour later Grace still lay on the floor in the
hall, but with a pillow under her head and a rug keeping
her warm.

Dexter Cranfield had come back from watching the
horses work and walked unprepared into the aftermath of
drama. His wife's semihysterical explanations hadn't
helped him much.

Roberta told him that Grace had come to kill him
because he had his license back and that she was the
cause of his losing it in the first place, and he stamped
around in a fury which I gathered was mostly because the
source of our troubles was a woman. He basically didn't
like women. She should have been locked up years ago, he
said. Spiteful, petty-minded, scheming, interfering . . . just
like a woman, he said. I listened to him gravely and
concluded he had suffered from a bossy nanny.

The doctor had done some intensive telephoning, and
presently an ambulance arrived with two compassionate-
looking men and a good deal of special equipment. The
front door stood wide open and the prospect of Grace's
imminent departure was a relief to everyone.

Into this active bustling scene drove Jack Roxford.

He scrambled out of his car, took a horrified look at the
ambulance, and plowed in through the front door. When
he saw Grace lying there, with the ambulance men
preparing to lift her onto a stretcher, he went down on his
knees beside her.

"Grace, dear . . ." He looked at her more closely. She
was still unconscious, very pale now, looking wizened and

sixty. "Grace, dear!" There was anguish in his voice. "What's the matter with her!"

The doctor started to break it to him. Cranfield interrupted the gentle words and said brutally, "She's raving mad. She came here trying to kill me, and she could have killed my wife and daughter. It's absolutely disgraceful that she should have been running around free in that state. I'm going to see my solicitors about it."

Jack Roxford only heard the first part. His eyes went to the cut on Roberta's neck and the bloodstain on her jersey, and he put his hand over his mouth and looked sick.

"Grace," he said. "Oh, Grace . . ."

There was no doubt he loved her. He leant over her, stroking the hair away from her forehead, murmuring to her, and when he finally looked up there were tears in his eyes and on his cheeks.

"She'll be all right, won't she?"

The doctor shifted uncomfortably and said one would have to see, only time would tell, there were marvelous treatments nowadays . . .

The ambulance men loaded her gently onto the stretcher and picked it up.

"Let me go with her," Jack Roxford said. "Where are you taking her? Let me go with her."

One of the ambulance men told him the name of the hospital and advised him not to come.

"Better try this evening, sir. No use you waiting all day, now, is it?" And the doctor added that Grace would be unconscious for some time yet and under heavy sedation after that, and it was true, it would be better if Roxford didn't go with her.

The uniformed men carried Grace out into the sunshine and loaded her into the ambulance, and we all followed them out into the drive. Jack Roxford stood there looking utterly forlorn as they shut the doors, consulted finally with the doctor, and drove away.

Roberta touched his arm. "Can't I get you a drink, Mr. Roxford?"

He looked at her vaguely, and then his whole face crumpled and he couldn't speak.

"Don't, Mr. Roxford," Roberta said with pity. "She isn't in any pain, or anything."

He shook his head. Roberta put her arm across his shoulders and steered him back into the house.

"Now, what?" Tony said. "I've really got to get on to Reading, pal. Those runners of mine have to be declared for the second race."

I looked at my watch. "You could spare another quarter of an hour. I think we should take Jack Roxford with us. He's got a runner, too, incidentally, though I imagine he doesn't much care about that. . . . Except that it's one of Edwin Byler's. But he's not fit to drive anywhere himself, and the races would help to keep him from brooding too much about Grace."

"Yeah. A passable idea." Tony grinned.

"Go into the house and see if you can persuade him to let you take him."

"O.K." He went off amiably, and I passed the time swinging around the drive on my crutches and peering into the cars parked there. I'd be needing a new one . . . probably choose the same again, though.

I leant against Tony's car and thought about Grace. She'd left on me a fair legacy of bruises from her pinches to add to the crop grown by Oakley. Also, my coat would cost a fortune at the invisible menders, and my throat felt like a well-developed case of septic tonsils. I looked gloomily down at my plastered leg. The dangers of detecting seemed to be twice as high as steeplechasing. With luck, I thought with a sigh, I could now go back to the usual but less frequent form of battery.

Tony came out of the house with Roberta and Jack Roxford. Jack looked dazed, and let Tony help him into the front of the station wagon as if his thoughts were miles away. As indeed they probably were.

I scrunched across the gravel toward Roberta.

"Is your neck all right?" I asked.

"Is yours?"

I investigated her cut more closely. It wasn't deep. Little more than an inch long.

"There won't be much of a scar," I said.

"No," she agreed.

Her face was close to mine. Her eyes were amber with dark flecks.

"Stay here," she said abruptly. "You don't have to go to the races."

"I've an appointment with Lord Ferth. . . . Best to get this business thoroughly wrapped up."

"I suppose so." She looked suddenly very tired. She'd had a wearing Saturday morning.

"If you've nothing better to do," I suggested, "would you come over tomorrow . . . and cook me some lunch?"

A small smile tugged at her mouth and wrinkled her eyes.

"I fell hopelessly in love with you," she said, "when I was twelve."

"And then it wore off?"

"Yes."

"Pity," I said.

Her smile broadened.

"Who is Bobbie?" I asked.

"Bobbie? Oh . . . he's Lord Iceland's son."

"He would be."

She laughed. "Father wants me to marry him."

"That figures."

"But Father is going to be disappointed."

"Good," I said.

"Kelly!" yelled Tony. "Come one, for hell's sakes, or I'll be late."

"Good-bye," she said calmly. "See you tomorrow."

Tony drove to Reading races with due care and attention and Jack Roxford sat sunk in gloomy silence from start to finish. When we stopped in the car park, he stepped out of the car and walked dazedly away toward the entrance without a word of thanks or explanation.

Tony watched him go and clicked his tongue. "That woman isn't worth it."

"She is, to him," I said.

Tony hurried off to declare his horses, and I went more slowly through the gate looking out for Lord Ferth.

It felt extraordinary being back on a racecourse. Like being let out of prison. The same people who had looked sideways at me at the Jockeys' Fund dance now slapped me familiarly on the back and said they were delighted to see me. Oh, yeah, I thought ungratefully. Never kick a man once he's up.

Lord Ferth was standing outside the weighing room in a knot of people from which he detached himself when he saw me coming.

"Come along to the Stewards' dining room," he said. "We can find a quiet corner there."

"Can we postpone it until after the third race?" I asked. "I want my cousin Tony to be there as well, and he has some runners. . . ."

"Of course," he agreed. "Later would be best for me, too, as it happens. After the third, then."

I watched the first three races with the hunger of an exile returned. Tony's horse, my sometime mount, finished a fast fourth, which augured well for next time out, and Byler's horse won the third. As I hurried round to see how Jack Roxford would make out in the winner's enclosure, I almost crashed into Jessel. He looked me over, took in the plaster and crutches, and said nothing at all. I watched his cold expressionless face with one to match. After ramming home the point that he had no intention of apologizing, he turned brusquely on his heel and walked away.

"Get that," Tony said in my ear. "You could sue him for defamation."

"He's not worth the effort."

From Charlie West, too, I'd had much the same reaction. Defiance, slightly sullen variety. I shrugged resignedly. That was my own fault, and only time would tell.

Tony walked with me to the winner's enclosure. Byler was there, beaming. Jack Roxford still looked lost. We watched Byler suggest a celebration drink, and Jack shook his head vaguely as if he hadn't understood.

"Go and fish Jack out," I said to Tony. "Tell him you're still looking after him."

"If you say so, pal." He obligingly edged through the crowd, took Jack by the elbow, said a few explanatory words to Byler, and steered Jack out.

I joined them and said neutrally, "This way," and led them along toward the Stewards' dining room. They both went through the door taking off their hats and hanging them on the pegs inside.

The long tables in the Stewards' dining room had been cleared from lunch and laid for tea, but there was no one there except Lord Ferth. He shook hands with Tony and Jack and invited them to sit down around one end of a table.

"Kelly . . . ?" he said.

"I'll stand," I said. "Easier."

"Well, now," Ferth said, glancing curiously at Tony and Jack. "You told me, Kelly, that you knew who had framed you and Dexter Cranfield."

I nodded.

Tony said regretfully, "Grace Roxford. Jack's wife."

Jack looked vaguely down at the tablecloth and said nothing at all.

Tony explained to Lord Ferth just what had happened at Cranfield's and he looked more and more upset.

"My dear Roxford," he said uncomfortably, "I'm so sorry. So very sorry." He looked up at me. "One could never have imagined that she . . . that Grace Roxford of all people . . . could have framed you."

"That's right," I said mildly. "She didn't."

Chapter 16

Both Tony and Jack sat up as if electrified.

Lord Ferth said, "But you said . . ." And Tony answered, "I thought there was no doubt. . . . She tried to kill Kelly . . . she was going to kill Cranfield, too."

"She tried to kill me this time," I agreed. "But not the time before. It wasn't she who fiddled with my car."

"Then *who?*" Lord Ferth demanded.

"Her husband."

Jack stood up. He looked a lot less lost.

I poked Tony on the shoulder with my crutch, and he took the hint and stood up, too. He was sitting between Jack and the door.

"Sit down, Mr. Roxford," Ferth said authoritatively, and after a pause, slowly, Jack obeyed.

"That's nonsense," he protested. "I didn't touch Kelly's car. No one could have arranged that accident."

"You couldn't have imagined I would be hit by a train," I agreed. "But some sort of smash, yes, definitely."

"But Grace——" began Tony, still bewildered.

"Grace," I said with deliberateness, "has in most respects displayed exactly opposite qualities to the person who engineered Cranfield's and my suspension. Grace has been wild, accusing, uncontrolled, and emotional. The planning which went into getting us warned off was cool, careful, efficient, and brutal."

"Mad people are very cunning," Tony said doubtfully.

"It wasn't Grace," I said positively. "It was Jack."

There was a pause. Then Jack said in a rising wail,

201

"Why ever did she have to go to Cranfield's this morning? Why couldn't she leave things alone?"

"It wouldn't have done any good," I said. "I already knew it was you."

"That's impossible."

Ferth cleared his throat. "I think—er—you'd better tell us, Kelly, what your grounds are for making this very serious accusation."

"It began," I said, "when Dexter Cranfield persuaded Edwin Byler to take his horses away from Roxford and send them to him. Cranfield did no doubt persuade Byler, as Grace maintained, that he was a more highly regarded trainer socially than Roxford. Social standing means a great deal to Mr. Cranfield, and he is apt to expect that it does to everyone else. And in Edwin Byler's case, he was very likely right. But Jack had trained Byler's horses from the day he bought his first, and as Byler's fortune and string grew, so did Jack's prosperity and prestige. To lose Byler was to him a total disaster. A return to obscurity. The end of everything. Jack isn't a bad trainer, but he hasn't the personality to make the top ranks. Not without an accident—a gift from heaven—like Byler. And you don't find two Bylers in your yard in one lifetime. So almost from the start I wondered about Jack; from as soon as Cranfield told me, two days after the Enquiry, that Byler had been going to transfer his horses. Because I felt such a wrench of regret, you see, that I was not going to ride them . . . and I realized that that was nothing compared to what Jack would have felt if he'd lost them."

"It wasn't fair, you know. Not fair," said Jack dully.

"I had an open mind," I said, "because Pat Nikita had much the same motive, only the other way round. He and Cranfield detest each other. He had been trying to coax Jessel away from Cranfield for years, and getting Cranfield warned off was one way of clinching things. Then there were various people with smaller motives, like Charlie West, who might have hoped to ride Squelch for Nikita if I were out of the way. And there was a big possibility that it was someone else altogether, someone I hadn't come across, whose motive I couldn't even suspect."

"So why must it be Mr. Roxford?" Ferth said.

I took the paper Teddy Dewar had sent me out of my pocket and handed it to him, explaining what it meant.

"That shows a direct link between Oakley and the people in the circles. One of those people is Jack Roxford. He did, you see, know of Oakley's existence. He knew Oakley would agree to provide faked evidence."

"But . . ." Lord Ferth began.

"Yes, I know," I said. "Circumstantial. Then there's this list of people from George Newtonnards." I gave him the list, and pointed. "These are the people who definitely knew that Cranfield had backed Cherry Pie with Newtonnards. Again this is not conclusive, because other people might have known who are not on this list. But that man"—I pointed to the name in Herbie Subbing's list of contacts—"that man is Grace Roxford's brother. Jack's brother-in-law."

Ferth looked at me levelly. "You've taken a lot of trouble."

"It was taken for me," I said, "by Teddy Dewar and his friend, and by George Newtonnards."

"They acted on your suggestions, though."

"Yes."

"Anything else?"

"Well," I said, "there are those neatly typed sheets of accusations which were sent to Lord Gowery. So untypical, by the way, of Grace. We could compare the typewriter with Jack's. . . . Typewriters are about as distinctive as fingerprints. I haven't had an opportunity to do that yet."

Jack looked up wildly. The typewriter made sense to him. He hadn't followed the significance of the lists.

Ferth said slowly, "I obtained from the Stewards' Secretaries the letter which pointed out to them that a disqualified person was living in a racing stable. As far as I remember, the typing is the same as in the original accusations."

"Very catty, that," I said. "More like Grace. Revengeful, and without much point."

"I never wrote to the Stewards' Secretaries," Jack said.

"Did Grace?"

He shook his head. I thought perhaps he didn't know. It didn't seem to be of any great importance. I said instead, "I looked inside the boot of Jack's car this morning, while he was in Mr. Cranfield's house. He carries a great big tool kit, including a hand drill."

"No," Jack said.

"Yes, indeed. Also you have an old gray Volkswagen, the one Grace drove today. That car was seen by the mechanic from my garage when you went to pick over the remains of my car. I imagine you were hoping to remove any telltale drill holes which might have led the insurance company to suspect attempted murder, but Derek was there before you. And you either followed him or asked the garage whether he'd taken anything from the wreckage, because you sent David Oakley to my flat to get it back. Oakley didn't know the significance of what he was looking for. A chunk of metal with a hole in it. That was all he knew. He was there to earn a fee."

"Did he find it?" Ferth asked.

"No. I still have it. Can one prove that a certain drill made a certain hole?"

Ferth didn't know. Jack didn't speak.

"When you heard, at the dance," I said, "that I was trying to find out who had framed Cranfield and me, you thought you would get rid of me, in case I managed it. Because if I managed it, you'd lose far more than Byler's horses . . . so while I was talking to Lord Ferth and dancing with Roberta, you were out at the back of the car park rigging up your booby trap. Which," I added calmly, remembering the blazing hell of the dislocations, "I find hard to forgive."

"I'll strangle him," Tony said forcefully.

"What happens to him"—I shook my head—"depends on Lord Ferth."

Ferth regarded me squarely. "You find him. I deal with him."

"That was the agreement."

"To your satisfaction."

"Yes."

"And what *is* your satisfaction?"

I didn't know.

Tony moved restlessly, looking at his watch. "Lord Ferth, Kelly, look, I'm sorry, but I've got a horse to saddle for the last race. . . . I'll have to go now."

"Yes, of course," said Lord Ferth. "But we'd all be obliged if you wouldn't talk about what you've learned in here."

Tony looked startled. "Sure. If you say so. Not a word." He stood up and went over to the door. "See you after," he said to me. "You secretive so-and-so."

As he went out, a bunch of Stewards and their wives came in chattering for their tea. Lord Ferth went over to them and exerted the flashing eyes, and they all went into reverse. A waiter who had materialized behind them was stationed outside the door with instructions to send all customers along to the members' tearoom.

While this was going on, Jack looked steadfastly down at the tablecloth and said not a word. I didn't feel like chatting to him idly, either. He'd cost me too much.

Lord Ferth came briskly back and sat down.

"Now, then, Roxford," he said in his most businesslike way, "we've heard Kelly's accusations. It's your turn now to speak up in your defense."

Jack slowly lifted his head. The deep habitual lines of worry were running with sweat.

"It was someone else." His voice was dead.

"It certainly wasn't Grace," I said, "because Lord Gowery was quite clear that the person who tried to blackmail him on the telephone was a man." So was the person who had got at Charlie West a man, or so he'd said.

Jack Roxford jerked.

"Yes, Roxford, we know about Lord Gowery," Ferth said.

"You *can't* . . ."

"You belong to the same club," I said assertively, as if I knew.

For Jack Roxford, too, the thought of that club was the lever which opened the floodgates. Like Gowery before him, he broke into wretched pieces.

"You don't understand. . . ."

"Tell us, then," Ferth said. "And we'll try."

"Grace . . . we . . . I . . . Grace didn't like . . ." He petered out.

I gave him a shove. "Grace liked her sex natural and wouldn't stand for what you wanted."

He gulped. "Soon after we were married, we were having rows all the time, and I hated that. I loved her, really I did. I've always loved her. And I felt . . . all tangled up. . . . She didn't understand that when I beat her it was because of love . . . she said she'd leave me and divorce me for cruelty . . . so I asked a girl I'd known . . . a street girl, who didn't mind . . . I mean . . . she let you, if you paid well enough . . . if I could go on seeing her . . . but she said she'd given that up now . . . but there was a club in London . . . and I went there . . . and it was a terrific relief . . . and then I was all right with Grace . . . but of course we didn't . . . well, hardly ever . . . but somehow . . . we could go on being married."

Lord Ferth looked revolted.

"I couldn't believe it at first," Jack said more coherently, "when I saw Lord Gowery there. I saw him in the street, just outside. I thought it was just a coincidence. But then, one night, inside the club, I was sure it was him, and I saw him again in the street another time . . . but I didn't say anything. I mean, how could I? And anyway, I knew how he felt . . . you don't go there unless you must . . . and you can't keep away."

"How long have you known that Lord Gowery went to the same club?" I asked.

"Oh . . . two or three years. A long time. I don't know exactly."

"Did he know you were a member?"

"No. He hadn't a clue. I spoke to him once or twice on

the racecourse about official things. . . . He didn't have any idea."

"And then," Ferth said thoughtfully, "you read that he had been appointed in Colonel Midgely's place to officiate at the Cranfield-Hughes Enquiry, and you saw what you thought was a good chance of getting Cranfield out of racing, and keeping Byler's horses yourself."

Jack sat huddled in his chair, not denying it.

"And when Lord Gowery declined to be blackmailed, you couldn't bear to give up the idea, and you set about faking evidence that would achieve your ends."

A long silence. Then Jack said in a thick disjointed voice, "Grace minded so much . . . about Cranfield taking our horses. Well, so did I, too. It wasn't fair. It wasn't, really, not after all the work I've put into them. But she went on about it . . . morning, noon, and night. Couldn't stop. Talk, talk, talk. All the time. Saying she'd like to kill Cranfield . . . and things like that. I mean . . . she's always been a bit nervy . . . a bit strung up . . . but Cranfield was upsetting her. . . . I got a bit frightened for her sometimes, she was that violent about him. . . . Well, it was partly because of that that I tried to get Cranfield warned off. . . . Mostly, of course, it was so I could keep Byler's horses, but, well . . . I mean, Cranfield was better warned off than Grace trying to kill him."

"Did you truly believe she would?" I asked.

"She was ranting about it all the time. . . . I didn't know if she really would . . . but I was so afraid. . . . I didn't want her to get into trouble . . . dear dear Grace . . . I wanted to help her . . . and make things right again . . . and keep the horses myself. . . . They were mine by rights, weren't they? . . . So I set about it . . . and it wasn't too difficult, really, not once I'd set my mind to it."

Ferth gave me a twisted smile. I gave him a similar one back and reflected that marriage could be a deadly institution. Grace's strung-up state would have been aggravated by the strain of living with a sexually odd man, and Jack would have felt guilty about it and wanted to make it up to her. Neither of them had been rationally inclined, and the whole situation had boiled up claustrophobically inside their agonized private world. Having "dear Grace" harping on endlessly would have driven many a stronger man to explosive action; but Jack couldn't desert her, because he had to stay with his horses, and he couldn't drive her away, because he loved her.

He wanted desperately to keep Byler's horses for his own sake as much as hers, and the only way he had seen to achieve it had been to ruin Cranfield.

"Why me?" I said, trying to keep out the bitterness. "Why me, too?"

"Eh?" He squinted at me, half focusing. "You . . . well . . . I haven't anything against you personally. . . . But I thought it was the only way to make it a certainty. . . . Cranfield couldn't have swindled that race without Squelch's jockey being in the know."

"That race was no swindle," I said.

"Oh . . . I know that. Those stupid Oxford Stewards . . . still, they gave me such an opportunity . . . when I heard about Lord Gowery being in charge. And then, when I'd fixed up with Charlie West and Oakley . . . Grace's brother told me, just told me casually, mind you, that his bookmaker had told him that Cranfield had backed Cherry Pie, and do you know what, I couldn't stop laughing. Just like Grace, I felt . . . dead funny, it was, that he really had backed Cherry Pie. . . ."

"What was that about Charlie West?" Ferth said sharply.

"I paid him . . . to say Kelly pulled Squelch back. I telephoned and asked him . . . if Kelly ever did anything like that . . . and he said once, in a novice chase, Kelly had said 'O.K. Brakes on, chaps,' and I told him to say Kelly had said that in the Lemonfizz Cup, because it sounded so convincing, didn't it, saying something Kelly really had said. . . ."

Ferth looked at me accusingly. "You shielded West."

I shrugged ruefully. Jack paid no attention, didn't hear.

He went on miserably: "Grace was all right before the dance. She was wonderfully calm again, after Cranfield was warned off. And then Edwin Byler said that we would be keeping his horses for always . . . and we were happy . . . in our way . . . and then we heard . . . that Kelly was at the dance . . . saying he'd been framed . . . and was just on the point of finding out who . . . and Grace saw Cranfield's daughter and just boiled over all over again, nearly as bad as before . . . and I thought . . . if Kelly was dead . . . it would be all right again. . . ."

Ferth slowly shook his head. The reasoning which had led Jack Roxford step by step from misfortune to crime defeated him.

"I thought he wouldn't feel anything," Jack said. "I thought that you just blacked out suddenly from carbon monoxide. I thought it would be like going to sleep. . . . He wouldn't know about it. Just wouldn't wake up."

"You didn't drill a big enough hole," I said without irony. "Not enough gas came through at once to knock me out."

"I couldn't find a large enough tube," he said macabrely. "Had to use a piece I had. It was a bit narrow. That was why."

"I see," I said gravely. So close. Only a few inches from the express train. One-eighth of an inch extra in the tube's diameter would have done it.

"And you went to look for the piece of manifold, afterward?"

"Yes . . . but you know about that. I asked at the garage and they told me the mechanic had taken it away and given it to you. I was furious with Oakley for not finding it. . . . I'd told him to *make* you give it to him . . . and he said he did try . . . but you wouldn't. . . ."

"Why didn't you ask *him* to kill me?" I said matter-of-factly.

"Oh, I did. He said he didn't kill. He said he would dispose of the body if I did it, but he never did the job himself. Not worth it, he said."

That sounded like the authentic Oakley. Straight from the agent's mouth.

"But you couldn't risk it?" I suggested.

"I didn't have any chance. I mean . . . I didn't like to leave Grace alone much . . . she was so upset . . . and

then, you were in hospital . . . and then you went back to
your flat . . . and I did try to shift you out into the open
somewhere . . . because I couldn't risk going there, not
into someone else's stable. . . . I would have had to ask
where you lived . . . and they would have known me. . . .
So I thought, in a hotel, or something. . . ."

"You did write to the Stewards' Secretaries," Ferth
exclaimed. "After all."

"Yes . . . but it was too late . . . wasn't it. . . . She really
meant it . . . poor Grace, poor Grace . . . why did I let her
go out . . . I would have managed it for her somehow . . .
I'd've found another way to keep the horses. . . . But she
seemed so much better this morning . . . and now . . . and
now . . ." His face screwed up and turned red as he tried
not to cry. The thought of Grace as he'd last seen her was
too much for him. The tears rolled. He sniffed into a
handkerchief.

I wondered how he would have felt if he'd seen Grace
as I'd seen her. But probably the uncritical love he had
would have survived even that.

"Just sit here quietly a moment, Roxford," Lord Ferth
directed, and he himself stood up and signed for me to
walk with him over to the door.

"So what do we do with him?" he said.

"It's gone too far now," I said reluctantly, "to be entirely hushed up. And he's—if anything—more dangerous
than Grace. He has no moral brakes. He attempted
blackmail, and progressed to fixing evidence, and as soon
as it seemed necessary to him, he was prepared to kill. He
had no hesitation, no compunction at all . . . and if he saw
the need again, he would react in the same way. People's
mind patterns solidify anyway, and if they're obsessive,
like this, they intensify as well. Grace will live, and he
will very likely from now on see anything in terms of her
happiness. Anyone who treats either of them badly in
any way could end up as a victim of his scheming. End up
ruined . . . or dead. People like nurses . . . or relations . . .
or even people like me, who did them no harm at all.
Anybody . . ."

Ferth said, "You seem to understand his mind. I must

say that I don't. But what you say makes sense. We cannot just take away his license and leave it at that. . . . It isn't a racing matter any more. But Lord Gowery . . ."

"Lord Gowery will have to take his chance," I said without satisfaction. "Very likely you can avoid busting open his reputation . . . but it's much more important to stop Jack Roxford doing the same sort of thing again."

"Yes," he said. "It is." He spread out his hands sideways in a pushing gesture as if wanting to step away from the decision. "All this is so *distressing.*"

I looked down the room at Jack, a huddled defeated figure with nervous eyes and an anxious forehead. He was picking at the tablecloth with his fingers, folding it into senseless little pleats. He didn't look like a villain. No hardened criminal. Just a tenacious little man with a fixed idea, to make up to dear Grace for being what he was.

Nothing was more useless than sending him to prison, and nothing could do him more harm; yet that, I imagined, was where he would go. Putting his body in a little cage wouldn't straighten the kinks in his mind. The system, for men like him, was ridiculous.

He stood up slowly and walked unsteadily toward us.

"I suppose," he said without much emotion, "that you are going to get the police. I was wondering . . . please . . . don't tell them about the club. . . . I won't say Lord Gowery goes there . . . I won't tell anybody ever . . . I never really wanted to . . . it wouldn't have done any good, would it? I mean, it wouldn't have kept these horses in my yard . . . wouldn't have made a scrap of difference. . . . So do you think anyone need know about . . . the club?"

"No," said Ferth with well-disguised relief. "They need not."

A faint smile set up a rival set of creases to the lines of anxiety. "Thank you." The smile faded away. The lost look deepened. "How long . . . do you think I'll get?"

Ferth moved uncomfortably. "No point in worrying about that until you have to."

"You could probably halve it," I said.

"How?" He was pathetically hopeful. I flung him the rope.

"By giving evidence at another trial I have in mind, and taking David Oakley down with you."

Part Three

MARCH EPILOGUE

Yesterday I rode Breadwinner in the Cheltenham Gold Cup.

A horse of raw talent with more future than past. A shambling washy chestnut carrying his head low. No one's idea of equine beauty.

Old Strepson had watched him slop round the parade ring and said with a sigh, "He looks half asleep."

"Hughes will wake him up," Cranfield said condescendingly.

Cranfield stood in the chilly March sunshine making his usual good stab at arrogance. The mean calculating lines round his mouth seemed to have deepened during the past month, and his manner to me was if anything more distant, more master-servant, than ever before. Roberta said she had told him that I had in some way managed to get our licenses back, but he saw no reason to believe her and preferred the thought of divine intervention.

Old Strepson said conversationally, "Kelly says Breadwinner was a late foal and a late developer, and won't reach his true strength until about this time next year."

Cranfield gave me a mouth-tightening mind-your-own-business glare, and didn't seem to realize that I'd given him an alibi if the horse didn't win and built him up into one heck of a good trainer if it did. Whatever low opinion Cranfield held of me, I reciprocated it in full.

Further along the parade ring stood a silent little group: Jessel, Pat Nikita, and their stable jockey, Al Roach. They were engaged in running poor old Squelch, and their interest lay not so fiercely in winning as in finishing at all costs in front of Breadwinner. Jessel him-

self radiated so much hatred that I thought it was probably giving him a headache. Hating did that. The day I
found it out, I gave up hating.

Grace's hatred headache must have been unbearable. . . .

Grace's recovery was still uncertain. Ferth had somehow wangled the best available psychiatrist onto her case,
and had also arranged for him to see Jack. Outside the
weighing room when I had arrived, Ferth had jerked his
head for me to join him, and told me what the psychiatrist
had reported.

"He says Jack is sane according to legal standards, and
will have to stand trial. He wouldn't commit himself
about Grace's chances. He did say, though, that from all
points of view their enforced separation was a godsend. He
said he thought their only chance of leading fairly normal
lives in the future was to make the separation total and
permanent. He said a return to the same circumstances
could mean a repeat of the whole cycle."

I looked at Ferth gloomily. "What a cold, sad, depress-
ing solution."

"You never know," he said optimistically. "Once they
get over it, they might both feel—well—released."

I smiled at him. He said abruptly, "Your outlook is
catching, damn it. . . . How about that dinner?"

"Any time," I said.

"Tomorrow, then? Eight o'clock. The Caprice, round
the corner from the Ritz. . . . The food's better there than
at my club."

"Fine," I said.

"And you can tell me how the police are getting on
with David Oakley. . . ."

I'd had the Birmingham police on my telephone and
doorstep for much of the past week. They had almost
fallen on my neck and sobbed when I first went to them
with enough to make an accusation stick, and had later
promised to deliver to me, framed, one of the first fruits
of their search warrant: a note from Cranfield to Jack
Roxford dated ten months earlier, thanking him for not
bidding him up at an auction after a selling race and
enclosing a check for fifty pounds. Across the bottom of

the page, Cranfield had written, "As agreed. Thanks. D.C."

It was the note Oakley had photographed in my flat.

Supplied by Roxford, who had suggested the photograph.

Kept by Oakley, as a hold over Roxford.

The police also told me that Jack Roxford had drawn six hundred pounds in new notes out of his bank during the two weeks before the Enquiry, and that David Oakley had paid three hundred of the same notes into his own account five days later.

Clever, slippery Mr. Oakley had been heard to remark that he regretted not having slaughtered Kelly Hughes.

The bell rang for the jockeys to mount, and Cranfield and old Strepson and I walked over to where Breadwinner waited.

The one jockey missing from the day's proceedings was Charlie West, whose license had been suspended for the rest of the season. And it was only thanks to Hughes's intervention, Ferth had told him forcefully, that he hadn't got his deserts and been warned off for life. Whether Charlie West would feel an atom of gratitude was another matter.

I swung up easily onto Breadwinner and fitted my right foot carefully into the stirrup. A compromise between me and the orthopedist had seen the plaster off seven days previously, but the great surgeon's kind parting words had been "You haven't given that leg enough time, and if it dislocates again it's your own bloody fault."

I had told him that I couldn't afford to have Cranfield engage another jockey for Breadwinner with all the horse's future races at stake. Old Strepson was the grateful type who didn't dislodge a jockey who had won for him, and if some other jockey won the Gold Cup on Breadwinner I would lose the mount for life; and it was only this argument which had made him grudgingly bring out the saw.

I gathered up the reins and walked the horse quietly round the ring while everyone sorted out into the right order for the parade down the course. Apart from the Grand National, the Cheltenham Gold Cup was the biggest steeplechase of the year. In prestige, probably the greatest of all. All the stars turned out for it, meeting each other on level terms. Bad horses hadn't a hope.

There were nine runners yesterday. Breadwinner was the youngest, Squelch the most experienced, and a bad-tempered gray called Ironclad the favorite.

Al Roach, uninfected by Jessel, lined up beside me at the start and gave me his usual wide friendly Irish grin. "Now, Kelly me bhoy," he said, "tell me how you ride this little fellow, now."

"You want to be warned off?" I said.

He chuckled. "What's the owner got against you, Kelly me bhoy?"

"I was right and he was wrong, and he can't forgive that."

"Peculiar fellow, he is, that Jessel. . . ."

The tapes went up and we were away. Three and a quarter miles, twenty-one jumps, two whole circuits of the course.

Nothing much happened on the first circuit. No horses fell and no jockeys got excited, and going past the stands and outward bound for the second time, a fair-sized sheet would have covered the lot. The next mile sorted the men from the boys, and the bunch flattened out into the relentless, thundering, muscle-straining procession in which hope and sweat and tactics merged into a rushing private world of conflict. Speed . . . jumping at near disaster rate . . . gambling on the horse's coordination . . . stretching your own . . . a race like the Gold Cup showed you what you were made of. . . .

Coming to the second to the last fence, Ironclad was leading Squelch by three lengths which could have been ten, and he set himself right with all the time in the world. Squelch followed him over, and four lengths behind Breadwinner strained forward to be third.

Between the last two fences the positions were unchanged, Breadwinner making no impression on Squelch, or Squelch on Ironclad. Oh, well, I thought resignedly. Third. That wasn't really too bad for such a young horse. One couldn't have everything. And there was always Pound Postage in the Grand National, two weeks from Saturday. . . .

Ironclad set himself right for the last fence, launched himself muscularly into the air, crossed the birch with a good foot of air beneath him . . . and pitched forward onto his nose on landing.

I couldn't believe it. Shook up Breadwinner with a bang of renewed hope and drove him into the last fence for the jump of his young life.

Squelch was over it first, of course. Squelch the sure-footed trained-to-the-minute familiar old rascal . . . Irony of ironies, to be beaten to the Gold Cup by Squelch.

Breadwinner did the best he could to catch him, and I saw that, as in the Lemonfizz, Squelch was dying from tiredness. Length by length, my gangling chestnut pegged back the gap, straining, stretching, quivering to get past . . . but the winning post was too near . . . it was no good . . . there wasn't time. . . .

Al Roach looked round to see who was pressing him. Saw me. Knew that Breadwinner was, of all others, the one he had to beat. Was seized with panic. If he had sat still, he would have won by two lengths. Instead, he picked up his whip and hit Squelch twice down the flank.

You stupid ass, I thought breathlessly. He hates that. He'll stop. He always stops if you hit him. . . .

Squelch's tail swished in fury. His rhythmic stride broke up into bumps. He shook his head violently from side to side.

I saw Al's desperate face as Breadwinner caught him . . . and the winning post was there and gone in a flash . . . and neither of us knew even then which had won.

The photograph gave it to Breadwinner by a nostril. And if I got booed by the crowd after the Lemonfizz they made up for it after the Gold Cup.

Jessel, predictably, was purple with fury, and he seemed on the brink of explosion when someone remarked loudly that Squelch would have won if

Hughes had been riding him. I laughed. Jessel looked almost as murderous as Grace.

Old Strepson was pale with emotion, but even the Gold Cup did not raise much observable joy in Cranfield; and I found out later that Edwin Byler had just told him he wouldn't be sending him his horses after all. Grace's psychiatrist had written to say that Grace's ultimate sanity might depend on Cranfield not having the horses, and Byler said that he felt he owed the Roxfords something. . . . Sorry and all that, but there it was.

Roberta, with her mother, had been there patting Breadwinner in the winner's enclosure, and when I came out of the weighing room twenty minutes later after changing into street clothes, she was leaning against the rails, waiting.

"You're limping," she said calmly.

"Unfit, that's all."

"Coffee?" she suggested.

"Yes," I said.

She walked sedately ahead of me into the coffee room. Her copper hair still shone after she'd stepped out of the sunshine, and I liked the simple string-colored coat which went underneath it.

I bought her some coffee and we sat at a little plastic-topped table and looked at the litter left by the last occupants: empty coffee cups, plates with crumbs, cigarette butts, and a froth-lined beer glass. Roberta packed them coolly to one side and ignored them.

"Winning and losing," she said. "That's what it's all about."

"Racing?"

"Life."

I looked at her.

She said, "Today is marvelous, and being warned off was terrible. I suppose everything goes on like that . . . up and down . . . always."

"I suppose so," I agreed.

"I've learned a lot, since the Enquiry."

"So have I . . . about you."

"Father says I must remember your background. . . ."

"That's true," I said. "You must."

"Father's mind has chains on. Iron bars in his soul. His head's chock-a-block with ideas half a century out of date." She mimicked my own words with pompous mischief.

I laughed. "Roberta . . ."

"Please tell me . . ." She hesitated. "At the level crossing . . . when you called me Rosalind . . . was it her you wanted?"

"No," I said slowly, "it was you. . . . In her place."

She sighed contentedly.

"That's all right, then," she said. "Isn't it?"

Agatha Christie's *favorite*

THE REMARKABLE MISS MARPLE

Everyone knows MISS JANE MARPLE—she's that elderly spinster lady whose innocent china-blue eyes hide a mind of steel. A mind that solves crimes—in all sorts of surprising ways.

Put a little mystery into your life—a Miss Jane Marple murder mystery by Agatha Christie from Pocket Books.

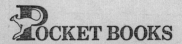

POCKET BOOKS